ONLY MONSTERS REMAIN

William J. Donahue

JOURNALSTONE
YOUR LINK TO ARTIST TALENT

ISBN: 978-1-68510-110-7 (trade paper)
ISBN: 978-1-68510-111-4 (ebook)
Library of Congress Catalog Number: 2023943902

First printing edition August 25, 2023
Published by JournalStone Publishing in the United States of America.
Cover Artwork and Design: Don Noble
Edited by Sean Leonard
Proofreading and Cover/Interior Layout by Scarlett R. Algee

JournalStone Publishing
3205 Sassafras Trail
Carbondale, Illinois 62901

JournalStone books may be ordered through booksellers or by contacting:
JournalStone | www.journalstone.com

For Jake, Killer Khan, and the late, great Kamala.

Death waits inside us for a door to open.
—Jim Harrison

Chapter 1
Mountains in the Sky

Samantha hoped to die on this godforsaken footpath, in the grisliest manner possible, purely to hold the grotesqueness of her demise over her husband's head for all eternity.

The muscles in her lower back spasmed from the persistent insult of a backpack weighed down with thirty-plus pounds of tent, sleeping bag, and other useless crap she hoped to never see again — and the cruelties kept coming. At the very least, death would put an end to this junket of nonstop self-abuse.

"I've got another goddamn bug in my ear!"

She tilted her head and thudded a palm against the side of her head, as if trying to coax a slurry of wax and river water from her ear canal. She toppled forward as her boot clipped the edge of a rock sunken into the trail. The filthiest curse word she could think of tumbled from her lips.

"I might suggest a few ways to take your mind off the problem," said Paul, her husband. "Nudge-nudge, wink-wink."

"Very subtle, Paul." She wiped the sweat from her brow. "Now make yourself useful and jab a sharp stick in my ear. Shake loose whatever's making a home sweet home in there."

She bristled at hubby's all-too-obvious hints at sex, probably the sixth or seventh entendre he'd snuck into their one-sided conversations over the past two days. If she were to indulge his urges — a *big* if — it would not be the first time in their more than twenty years together that they copulated in the woods, though this time would likely be the most unpleasant. Three days had passed since her last shower, and his too, for that matter, so the sweat, filth, muck, and grime, maybe even a deer tick or two, had made her body about as pristine as a bowling-alley ashtray.

Who in his right mind would want to smell, taste, and touch such things?

But yes, she would oblige if he kept pressing. In a way, she felt as if she owed him, as compensation for her many outbursts of panic, berating, and pouting on the ground with her knees tight to her chest. She regretted reminding him that his recklessness and stupid decisions and unfamiliarity with the terrain had gotten them lost in the middle of the deep, dark forest somewhere between Albany and Montreal, and that his dumb idea to come out here at all, tramping an ankle-breaking river of rocks for no good reason, was going to get them both killed.

All those things were true, of course, but some truths deserved to go unspoken. He must have felt bad enough already.

She longed for the exhaust of a motor vehicle, the ping of a delivered text message, and every other irritation of the civilized world. Hiking in the backcountry probably had a lower risk of death than walking around the block in her suburban New England neighborhood, but the thought of her inert body decomposing in a remote stretch of woods, alone, with furry critters and cold-blooded creepy crawlers carrying her away one bite at a time — she couldn't bear imagining such a fate. While she had accepted the idea that death would come for her one day, she had other circumstances in mind for her final moments. Given the option, she would want her last breath to come one of two ways: either in a warm bed as a tired old lady, all too ready for the curtain to come down; or in a freak accident while hang-gliding, skydiving, or some other exhilarating activity, a spectacular tragedy that would make her friends and family say, "At least she went out with a bang."

The first day on the trail had gone smoothly enough. After gallivanting a dozen or more miles through a well-marked stretch of upstate New York's Adirondack Park, they had spent the night in a cozy little lean-to, just as planned. She washed down a dinner of reconstituted chicken tikka masala with two mugs of weak chamomile, and then snuggled into her sleeping bag atop soft wooden planks that made a surprisingly comfortable bed. She nodded off with her head tilted toward the lean-to's mouth, studying an unpolluted sky abloom with a million stars.

Their fortunes had taken a turn on day two. Night came quickly, so they had to make camp in a rocky clearing about twenty yards from an overgrown trail that had taken them wildly off course. The worst of it: They had missed the brook where they were supposed to have replenished their water reserves, so she went to sleep with a parched mouth and the beginnings of a dehydration headache.

In the morning, less than an hour into their hike out, they happened upon a clear-as-glass pool at the base of a cataract. Paul hurriedly pumped parasite-sieved water into their Nalgenes. Never had she imbibed a liquid so delicious; she drank enough to make her stomach hurt. Hours later, she had yet to empty her bladder, a sign of how perilously close to the brink of dehydration her body had crept.

A third night of sleeping out of doors, where an itinerant brown recluse could lay its eggs in an unguarded orifice, where black bears could raid their campsite in search of sustenance more tempting than freeze-dried beef stew, and where trail-roving psychopaths could disembowel Paul and do worse to her — each scenario seemed entirely plausible, if not likely.

Paul had spent the whole morning poring over the topographical maps and made a good guess that ran them into a kindly ranger. The young man had steered them onto a trail leading toward the backwoods HQ of the Adirondack Park Mountain Club. "Salvation," she had whispered. But now, with so many miles already behind them, salvation seemed a distance too far to go.

A wooden trail marker suggested, in fading yellow paint made dull by the silk of some critter's cocoon, that they would arrive at the APMC lodge in a little more than three miles. Paul slapped the sign with the face of his palm.

"See, Sam? You can do anything for three miles."

He had uttered the remark with the best of intentions, but damn him, his optimism made Samantha want to push him off the nearest cliff.

She dug her pinkie into her ear canal, trying to rouse the insect, spider, or other many-legged invader from its roost. What she wouldn't give for a Q-tip or a metal coat hanger glowing red in the flame of a blowtorch.

Her math suggested they would reach the APMC lodge within the hour, and they would need to hoof it another two hours back to the primitive parking lot where they'd left the car. Bottom line: The comforts of the hotel in Lake Placid were within their grasp — four hours, more or less, including drive time, putting them at their final destination right at the edge of sundown. Once there, she would soak her sore ass and aching arches in a tub of scalding water, while a glass of chilled Pinot Grigio sweated on the tub's porcelain edge.

Paul stopped in the middle of the trail and asked if she needed a break for "stress relief." Still trawling for trail sex, she knew, oral first — his and hers — followed by two to three minutes of clumsy, violent thrashing.

"Keep walking."

After twenty years, she could read him. His overtures were insincere, him just trying to busy her mind with cotton-candy thoughts, to remind her of his status as a sexual being, or possibly as a kindness to let her know he still found her desirable at fifty-five, even though she had retained most of the "winter weight" she had packed on three years earlier. If she thought he truly wanted to have a go, *au natural*, she would certainly entertain him — just veer off the trail, peel off her shorts and sweat-drenched underwear, find a tree to lean against, and spread her legs so he could do his worst. The whole affair would take ten minutes or less. Far less, in fact.

And he knew all that too, she figured, which explained why he chose to keep walking.

The day grew hot and gray, close. Rivulets of sweat trickled down the vertical crease between her eyebrows and slid into her eyes. She squinted away the sting. Thoughts of the hotel consumed her, of the opportunity to scrub off the grime and salt and any blood-sucking pests she had acquired and, once she had succeeded in that task, take pleasure in watching the dirty bathwater spiral down the drain. She envisioned the two of them walking — limping, more likely — into town for martinis and a plate of French cheeses to start, maybe a nice piece of salmon to follow, a bottle of citrusy white to bring out the vibrancy in each morsel to touch her tongue.

A sharp pain in her big toe erased the hotel fantasy from the chalkboard in her brain. She hoped she wasn't about to forfeit a toenail in tribute to this doomed trek.

"Never again," she said under her breath.

The grumbling sky turned a peculiar shade of green, or was it red? A deafening crack, as loud as a gunshot by her ear, chased a pair of warblers from the brush. Instinct forced her into a defensive crouch.

"Thunder?"

"Relax, Sam. What else could it be?"

"You said the skies would be clear."

"You know what they say about weather in the mountains. You don't like it the way it is, wait five minutes."

"But we're not on the peaks anymore."

"We're close enough. Onward, troops!"

She hurried her steps to get within a yard of Paul, close enough to read the label on his overstuffed backpack. The air felt different somehow, charged. It felt, in a word, wrong.

Droplets of rain speckled her cheeks.

Another crack of thunder split the sky. The rain turned heavy, soaking, as loud as footsteps. A gust of wind pushed her forward. The violence of it all frightened her. She squinted in the rain, and the drops stung her eyes. Salt from her sweaty brow, she figured, though the sting turned into a pronounced burn.

"There should be a lean-to between here and the lodge," Paul hollered.

His boot steps quickened. She struggled to keep up.

Rain slicked her arms, legs, and neck. Each drop felt slimy on her skin. She could barely keep her eyes open from the burn.

"Paul!" she yelled, reaching out for him.

She felt his hands on hers, leading her half blind. She sensed the outline of the structure, an old lean-to covered in moss and lichen. They dropped their packs onto the raised floor and stirred up a film of dust. She immediately went about wiping the sting from her eyes.

"Feels like someone tossed lye in my face," she told him matter-of-factly. "My frickin' retinas are on fire."

"Don't be so dramatic," Paul responded. "It's not *that* bad."

"It stings like a son of a bitch, Paul."

"Acid rain, maybe?"

"Is that actually a thing?"

From a kneeling position, she blinked until Paul came into focus. He stood tall, arms above his head and his hands clutching one of the beams that held up the ceiling. A smile creased his grizzled face.

"I can't believe you're enjoying this," she said.

"Beats a day at the office. What's not to like?"

Everything, she thought. *Every-fucking-thing.*

Not a single aspect of this experience had been enjoyable, and it kept getting worse. The downpour would extend their hike out — and, more importantly, delay the scalding-hot bath, the chilled bottle of white, and the chance to roll around on a real bed with real pillows, a real comforter, and real cotton sheets with an ultra-high thread count.

Some day in the distant future, if Paul asked her to go backpacking again — *when* he asked — she would remember this miserable hell and be sure to remind him of the torture he had put her through. The realization that she would never have to endure this bullshit ever again filled her with joy, made her playful.

Raindrops beat upon the mossy wood. Something heavy smacked the roof. A tree branch shaken loose, perhaps.

"Looks like we might be here for a while," he said. "Unless you want to run for it and get wet."

"I'm already wet." She showed a devilish smile.

"Don't tease me now."

"More than moist," she said, playing along. "Dripping, in fact. Sopping, like a damp sponge in need of wringing out."

"You know," he said as he clapped the plank floor with the heel of his boot, "you don't find too many flat surfaces in the Adirondacks."

"Okay," she said. "Let's get sloppy. Drop 'em."

"Really?"

"Yes, but make it quick."

"As always," he said.

She stood to greet him, with the full knowledge of the odors her body exuded, of how atrocious her breath must be. She tried to cast such thoughts from her mind and just enjoy the moment as best she could. After all, how many more opportunities would she have to make love to her husband in the mountains, during a rainstorm no less? If nothing else, the experience would give her a good story to tell, once they got out of this mess and back home on the outskirts of Hartford, among the girlfriends who could appreciate real-life erotica.

Her pants found a way open, the zipper undone, with Paul's hand checking to see if she was ready for him. Her hiking shorts slid to the floor. She stepped out of them and kicked them aside. Her hands were in the process of liberating him from his shorts when an odd noise stopped her. She would have described it as a quiet — the word eluded her — *slurping*. The sound reminded her of an old man breathing through diseased lungs, thick with mucus. Nothing but the rain, she told herself, scrubbing weeks or months of determined moss from the lean-to's roof. When the noise grew more insistent, she peered into the structure's darkened corner, where the near wall met the ceiling.

"What is that?" she asked.

"What's what?"

"Something's in here with us." She turned him around and nudged him toward the corner.

He gave the space a cursory glance and then turned back to her, eager to resume their foreplay. "I don't see anything. Don't hear anything either."

"That's because you've gone deaf, dumb, and blind from all the blood rushing to the space between your legs. Go check."

She urged him forward with a knee to his buttocks. He bent to grab one of his hiking poles. He took a tentative step forward, followed by another, even more cautious, as if he saw something that did not belong.

"What is it?" she asked.

Slowly, the thing emerged. Long and rope-like — slimy, muscular. Dangerous. It reared back, as if threatening to strike.

"Snake!" she screamed. "A goddamn boa constrictor!"

Paul held the pole as if it were an epee — a fencing sword — and poked the snake-like thing with the metal tip. The thing recoiled and then nudged forward, sightless, as if tasting the air.

"That's no snake," he said. "I don't know what it is, but it's—"

As he spoke, another snake-like thing materialized from the darkened corner, followed by another. Three slimy stalks swayed in the air. As Samantha backed up, she toppled off the edge of the lean-to and splashed into the muck of a muddy puddle.

"You all right?" Paul turned away from the corner toward her. "Let's hope that's our worst spill of the day."

"Paul!"

Her warning came too late.

A writhing stalk latched onto Paul's cheek and, after the briefest of fights, dragged him into the darkness. She screamed his name, but the pouring rain and the shrill of her own voice kept her from hearing any response.

As she sat up, Paul stumbled from the shadows and spilled off the edge of the lean-to. He landed beside her, thrashing wildly, his face an obscene mask of blood and writhing flesh. As she reached for him, one of the stalks — *a tentacle!* — snatched her by the wrist. Her skin reacted as if burned. She howled and wrenched her wrist free.

Paul coughed up black blood, gurgled, and then went still. The thing — a scarlet-red octopus, no bigger than a handbag — slithered off his face, or what remained of it. His nose was absent, his eyes cored out. Two tentacles encircled his neck. Two more invaded his mouth, plucking out his tongue.

She backed away and found her feet, escaping, abandoning her husband, to outpace this terrible nightmare. Wet pine branches raked her face as she raced blindly through the woods. After a moment she had the sense to stop and recalculate, crossing a patch of soft earth covered in fallen pine needles, in search of the trail that had led them to the lean-to where...

Paul.

She turned, realizing she was, in the barest sense, near naked and alone — no backpack, no food or water, no hiking poles, no Paul. The cool air made her look down and regard her lavender underwear, a streak of blood on the curve of her porcelain belly. Her eyes studied her wrist where the tentacle had bitten into her flesh — and that's exactly what it had felt like, a bite, stone-hard fangs stabbing her skin and infecting her with only God knows what.

"What the fuck is happening?"

She took two cautious steps onto the trail that would lead her back to the lean-to. A bend in the trail obscured her view. She saw no body, no sign of her husband.

"Paul?" she said, her voice soft and broken. She repeated his name, her voice quieter this time, thinner, resigned.

She knew.

"Paul."

She had the presence of mind to realize the rain had stopped, and noticed a pronounced change in the light. The sky glowed an obscene shade of red. The clouds seemed alive.

Then came the unmistakable crack of a felled tree. Followed by another. The canopy shuddered. Towering ash trees and pines toppled like pushed dominoes, their crowns falling to the forest floor.

Something was coming for her.

She turned and ran down the trail, away from the husband she had left behind, his face savaged by an octopus in the middle of the woods.

As she ran, she heard a rush of air, felt it, as if a giant inflated its lungs with a bottomless breath. A steel grip crushed her middle, from breast to waist. Daggers impaled her bones and precious organs. An electric current coursed through her body. As she left her feet, she forgot everything she had ever learned.

Only the pain mattered.

Samantha passed over the tops of trees and craggy peaks as the massive tentacle carried her into the underbelly of a roiling scarlet cloud. In the distance she saw dozens of colossal objects — mountains in the sky — drooping from the bellies of clouds and hurtling toward the earth.

Her view turned upside down. A moment later, as the world righted itself, she faced a massive parrot-like beak. The beak snapped twice and then yawned wide, groaning like a rusty hinge. The cavity reminded her of an unguarded manhole, empty save the enormous tongue lurking in the dark space just beyond. A strange peacefulness overcame her. An entirety of numbness. No cares or worries. No trace of pain in her ruined body. She laughed at the hungry beak, each of its bony mandibles rimmed with serrated ivory teeth.

Then, in a blink, her blood-red world turned black.

Chapter 2
Fragile Peace

Jillian Futch adjusted the microphone and swiped the thin coating of dust from the edge of the lectern. She backed up a step and strode past the all-black casket, its bridge closed to hide its secretive contents. The attendees could only guess at the dreadfulness lurking within the shiny black box. Jillian knew. She had seen — and smelled — the horror firsthand, had shoveled all the glistening bits of gristle into green trash bags bound for the casket. Some of the offal had leached through the plastic and stained the casket's silky interior.

From the corner of the room, beneath a patch of water-stained ceiling, Jillian watched as a thickset woman, thirty-eight, maybe forty, approached the lectern and leaned forward until her plump, over-glossed lips came within a few millimeters of the just-for-show microphone. The woman wore too much eye makeup, her clothes too revealing, her gray-streaked hair pulled back into a severe bun. The thin fabric of her blouse accentuated the contours of her obscenely full breasts. The woman lifted her eyes from a scribbled-over napkin and scanned the cavernous room.

Five people sat amid the eight rows of folding chairs. Sparse, but a good crowd, all things considered.

"Most people knew her as Jessica Twin Peaks," the woman began. "There's a different name on her birth certificate, but that's the name she had them print on her driver's license. She went by other names too, a.k.a. the Lap Queen, a.k.a. Messy Jessie, a.k.a. the Pride of Dixie Cups Saloon for Scoundrels and Gentlemen on the outskirts of Pell, open ten a.m. to two a.m., including Sundays — or at least it used to be, before all this bullshit started."

She turned away from the microphone and coughed. A smoker's cough.

"She was thirty-six when she died, same age as me, and she lived every day like it was the best day of her life," she continued. "Most people who have known me over the past ten years have known me by my stage name, Savannah, but Jess knew me by the name my momma gave me, Ellen. Jess was something else. Everyone likes to think of every exotic dancer as a gentle sweetheart with a heart of gold and a stiletto strapped to her thigh, just in case, and I suppose some of those women do exist. I've met them. I've known them. Jess wasn't one of them. She could be mean as a cottonmouth — that's a snake, for you northerners — and that was on her better days, but she would do almost anything for you if you were lucky enough to have earned her trust."

Another cough.

"I would know," Ellen added. "I worked with her for nine years before all of this madness started."

Before the world ended, Jillian figured she meant.

"We met at Night Whispers in Biloxi, Mississippi, where we stayed for a good year," Ellen said. "She convinced me to head north, because that's where the opportunity was, she said, where the money was. I've lost track of how many stops we made along the way from there to here, most of them forgettable. Candy Cane's in Charleston, where we took do-nothing dayshifts for a few months. Jiggles, just outside of Asheville, North Carolina, where we stayed for a solid two years. Tops 'N' Bottoms, just outside of Philly, which is nicer than most people think. Ride 'Em Cowboys in Wilkes-Barre, Pennsylvania, for a cup of coffee. The Flesh Parade in Binghamton, New York. The Love Shack in Hartford. Then we ended up at Dixie Cups, here in Pell, Rhode Island, to preside over the end of all things under God's distant Heaven."

Jillian loved eulogies, always had. They seemed to say more about those who were left behind than they did about the folks who had passed on. To her delight, the eulogies had gotten even more colorful in the months since...well, in the months since a horde of tentacled monsters descended from the sky and tore the mortal world asunder.

"I followed Jess each time, without fail," Ellen said. "'This is the one, El,' she'd tell me. 'The owner treats us good, and there's money to be had.' Each time she'd be wrong, of course, but you can't blame Jess for her optimism. I think that's what I'll miss most about her. That glass-half-full mentality is what drove her to break out a map, point to a new place, and say, 'Let's see what happens.' And that same devil-may-care attitude is what sent her outside on that fateful day last week, right into the slime-slathered clutches of the demon that tore her in two."

She wiped her nose on her sleeve.

"I only wish someone could tell me what happened to the other half of her."

***

Once the ceremony had ended and she'd ushered the small gathering to the front door, Jillian sealed herself into the quiet of the empty funeral-home parlor. A dust-shagged grandfather clock tick-tocked in the far corner. She took a deep breath and forced herself to peek through the slit of a window.

Her eyes roved the underbellies of clouds. The sky had been back-to-normal blue for nearly a week, having slowly shed its obscene pallor, that of an overripe tomato. No signs of the colossal tentacles eager to scour the sidewalks for humans to hurl to their doom. Those horrid visions seemed like snapshots of some terrible, impossible dream. She knew better.

Misfortune had been Jillian's passenger for as long as she could remember, so she had been waiting most of her adult life for something like this to happen. The apocalypse had come just fine, though all along she had been expecting something small and personal, like ovarian cancer or a head-on collision with a hay baler driven by a high-on-meth hillbilly.

She left the parlor and returned to her task deep in the belly of the darkened funeral home. As she entered the embalming room, she remembered a trip she and her father had taken to visit his sister's family in Guillemot, a farming village in southern Maine, so she could become best friends with a trio of cousins she had never met. She'd been twelve, maybe thirteen years old, only a few weeks after she started bleeding for the first time.

***

"I guess you're not my little girl anymore," Dad told her one too many times during the drive north. She wished she had never told him her secret, because "becoming a woman" made her ashamed of something she had no control over — and something she would rather have gone without had anyone bothered to ask.

Dad had done his best raising a girl as a single parent. She just wished his best had been better. Maybe spending a full week with his sister and brother-in-law, meaning Jillian's aunt and uncle, would give him a crash course in how moms and dads of pubescent kids were supposed to behave.

"Take your cousin to the lake," her aunt, Sylvia, had told her three kids, a daughter about Jillian's age, and twin sons a few years younger.

At her father's urging, Jillian agreed to go even though she had left her swimsuit back home in Dracut, Massachusetts, north of Boston. She had never been a particularly strong swimmer, having had few opportunities to learn, and even fewer friends to swim with. She surprised herself by wading into the tea-colored lake, icy even in July.

"It's a thousand feet deep," one of the boys assured as he breaststroked toward the lake's middle.

She felt all right as long as she could touch the bottom. Her cousins kept going farther out, and she followed. The water rose to her waist and soft belly, and then her undeveloped chest, and then her shoulders and chin. Then the bottom gave way, and Jillian found herself floating, flailing, her lungs heaving, and her toes stretching for firm ground. She dipped her face below the surface to make sure the blurry bottom was still down there, somewhere. After the fifth or sixth time, she decided to stop looking, afraid of what she might see: a giant freshwater shark, a prehistoric snapping turtle, or an ancient monster with bony claws outstretched, sniffing her out and grabbing her ankle, then yanking her under and holding her there until her lungs filled with water. Her vision went funny. She imagined some half-man, half-fish abomination clutching her in a vise-like embrace until she stopped thrashing, and then stowing her lifeless body beneath a sunken log, as crocodiles did, where her corpse would rot until it was good enough to eat.

"I don't like this," she told her cousins, who were yards away from her, splashing and dunking each other. She swallowed a mouthful of lake water, followed by another. And then she blacked out.

She had no other memories of that trip, good or bad. But she had been right to be fearful out on that lake in southern Maine. The monsters had finally come for her and the rest of humanity. The reckoning had just taken longer than she'd anticipated.

***

Cold from so many hours without the balm of sunlight, and the muscles in her hands aching from overuse, Jillian steadied herself against the stainless-steel table. A sigh escaped her lips as she positioned the half-naked corpse. A second body waited patiently on the gurney by the door, seeming to crave her peculiar brand of magic.

Only a pair this week, she thought. *Not bad considering the procession of bodies that rolled in on Pell's darkest days, the crematory furnace working overtime. Maybe things have reached a turning point.*

She hoped so, because the LPG tanks would take her only so far, and who knew how much juice the generator out back had left. Perhaps the remaining humans within Pell's borders had gotten better at hiding, at evading *those things.* Or maybe there were fewer humans left to hunt. No one in Pell had seen the beasts for days, but she figured they would eventually come back. Because they always came back.

She inserted the cannula and turned on the suction machine. Little blood remained in the body — the contorted shell of a balding and gray grandfather, somewhere on the timeline between sixty and seventy — meaning a mercifully quick job, for a change. As the machine made its hungry noise, she wandered back to the sitting room and stared through the bay window, long since reduced to an inch-wide slit between two slabs of tacked-up plywood.

A figure moved into the light. A pair of eyes — human eyes — stared back.

"Boo!"

A jolted Jillian stepped back from the window slit.

"Let me in, Jill," said a familiar voice.

"Christ, you scared the shit out of me."

Jillian hurried to the front door. She removed the wooden brace, undid the deadbolt, and swung open the door.

"Hurry up, jackass."

Laurie Woolly stepped through the door into the cavernous sitting room.

"You need to be more careful," Jillian said. "It's almost dark."

She closed the door behind her and refastened the lock.

"Stay here."

She returned to the embalming room and turned off the suction — the body dry, the machine's dutiful work complete. The heavy door closed behind her.

Jillian had met Laurie two months earlier, perhaps three; days bled into each other, robbing time of its meaning. Jillian remembered almost every detail of their first interaction, during a rare break in the tentacled beasts' ongoing assault on Pell. She had been in the stairwell leading to the basement, in the depths of a depressive state, when an insistent knocking rattled the front door. At the time, she hadn't seen another living human being in weeks. She opened the door to find this woman: big, thick, no emotion to light up her round yet pretty face.

"Oh," the woman had said. "I was expecting Bart."

Bartholomew Cozen, second-generation owner and operator of the Cozen Family Funeral Home and Crematory.

"Bart's gone — dead," Jillian had responded. "I work for him — *worked* for him."

Then came the difficulty of describing Bart Cozen's grisly death. She hadn't revisited the story since the day Bart died. Remembering how it happened, why it happened, would have produced too much pain.

"Well, isn't that a fine fuck-me-in-the-ass," the woman said. She extended an open palm and introduced herself as, "Laurie like Hugh, Woolly like the mammoth. I live just up the street, or what's left of the street. From the outside my house looks like it got skull-fucked by an atomic bomb. Inside isn't much better. Worse, actually."

As much as Jillian had been shocked by Laurie's colorful vocabulary, she appreciated anyone with a perverse sense of humor. Laurie had stopped by the funeral home almost every day thereafter — any day those enormous tentacles weren't dangling from the blood-red sky. The true Laurie came out all at once during those visits — boisterous, crass, carefree — so unlike the sullen woman who first appeared on Jillian's doorstep. It felt good to have a friend, a human friend, and a female friend to boot, meaning a creature other than a beloved pet or the voles, brown snakes, and other wild critters she'd discovered in the weed-choked alley behind her childhood home, or the stinkbugs that seemed to crawl out of every crack in her father's drafty old living room.

Laurie had given Jillian what she craved most: a cure to her misfit pathology. Through no fault of her own, Jillian had long struggled to believe she belonged to the same species as her fellow humans. She had gotten so good at playing the outcast that she felt like a pretender on the rare occasion she did try to conform. It was almost like people could smell something on her that didn't quite fit. She wondered if she had lost or broken or perhaps never been given one small but crucial element that would have made her "one of us."

Laurie, no matter how many times Jillian had tried to turn her away in the weeks since their awkward first meeting, had refused to give up on their fledgling friendship. And here she was again, back for more.

"The coast seemed clear," she said. "Not a blessed sign of those bastard things. Besides, I had to get the fuck out of the house."

"You always say that."

"It's always true. Be glad you never got married."

"I'm sure Frank is thankful for the reprieve too," Jillian said, referring to Laurie's husband. She had yet to meet the man, yet to determine if he was as bad as Laurie made him out to be.

"Guess what: We're practically neighbors now," Laurie added. "We're only five doors away from each other now. The hovel next to mine finally collapsed."

"Lucky me."

Six months ago, the Cozen Family Funeral Home and Crematory, located in one of Pell's grittier neighborhoods, or at least one of the least charming, had likely been a dozen doors away from Laurie's house. The monsters had claimed the rest — total annihilation.

Jillian was glad for the distraction. She hadn't known any of the neighbors prior to the invasion, because the funeral home had been nothing more than a workplace; it had since become her one and only dwelling. Laurie said she had noticed Jillian's comings and goings during her every-other-day jaunts to the town's outer rim.

Looking for Albert.

No sign of him so far. Jillian wondered if he had made it, if he had survived the attacks. She wouldn't stop looking until she knew for sure. He had been in her life for six companionable years, and she wasn't yet ready to accept another goodbye.

Jillian had come to Pell — "New Orleans of the North, Portland of the East," as the locals called it, even though there was already another Portland farther up the coast — for a fresh start, and she'd found it. Years earlier, as she was coming of age, she figured she would leave New England in her wake, ending up either someplace exotic and warm yet slightly off-kilter, like Key West or Taos, New Mexico, or someplace dreary, like Seattle or San Francisco, and find work as a taxidermist-slash-artist. She had been enrolled in the program at Still Lakes Center for the Mortuary Arts in Providence when a late-May day trip in her beat-up Hyundai dropped her in this weird little place on Narragansett Bay. She had never experienced anything quite like Pell — a town that staged unicycle jousts in front of the mayor's house every Thursday afternoon, host of the largest commercial alligator farm north of the Carolinas, and, as an odd counterbalance, the birthplace of the country's most reputable nondenominational seminary — in other words, a town where oddballs, freaks, and castaways of every feather could make a home.

She had spent most of her time in Pell doing little more than studying her craft under the tutelage of Bart Cozen, the stingy fifty-something mortician. This version of her life had been going peaceably enough until...

Laurie held up a brown bottle with no label. "Sip?"

"More of your toilet wine? No thank you."

Laurie swilled from the bottle. She towered over Jillian by a good eight inches, which wasn't hard considering Jillian had stopped growing at sixteen, barely making it past the five-foot mark. Whereas Jillian was mostly quiet and sarcastic, Laurie was loud and direct, lacking any subtlety. They made a good pair.

"How many stiffs are you dressing up today?"

"Just two — two peas in a measly little pod. How do you think Frank would like it if you died and someone called you a stiff?"

"He wouldn't give a fuck. Words ain't going to make anyone's death any better or worse."

"Any news I need to know? Any gossip from around the water cooler?"

"Oh, I almost forgot! Get this: The world's still ending, Jill."

"Fine with me. I've been saying for years we could use a good apocalypse. All in all, I have few complaints. Those tentacled bastards have done the survivors a great service."

"Like hell. Somebody kill me already. Nothing to do anymore but eat, drink, and fuck, and I'm shit out of luck with Frank on that last one. If you're looking for fireworks in the bedroom, he's a sparkler at best."

Jillian could understand what her friend meant, considering how much human life had changed since the invasion. Still, she could not fathom why anyone would want to go back to such a pointless existence.

Ceaseless chirping from cellphones and, worse, their owners. Traffic. Mindless time sucks, such as endless photo scrolls on Instagram, live-streams about "super cute" makeup looks, and reality TV shows starring misbehaving idiots lacking an iota of cleverness, decorum, or intellect. Politics and politicians, and the acolytes who blindly follow them, adore them, pledge their willingness to kill and die for the cause. The scourge of roadside litter, since expanded to include the picked-clean skeletons of her former neighbors. Shitty pop music vomiting from the overheads of stores and restaurants, and from the speakers wired to her car radio. Rush-rush-rushing to fulfill every little obligation, while the real marrow of life went uneaten. Fireworks every weekend night from May through September. Sports stadiums packed with drunken revelers in face paint and plus-sized jerseys. Loud-as-fuck motorcycles, sports cars, or other self-indulgent noisemakers favored by men with fragile egos and, as the psychology suggested, microscopic ding-dongs. Growing threats of annihilation from thermonuclear, chemical, or biological means. Ambition. The twenty-four-seven news cycle. The embarrassment of family. And stuff — so much useless stuff.

Almost none of it was worth mourning, with few exceptions. *The Scream, Join Hands,* and *Juju* albums from Siouxsie and the Banshees. Cranberry scones from Necromancy Artisanal Bakery on the way to work, and seaweed salads from Ninjitsu Sushi on the way home. The convenience of tampons. And cat videos. She would forfeit anything she had left for the privilege of spending an hour or two gawking at the smudged screen of her smartphone, smiling and cooing as cats went about their business of being dicks to humans, dogs, and other cats. Everything else could be wiped clean.

"You think the government will ever get its shit together?" Laurie asked.

"I don't know if the government still exists; if it does, it doesn't know what to do with itself. How do you solve a problem like a thousand giant squid poking from holes in the sky and razing all of the world's Jamba Juices to the ground?"

"Easy. Nuke 'em."

"I imagine they've tried that," Jillian said. "I'd be willing to bet there's at least one Plains state that's been reduced to a glass sheet and dusted with radioactive ash, and I'll bet you the tentacles are still dangling from the bellies of the clouds overhead, no worse for wear."

"No one's seen any sign of the Army, Navy, Air Force, Marines. All standing around with their dicks in their hands. Not so much as a fart from a fighter jet or a tank since this whole shitstorm started."

"Coast Guard. Don't forget them."

Laurie took another pull from the brown bottle, sucking on air. She blew twice into the bottle's mouth. *Foop-foop.*

"Listen," Jillian said, "the sun's going down, and I don't want you wandering the streets when those things decide it's feeding time again."

"I'll go," Laurie said, "but not because I'm scared of those fuckers. I'm sick of living like a rat scurrying in the basement walls, just waiting for a man with a big stick to come along and break its back. I'll die on my feet, not on my knees."

"Funny, I thought you enjoyed spending time on your knees."

Laurie smiled at the joke and said, "Later, slut."

Jillian showed Laurie to the door. Laurie filed out slowly and found the asphalt, her eyes scanning the drooping purple sky. Jillian watched as Laurie pitched the bottle into the street. Glass shattered. She sighed as Laurie turned the corner and disappeared behind a pile of rubble and rebar.

Chapter 3
The Outsider

Don't be a callous prick.

The phrase jumped into Jillian's head every time she stood in front of a shell-shocked widow or a grown man slobbering snot over the paperwork to send the remains of his dear departed mother off to a hole in the ground or the rattling bed of a two-thousand-degree furnace. Rote, like the multiplication tables — *seven times seven equals forty-nine.*

She had heard this pearl of wisdom during the first two minutes of "Mastering Empathy," a day-long class from her first semester at Still Lakes Center for the Mortuary Arts. The instructor, a pale and balding stick of a man with a John Waters mustache, had droned on for three and a half hours, but Jillian thought he could have cut it after those five telling words — *Don't be a callous prick.*

Translation: When interacting with grieving families, give a shit, or at least pretend to.

She had taken the instructor's meaning to heart as she moved through her classes and stood in front of families of limited means who came to Still Lakes solely because most of the mortuary services were free, so the students could practice their craft. She got so proficient at not being a callous prick, in fact, that her classmates had dubbed her "Faker Futch." She could produce tears on command, make her voice tremble as if distraught, and offer some well-placed words of comfort that might make someone who had lost everything feel as though the walls were not coming down around them.

Manufacturing sympathy was her superpower. She saw herself as an actor on a stage, playing a role, much like the spandex-clad heroes of her youth.

She put this skill to good use as she stood in front of Betty DeWeese.

"He'd just gone out for a run," Betty said. "We told him not to go, because of those damned things. We said, 'Dad, stay inside and run the stairs.' But he insisted, said he wasn't going to live like a caged animal. He thought it was safe."

One of Betty's sisters had found their father an hour later at the foot of the backyard rose garden, she explained, his face blue, the victim of an apparent heart attack. They weren't sure if he'd even gotten the chance to get his miles in.

"Was he religious?" Jillian asked.

Betty wagged her head. "None of us are," she said. "Especially not now."

"Can you get him here so we can prepare him for the viewing?"

"How would I do that?" Betty said. "Strap him to a goddamn skateboard?"

Laurie sniggered from the corner.

Shut up, Jillian mouthed to her friend.

"Don't you worry, Betty," Jillian said. "I'll come get him. Just give me your address. Better yet, Laurie will show me the way. She'll help me."

"I will?" Laurie asked.

"You will," Jillian said, and then turned back to Betty. "And you and your family can come by tomorrow morning so everyone can say their goodbyes, celebrate the good things your dad did with his life. Just pick out something nice that I can dress him in. He'll want to look his best."

Funny thing about the apocalypse, or at least funny about this apocalypse in particular: People still wanted to mourn their loved ones properly, even though they themselves could easily end up on the slab later the same day. Something about the sacredness of tradition, Jillian figured, the expectation, the fact that it was the normal course of business, the way the world was supposed to work. Surely not everyone in town who lost someone came to Jillian to send off their deceased loved ones, but she was surprised by the number of folks who did. Astounded, in fact. Word of her "services" had traveled from mouth to ear, and Laurie — her one-person marketing department — had a big mouth...the biggest, in fact.

Not that Jillian had anything to gain from her generosity. She asked for money from no one, because dollars and cents no longer had any value. She supposed she did what she did purely out of tradition too, because it was what she had been programmed to do. Besides, she loved to lose herself in the work, the art of it all.

Jillian walked Betty to the front door. A bubble rose in her stomach as she scanned the leaden sky, praying her eyes would not show her something horrid. No reddish hue, the apparent presage of the tentacled monsters' arrival — just a normal, cloud-puffed sky.

After Betty's departure, Jillian cataloged her needs in preparation for the excursion to the DeWeeses' home: a cadaver bag, for obvious reasons; a reasonably sharp blade, for defense; and a bottle of water, in case she got caught out in the open for longer than she wanted. She readied the gurney for the road while Laurie looked on.

"It's, what, four blocks or so?" Jillian peered out the window again. "The coast seems clear."

"Relax," Laurie said. "Ain't no one around here going to rustle your feathers while *I'm* around."

"Twenty minutes there," Jillian estimated. "Thirty minutes back, giving ten minutes for drag. No sweat."

Jillian had another superpower to her credit: the power over death itself. Through the magic of postmorbid cosmetology, she could make the dead look as though they were still alive. Close enough, anyway. In her mind, making corpses look half-human — fit for a send-off — was probably the only thing she did well, and she'd keep doing it until an internal governor spoke up and hollered, "Enough!"

The image of her high school "soulmate," Timmy Labreque, flashed through her mind. He hadn't been a boyfriend, per se, but he had been her first, and her only until her twenty-second birthday, when she had finally let him go.

Like all proper goth kids, she and Timmy wore so-called corpse paint nearly every day of their senior year at Greater Dracut Public High School: an all-white mask with hollows of black circling the eyes, suggesting the empty sockets of the newly skeletonized, and jagged black lines around the mouth, to mimic teeth freed from the prison of fleshy lips. Maybe she should adopt her old look again, given her dark work. If only she knew where to get her hands on some decent corpse paint...

Sometimes, in matters of trauma, no amount of makeup could tidy up a corpse, the damage just too severe. Even then she found ways to surprise herself.

Molly Gerber came to mind.

Molly had lived a few streets over, until a many-toothed sucker from one of those things' tentacles removed half of her face. When her husband, Crispin, came to Jillian and asked her to "restore Molly's beauty" for the funeral, she felt obligated to help. She even went to the Gerbers' home, and spent hours talking to Crispin about the things in Molly's life she held dear. His wife loved exotic animals, he'd told her — big cats, mainly, and the Bengal tiger in particular — so Jillian decided to hide Molly's wounds by tilting her head away from the casket opening and painting the rest of her face with orange and black tiger stripes, the wisps of whiskers added for effect. Crispin's jaw dropped when Jillian lifted the casket to show him, and then he started crying.

Perhaps she had done too good a job.

After the brief ceremony in the parlor, after everyone but Crispin had gone home, Jillian returned to find him curled up in the casket with his dead wife, nuzzling her, one hand up her blouse and doing God knows what else with the hand she couldn't see. She gasped, horrified, but who was she to judge how people grieved?

Sometimes she worried about her mental state, because she felt nothing — *nothing* — when a fresh corpse rolled into her prep room. In mortuary school, the smells wafting from a corpse's interior bothered her at first, and some of the more complex anatomy turned her stomach, but she learned to cope. Thoughts of death, her own or otherwise, did not absorb her; once they took root, she knew she wouldn't be able to shake them. Numbness made her good at her job, she figured. It's why she was willing to tramp halfway across a torn-to-pieces town to retrieve the corpse of a man she had never met.

She opened the funeral home's back door and slid the gurney down the ramp. The wheels squealed more loudly than she would have liked. With Laurie leading the way, Jillian lifted the gurney over the calf-deep crater in the driveway, evidence of a mammoth tentacle that had hit its mark. Off the sidewalk, into the street, rubber tires rattled across small divots in the macadam.

Into the warzone.

The skeletons of abandoned vehicles lined the street. Ford pickups. Saabs. Subarus. Some were charred or flattened — doors ajar, gas caps yawning open, the tanks sucked dry. Glass from shattered windshields and side windows crunched underfoot.

At the first intersection with a cross street, they surprised a skinny border collie picking meat off a human leg. The domino-patterned dog growled as they squeaked past. No trace of the leg's owner.

"It's so quiet," Jillian said. The gurney's racket seemed deafening.

Laurie gave no reply, making Jillian think her friend was nervous too.

Low, gray clouds hid the sky. With the threat of the monsters removed, or at least on hiatus, she suspected other threats would arise.

Smaller monsters — other humans, mostly.

Wind rustled the switch grass as they approached the salt marsh. A red-winged blackbird alighted on the spine of a bulrush plant. Jillian hadn't been this far south in months, since the time before monsters became real.

"How much farther?" she asked.

"Look," Laurie said. She nodded her head toward a stilted house on the marsh side of the street. A shirtless man stood in the doorway. He stepped outside, revealing his nakedness, and then pissed into the still water beneath his deck.

"It's supposed to shrink when it gets cold, right?" Laurie said. "Temp's got to be eighty degrees today, so what's his excuse?"

"Shut up and keep your head down."

A few turns later they arrived at the DeWeese home. The body of Doug DeWeese lay beneath a thin powder-blue blanket by the side of the porch, his feet still snug in their Nikes. Jillian knocked on the front door. Betty answered, and then made a point to introduce her two sisters, Bella and Bonnie. Neither was older than thirty, each showing tired eyes rimmed with red. Jillian offered her condolences to each sister, trying to sound sincere. Betty handed over a garment bag.

"Dad's favorite suit, shoes, shirt, tie," she said. "He didn't wear socks. Never wore socks." Fresh tears filled her eyes.

"You should go back inside," Jillian said. "I'll take care of everything this evening. Stop by the funeral home tomorrow, whenever you're ready."

She and Laurie then zipped Doug DeWeese's remains into the gray vinyl cadaver bag and — "on three" — hoisted him onto the gurney.

"I want to watch what you do with him," Laurie said as they wheeled the gurney back to the funeral home.

"No chance."

"All this hassle and I don't even get to watch the horror show?"

"Show some respect, Laurie. Besides, I know a fainter when I see one. My scalpel comes out, you won't last three seconds."

***

Like the pelt of a skinned mink, the man's running pants dangled from Jillian's gloved hand. They reeked of piss and shit. She dropped them unceremoniously into a stainless-steel trashcan.

She eyed the naked corpse that had once been Doug DeWeese III, the last principal in Blunk, Brown, and DeWeese P.C., Pell's only native law firm devoted to business and real estate transactions. The firm's three partners had gone down in order, according to Betty DeWeese — first Blunk, flattened to the width of a ham sandwich by a gargantuan tentacle in the first wave of attacks; then Brown, just a week later, crushed by the collapsed roof of his smashed-to-bits estate home on the outskirts of town; and, finally, the elusive DeWeese, Betty's father, apparently done in by a boring old heart attack while out for a run.

"What a shame," Jillian told DeWeese's graying corpse, "to have such an unremarkable end in such a remarkable moment in history."

She thought of her own father, another old man, wondering if he had managed to survive the topsy-turvy times. Years had passed between them. She hadn't seen him since the day she left for Pell. A cousin's text from a year earlier had described her father as sickly and frail, with a nasty cough and yellowed skin. She couldn't imagine he had endured — hoped against it, in fact, purely out of compassion. If he didn't have a TV to watch and cold beer to swill through all this mess, he'd probably rather be dead.

A memory came to her.

She was five, maybe six, sitting on her father's lap, their eyes glued to the flickering screen. A can of Pabst sweated on the folding table next to Dad's plaid recliner. Like every other Saturday night, they sat in awed silence, watching public-access reruns of delightfully amateurish wrestling matches put on by the Bay State Grapplers Alliance. She basked in the boot-stomping brilliance of her heroes, done up in neon spandex, luchador masks, and, when the need arose, ample amounts of stage blood.

A tag-team match featured two plain-as-white-bread do-gooders — Pioneer Boone, who wore a fringed jacket, beaded moccasins, and a coonskin cap to the ring, and the unremarkable, overweight Buddy

Ray Smith, who wore snug purple tights that did him no favors — versus Igor Nemchinov and Raul Santiago, a pair of mustache-twirling baddies known collectively as The Reds. The bad guys cheated every chance they got, but the good guys scored the pinfall.

Makes perfect sense, she remembered thinking.

The main event pitted her two favorite grapplers against one another: The Dying Man, a black-clad nihilist famous for his intense pre-match interviews, during which he rambled about the duality of the human animal and the pointlessness of life, existential concepts a five- or six-year-old couldn't possibly grasp, though she savored his diatribe's every word; and his opposite, The Quarterback, a blond-haired, blue-eyed hunk in shoulder pads and a numbered half-shirt, the pretty-boy darling who always found a way to get the W.

She couldn't remember how The Quarterback had won the match, and she supposed it didn't matter.

Those muscle-bound men, not to mention a handful of female bruisers whose "wrestling" repertoire consisted solely of pulling hair and scratching each other's eyes out, seemed to live in an alternate reality where every quarrel could be settled by tossing a fistful of salt in someone's eyes or clobbering him with a folding chair. The only thing in the world of any value was a flimsy strap of plastic and leather, better known as the BSGA Championship Belt. She had imagined herself alongside them, among them, wearing a tattered black wedding dress, a chaotic mask of corpse paint, and a malignant smile. Her in-ring character: The Wicked Widow. In her most vivid fantasies, she would lead The Dying Man to the wrestling ring on a dog leash and then linger. Her sole task: to prowl the ring's outskirts and distract the referee or sneakily hand over a "foreign object" *du jour* — a small blade or brass knuckles, perhaps, or a tidy bag of white powder fit for blistering an opponent's face or blinding his eyes — anything to help The Dying Man in his cause.

She shook the memory from her head; no point in ruminating on such things. Her father, as well as each of her childhood heroes from the BSGA, was likely long dead.

Heroes had gone extinct. Only monsters remained.

Jillian gloved up and placed her instruments on the stainless-steel tray — forceps, retractors, a trio of blades, a spool of suture. She then picked up a grease pencil and etched a mark onto a whiteboard, this one for Doug DeWeese III, in a column accounting for folks who had succumbed to seemingly natural causes over the past several months. Only three marks there, now four.

A second column kept a running tally of each citizen who had been crushed, trampled, torn apart, or otherwise annihilated by the invaders. Fifty-six, by her count. A third column, bearing the "A/S" designation, short for "assumed swallowed," accounted for Pell natives rumored to have been consumed and digested by one or more of those *things*. She counted seventy-one names there.

"Damn the Ochos," she whispered, her pet name for the eight-armed cephalopods that first appeared in the skies over Pell months earlier. At least she figured they had eight arms, like every other cephalopod. She'd never gotten close enough to count.

She saw it as her responsibility to keep a record of all those lost, so they could be properly mourned and honored once the human world righted itself — if it ever did. Likely, more than half of Pell's unaccounted for had either been swept into the sea or were rotting beneath tons of rubble.

She eyed her muddy reflection in the brushed-metal table. Given the apocalypse, dying alone seemed inevitable. She had no outstanding qualities other than sarcasm, disaffectedness, and a hand-me-down wardrobe borrowed from a bedroom on the funeral home's second floor — hardly enough to make her interesting to a member of the opposite sex, even in a place as broadminded as Pell.

Not that she needed anyone other than Albert, still unaccounted for.

Within a day, she would have to make yet another trek to the other side of town, where she had lived prior to the invasion, looking for Albert. The Ochos had reduced their former residence to another pile of detritus to be picked over, one shattered brick and broken timber at a time.

If Albert had survived, he would meet her there. He would know to stay put. If not, she would have her answer, and she could mourn him and move on. The question: How much more time would she give him?

An insistent knocking echoed through the prep room. She removed her gloves, exited the cool air, and entered the sitting room. She hurried to the front door and peered through the cloudy sidelight. Laurie stood on the welcome mat, looking somber.

"Miss me already?" Jillian asked as she turned the knob.

"Something like that," Laurie said through the glass.

The door sailed open. A gentle gust caressed Jillian's cheek.

"That was easier than I thought."

A man leaned into the doorway.

Jillian screamed in surprise.

"Sorry, Jill," Laurie said. "I didn't know how to warn you."

"May I come in?" the man said.

"Do I have a choice?" Jillian asked.

"We all have choices," he responded. "Let's talk."

Chapter 4
Meat on a Slab

The man leaned against the back of a plush couch in the sitting room, adjacent to the parlor. Ever polite, Jillian asked if he'd like something to drink. She didn't bother offering anything to Laurie. She fetched a lukewarm bottle of Crystal Spring from the pantry. She also tucked a dull steak knife into her underwear's waistband.

"Did Laurie tell you I'd be stopping by?" he asked.

"Must have slipped her mind," Jillian said.

Laurie looked ashamed.

"Do you know who I am?" the man said.

"Do you know who *I* am?" Jillian countered.

"I know everything that happens in Pell, and I've had my eye on you."

"Creepy."

"Kip Detto," he said, hand to his chest. "One of the principals of Detto Windows and Doors."

"How's business these days?"

A grin stretched across his face.

"Laurie was right about you — a real smartass," he added. "Honey, I'm the man who's going to keep you safe. The man who's going to keep us *all* safe, clear away the rubble, and rebuild."

Jillian knew the name. She also knew that Kip's twin brother, Kyle, had been taken by one of the Ochos early on — "A/S," assumed swallowed. Laurie had gabbed about the Dettos more than once, in the way people in small towns talk about their neighbors. Kyle had been the superior of the Detto boys at pretty much everything that mattered, she had said: smarter, better looking, harder working, ready with a kind word for anyone who deserved it; formerly a high-scoring winger and captain of Pell-Rask Municipal High School's ice hockey team, the Pell-Rask Titans, whereas Kip had been a third-pair defenseman better known as the team's hot-tempered goon; president of the family business to Kip's director of sales; and, Laurie had intimated with wide-eyed delight, Kyle had been the better endowed of the two.

"Praise the gods," Jillian said. "A big, strong *man* has come down from the mountain to save the day."

"Is that supposed to be funny?" he asked. "'Cause save the day is *exactly* what I'm going to do."

"Don't worry about little ol' me, here minding my own business."

"It's your funeral." His attempt at cleverness made him smile. "I'll just tell you what I came here to say: I'm taking the generator."

"Pardon me?"

"The generator. You don't need it, and frankly, it's probably going to get you killed anyway."

"*What?*"

"After five, six months of hell, no one has seen those tentacled fuckers in over a week. That shit's over. Now the tough part begins. The government's not coming to save our asses, and now that the threat has removed itself, anyone who survived is going to come crawling out of the mud, looking to find ways to move forward, and that includes taking what doesn't belong to them."

"Imagine that."

"So it's settled."

"You don't know the government's not coming."

"I was in the reserves, honey. I know. They would have shown up by now."

"Throwing on a pair of camouflage coveralls and rolling around in the bushes one weekend a month doesn't make you an expert. My guess is as good as yours, and I think it's too soon to wave the white flag on American democracy."

"I'm not going to argue with you," he said. "You want to live through the mess that's coming? You're going to have to keep quiet, not advertise our resources to every dipstick who rolls through town."

"Roving bands of murderous thugs and rapists? Is that what you're here to protect me from?"

"Maybe. Probably. Eventually. But this is my town, and I'm going to make sure our resources are safe: food, fuel, women."

"So I'm a resource now. Hear that, Laurie? Our vaginas make us as valuable as propane and Twinkies."

"Don't be so offended," he said. "You know what I mean. Every one of us brings something to the table. Yourself included."

"I'll keep my generator to myself... Kip, was it?"

"Look, you're lucky we let you stay at all, with you being from away and everything."

"I've lived here for seven years. Almost eight."

"A brief moment in time as far as I'm concerned. Look, I'm taking the damned generator, whether you like it or not. You're welcome to benefit from everything else we have to offer: community, safety, food, water, you name it. But the generator doesn't belong to you anymore. If you don't like it, start walking."

"What about the bodies?"

"Bodies?"

"This is a funeral home. People bring bodies here so they can have a civilized, structured goodbye. So they can have *some* normalcy in an abnormal time."

"Not anymore. Burn the bodies."

"I need the generator for that, genius."

"Drag them over to the bog. Torch 'em in the mud. I hate to break the news to you, but civilized funerals are a luxury Pell can no longer afford."

"I have a body on the table right now, preparing it for a ceremony I have to do tomorrow morning. What am I supposed to tell the family?"

"Not my problem."

"Who made you God's gift to Pell? It's my fucking generator."

"Really? The way I see it, you're a squatter. This is Bart Cozen's place."

Jillian got the sense she was about to lose more than just the generator.

"She works for Bart," Laurie interjected. "*Worked* for him, anyway. She was here the day everything went to shit. You know the story, Kip. She belongs here."

"Who is it?" he asked.

Jillian contorted her face in annoyance and asked, "Who is what?"

"Who's the stiff on the table back there?"

"I'm not telling you that."

"It's not a matter of doctor-patient confidentiality, toots. Whoever it is, he or she isn't going to care. It's meat on a slab."

"It's Doug DeWeese. The attorney."

"Fuck," he said under his breath. His demeanor softened and his swagger diminished. "He was my first coach. Practically taught me how to skate and take a wrist shot."

She could see him thinking through his next move, some slow-moving mechanism turning gears in his head.

"Look," she said. "Let me finish Mister DeWeese. I'll figure out other arrangements for anyone else who comes my way."

***

Ten minutes later, after she nudged Laurie and Kip toward the exit, Jillian slammed the door to the prep room and paced the perimeter. The overhead lights were still on, for now, but after tomorrow's viewing, everything was going to change if she didn't figure something out. She'd gotten used to the cold, dark nights, lost in her thoughts. The generator came into play only to facilitate her work. With that *resource* — Kip Detto's word — removed, she might as well be living in the Stone Age.

"Tomorrow problems," she told Doug DeWeese's corpse.

Almost in response, the body released a long, cacophonous burst of flatulence. It started low and built to the pitch of an elephant's trumpet. Postmortem flatulence was nothing new to Jillian, but she'd never heard a dead man's fart so loud and distinct.

The corpse's insides shifted. To Jillian, it looked like a finger poking out, pushing against the wall of the abdomen.

"Curious," she said.

She poised her scalpel over the spot and readied to make her incision.

Chapter 5
Cuts

Jillian slipped the obsidian blade into DeWeese's distended belly. She started the midline incision two inches beneath the xiphoid at the base of the sternum, skirted the belly button, and stopped a few inches north of the corpse's graying pubic bush. The pallid flesh opened to show a cushion of sickly yellow fat. She pried back the striated flaps of abdominal muscle, revealing the purple sac of stomach and gray tangle of intestine — ordinary, normal, peachy.

And then she saw something else, something...foreign.

It had an almost glandular appearance, the moist smoothness of a healthy liver. As she bent for a closer look, she noticed a faint pulse — and then the twitch of an eye.

A tentacle clamped onto Jillian's left wrist. First came surprise, and then pain. Barbs bit through her vinyl glove and sank into the skin beneath. The tentacle wound up her forearm. Small punctures, as if pricked by the spines of a cactus or the quills of a porcupine.

Slowly, the rest of the creature emerged from the slit in DeWeese's abdomen. The sound of its exit reminded Jillian of a shoe being liberated from thick mud. The octopus perched on the corpse's chest. Its tentacles fanned out and hugged the blue-tinted torso. Her wrist began to burn.

She tried to pull away, but the tentacle would not give — affixed, latched on, one with her flesh. She then remembered the scalpel. The blade sliced the air and made a clear cut through the tentacle, effortless, yet the severed arm maintained its hold on her wrist. The octopus wriggled off the table and dropped to the floor, trailing electric-blue blood, and slumped in the far corner where the stainless-steel storage freezers met the cinder-block wall.

Despite its separation from the rest of the body, the tentacle tightened around her wrist. She tossed the scalpel onto the metal tray. The blade rattled with a resonant clang. With as much care as she could, she grabbed the slimy tendril and tried to yank it free. The action sent bolts of pain coursing through her arm, from the tips of her fingers to the ball of her shoulder. Finally, the tentacle gave way, and she was surprised to see a small tooth — a glistening black tusk — in the center of each sucker. She dropped the severed limb to the floor and watched it thrash on the tile.

"You little shit," she seethed.

Primal anger swelled within her. She approached the octopus, still curled into a ball in the corner, leaking fluids. It looked like a normal octopus, as far as she could tell, though somehow more primitive — a trio of gnarled horns above each stalk-like eye, Braille-like protuberances dotting its alien flesh. She didn't want to kill it, didn't want to kill *anything*, and hadn't killed anything on purpose — a squirrel darting beneath her tire, she recalled, the ants she trampled from the simple act of walking the pavement, the millions of microscopic bugs she'd done in by scrubbing the dead flesh from her body in the shower — but this thing, a *fucking octopus*, had assaulted her in the sanctuary of her embalming room, a mile from the open ocean.

Of course, the creature had to be related to the Ochos, the destroyers of her world. Maybe, she thought, this was a baby Ocho. A cute, frightened baby Ocho.

Her scalpel would make quick work of it. Two or three slashes with the keen blade and it would be all over — calamari for the grill, not that she would eat it. Her lips hadn't tasted animal flesh in a decade.

Her wrist had gone numb. In fact, she could say the same of her whole hand and her arm up to the elbow. She exercised her fingers to make sure they still worked. She bled from a dozen or more pinpricks on her wrist and forearm.

"I'm too sober to deal with this shit," she said.

She emptied a small trashcan onto the floor and advanced on the octopus. As she stood before it, the creature held up two tentacles, almost in a defensive posture, as if pleading. She tossed the trashcan on top of it, catching one of its tentacles between the plastic rim and the floor until the appendage retreated, leaving a smear of translucent slime in its place. She then hunted for something heavy to weigh the trashcan down, so her captive could not escape. She settled on a head block, the dense plastic cradle she used to position a corpse's skull during the embalming process.

Her nerves danced. First Kip Detto came along and told her he was going to steal her generator, and then the son of a bitch threatened to make her leave town if she didn't "fall in line." And now this: an octopus the size of a Frisbee — with toothed tentacles, no less — crawling out of a corpse's abdominal cavity and assaulting her. What was the world coming to?

She eyed DeWeese's corpse on the table.

"Tomorrow problems," she said.

She hurried to the cabinet and rooted through the supplies, zeroing in on a half-empty bottle of rubbing alcohol. She poured the liquid onto the holes in her wrist and forearm. The sting made her wince. She stripped off her vinyl examination gloves and dropped them to the floor. She turned off the overhead lights. As she went to close the door, she turned back to the cute little baby Ocho trapped beneath the trashcan and said, "I want you to stay here and think about what you've done."

She paused for a moment and laughed, adding, "I must be losing my fucking mind."

***

She needed air. Or a shot of hard liquor. She had nearly depleted Bart Cozen's stores of spirits in the liquor cabinet — brandy, rye, vodka — over the past few months, so she decided to ration. Fresh air was a healthier choice anyway.

She went to the front door and peered through the sidelight glass. The gray sky bore no tint of red, the color that seemed to signal an attack from above. In the past, the skies would darken to that terribly bloody shade, and then, usually within a minute, devils would descend from the clouds: walls rattling, people screaming, earth shaking — tentacles laying Pell to waste. For now, anyway, the scene appeared to be safe.

It was late August, by her best guess, and the days had grown noticeably shorter, the nights cooler. Within a month, the world would turn dark and cold. She wondered if the Ochos had somehow sensed the looming seasonal change and made haste for someplace more hospitable to turn into a nightmarish hellscape — Miami,

Atlanta, Houston, Mercury. The thought tumbled from her mind. She had heard cephalopods, particularly octopuses, described as intelligent creatures, but she refused to accept that they were capable of actively plotting the overthrow of a rival civilization.

As far as she knew, only one species possessed such a diabolical mind.

Surely the invasion wasn't over, no matter what that Rambo wannabe Kip Detto said. Okay, so maybe cellphones no longer worked. And the electrical grid was offline. And no one could tap into the Internet. And televisions were useless. And no planes flew overhead, no cars traveled the road, and no signs of life came from the outside world. So what? It didn't necessarily mean this calamity had reached the rest of the globe.

Still, things didn't look promising.

At times she wished life would return to normal — semi-normal, anyway — but her gut told her not to get her hopes up. The terrestrial octopus in her embalming room was all the proof she needed. Maybe this new development marked stage two of the invasion.

She heaved her travel bag over her shoulder and exited through the back door so she could turn off the generator. She then climbed onto her bike — an ancient maroon ten-speed she had liberated from a neighbor's demolished shed — and rolled down the driveway, bunny-hopping over the foot-deep trench puddled with rainwater, and into the street. The asphalt wore a white crust, remnants of the salt rains that always seemed to accompany each Ocho attack. The bike's crank arm squealed and clicked with each rotation.

She made a hard right onto Terrapin Street and steered into a driveway a few houses down. She ditched the bike on an unkempt patch of lawn baked brown by the sun. She hurried to the front door and knocked insistently. Business to settle, she would say.

Laurie Woolly cracked the door open an inch, just enough so Jillian could see the guilt on her friend's face.

"So... What the fuck was that all about?" Jillian asked.

"Sorry, Jill. What Kip Detto wants, Kip Detto usually gets. When he asked me to help convince you to part ways with your generator, I knew there was no arguing with him. I had no choice but to go along with it."

"I find that hard to believe." Jillian eyed the clouds. "Aren't you going to invite me in?"

Laurie slipped through the opening and stepped outside. A horrid stink came with her.

"Sorry," she said. "Frank's been on the warpath again, and now he's sleeping it off. One too many pulls on the bottle."

Jillian noticed a heavy perfume. *Dead Flowers*, she would have named it.

"Don't sweat what happened, but you wouldn't believe what just happened to me..."

Laurie talked over her.

"Kip's not a total asshole," she said. "Just seventy-five percent of one. He means well — honestly, he does. He just doesn't know how to express himself without sounding like a complete jerk-off."

Jillian took the interruption as a sign, as the universe's way of telling her to keep quiet about the octopus in her embalming room. She knew it sounded crazy, and she knew the story would make *her* sound crazy.

"Between you and me, I have no intention of giving Kip my generator," she said. "I know his type: all bark."

Laurie cringed.

"He bites when he has to," she said. "I think he's just trying to bring everyone together. Believe it or not, he's trying to protect us. Trying to protect Pell."

"That's what all the fascists say."

Laurie checked over her shoulder, toward her front door.

"I'll let you go," Jillian said. "Just wanted you to know I'm heading home for a bit. Back to the old 'hood."

"Don't be too long," Laurie said. "It's going to be dark soon enough. Anyway, I hope you find him this time."

Jillian righted her bike and walked it into the road, stopping to lift the front tire over a downed telephone pole. Once clear, she pedaled off, leaving Laurie's dilapidated house in her wake.

She hoped to find him too. Albert.

Rubble and rubbish littered the streets: torn asphalt, bombed-out cars, blackened bodies slowly turning to skeletons, bags of fresh garbage left at the curb. She had been making this trip at least twice a week since the Ochos arrived, in rare moments of calm. She knew the road's every turn, every obstacle, but she ran into the occasional surprise — escapees from the alligator farm down the road, for example. Never had she expected to be hissed at by a six-foot-long alligator lounging on a neighbor's front lawn, baring its conical teeth and pale, pink tongue. Not in Rhode Island anyway.

Circumstances had somehow prepared her for the gauntlet of the apocalypse. She had gotten used to leading a life of abstinence and absence, so the biggest difference between then and now was having to flush the powder-room toilet with salty rainwater gathered from the rain barrel outback or do her business in a hole in the ground, hidden in the cellar. In some ways, Jillian's life had become better. She had a nicer place to call home now — the Cozen Family Funeral Home and Crematory, where she was "a squatter," as Kip had so dickishly pointed out — as opposed to her one-bedroom apartment, and she liked the respect and responsibilities that came from being Pell's chief mortician. It felt good to embalm again. In her apprenticeship, she had been doing mostly paperwork, assisting Bart Cozen in the undressing and dressing of corpses upon intake, and the postmorbid cosmetology, while Bart had done most of the heavy lifting, so to speak. She surprised herself at how much she remembered, how much she liked getting her hands dirty again — cutting, scooping, stitching, and then making the bodies pretty for the few friends and family who remained.

Minutes later she was back home, or where home had once been: a two-story apartment building since razed to the foundation, with the exception of a partial wall standing against the wind. The rest had been reduced to a hill of splintered timbers and shattered brick, with the tatters of left-behind possessions sprinkled throughout: torn clothes, decapitated dolls, ripped-to-shreds couch cushions, weathered and broken picture frames.

She had picked through the site dozens of times since the day the free world went to shit.

Chapter 6
Awake for the Nightmare

The last day of March — muggy and warm for early spring in Rhode Island, sixty-five degrees with a light wind coming in from the bay. She was driving to the funeral home after a quick bite at the luncheonette, tailing a blue Ford F-150 and thinking about her plans for the hot summer ahead.

Raindrops sprinkled the windshield, gentle at first and then in a torrent. She had just heard the weather forecast — no rain for the rest of the week, they said. A globular pink mass struck her windshield. The glass splintered.

The radio suddenly went dead, and the midday sky turned dark, the color of congealed blood. Roiling clouds stretched from the horizon's edge to the heavens' highest reach. Each cloud carried an absurd freight: a writhing green-and-black ball that slowly unfurled into what seemed like a hundred colossal tentacles.

Monsters.

Tentacles snaked down every street, flattening houses, crushing vehicles, hurling bystanders to their doom. A behemoth fell from the sky, and the ground shook as it landed. Jillian watched from her driver's seat. The largest octopus she had ever seen — a hundred feet long, maybe two hundred — reached upward, as if seeking help. Massive tentacles descended from the clouds and linked arms with those of its earthbound mate. The two creatures worked in tandem to return the fallen monster to its place in the blood-streaked sky.

The truck in front of Jillian squealed into reverse and slammed into her car's grille. Her face bounced off the steering wheel. Dazed, she barely reacted when a massive tentacle slapped her car's windshield. Suckers the size of dinner plates squeaked against the glass. Then, suddenly, she was airborne. Her head smacked the car's ceiling.

When she came to, with a sprinkling of glass in her lap, her eyes showed her a horrifying landscape: thousands of fluorescent tentacles dangling from the heavens, waving with the wind, and most of Pell reduced to piles of debris, ash, and the battered bodies of her former neighbors.

The driver's side door wouldn't budge, so she crawled through the door's glassless window. She was surprised to see the car half submerged in the salt marsh at the road's edge. She sank up to the knee in coal-dark mud, her heart racing, realizing every second out in the open increased the odds of a swift and violent death. Urine warmed her thigh and trickled down her leg. She clawed her way through the mud and stumbled onto asphalt. Through crippling fear, she ran. Her eyes zeroed in on the spire of the Cozen Family Funeral Home and Crematory. The edges of her vision went white.

Moments later she collapsed onto Cozen's porch, wishing she could dream herself into a nightmare of a less traumatic sort.

Chapter 7
Making Friends the Hard Way

Shadows lengthened as Jillian lingered at the site of her former home. She guessed she had less than an hour of daylight left.

Each building she had passed along the way looked cold and lifeless — broken. Months of death-from-above assaults had left nearly every structure in Pell impaired in some way. To Jillian's good fortune, the Cozen Family Funeral Home and Crematory remained almost fully intact, with only a toppled cupola, some torn-away roof shingles, and a few broken windows, plus the wrecked driveway she preferred not to think about. Rainwater dripped from the bowed ceiling and down the walls, and the parlor reeked of mildew. The place wouldn't last much longer without the proper repairs — skills she did not yet possess.

Still, she had lived in far worse places.

Jillian considered the random hand of fate, how some homes and businesses had been completely obliterated, while others had gotten through with only minor damage. She could say the same about people — the ones who were left anyway.

After the first few attacks, she would step outside to clear the porch of leaves, branches, and dead shorebirds, among other debris. Other survivors would do the same, even though they realized more attacks would come, purely for the normalcy of routine tasks, or perhaps for the comfort of seeing another human face. A few neighbors — the old lady next door, a young family across the street — consoled each other, asked if they needed food or water, wished each other well. Weeks, maybe months, had passed since she had last seen any of them, making her think they had either skipped town, become despondent, or joined the ranks of the "A/S."

Now, other than Laurie Woolly, everyone else she knew in the world was either dead or missing. The list included Albert, who had been home in their shared apartment the day of the Ochos' opening salvo. She had lost so much already, so she refused to accept that she had lost him too.

She leaned the bicycle onto the cracked sidewalk fronting her old apartment building and wandered the perimeter. She circled the wreckage twice, whispering his name with a singsong lilt — *"Allie-Allie-Albert"* — as if her voice might somehow coax him out of his hiding spot or give him the strength to burst through the rubble of his would-be tomb.

A door slammed nearby. Jillian turned to see a man tramping the lawn of a cream-colored rancher with a heavy branch jutting from a hole in the roof.

Beard, flannel shirt, tattered blue jeans. Thirty-three years old, by her best guess, maybe thirty-five. It was hard to tell anymore.

"Looking for someone special, sweetheart?" he asked.

"Friends of mine." Plural, she thought, smart.

"You can come inside my place and wait. It's not safe out here."

"I can see that."

"Let me help you. Don't be rude now."

"I can take care of myself."

"Prove it." He circled her, like a shark in open water.

"Oh, I don't think you want me to do that."

"You've made it this far. There's got to be something special about you."

He stopped circling and stepped toward her.

She reared into a crouch and reached behind her. Her fingertips found the wooden handle of a sharpened sickle. She waved the curved blade in furious arcs, aping the gestures she remembered from the grainy kung fu flicks of her youth.

"Not to be impolite," she said, "but step one inch closer and I'll slice your belly and introduce you to your lower intestine."

"Relax," he said, showing his empty palms. "Just making conversation. Just being friendly."

"Why?" she said, channeling her hero, The Dying Man, from his pre-match monologues during Saturday-night airings of Bay State Grapplers Alliance events. "Life is meaningless, yours and mine. If you don't believe me, this blade will shuffle you off this mortal coil. You'll be gone in the time it takes to blink."

Despite her calm façade, she was screaming inside. The Dying Man and The Quarterback had taught her many things, none more important than the value of false bravado.

She kept her eyes on the creep as she retreated to her bicycle. As she climbed aboard, her hand slapped the handlebars. The sickle clattered to the asphalt. A miserable laugh found her ears. Fury rose within her as she turned to see him wearing a wide smile. For a second she considered stepping off her bike and carving a hole in his face. Instead, she pedaled away, fighting off the numbness in her hand and the weakness in her fear-stricken legs.

***

Back at the Cozen Family Funeral Home and Crematory, Jillian slumped onto a couch no more than ten feet from the front door.

The creep in the flannel shirt had interrupted her search, but no sign of Albert, yet again. How many more times could she make that trip? If the emotional torture weren't enough, now there was the all-too-real threat presented by former neighbors who had backslid into would-be rapists, murderers, and foot fetishists — all because of one measly apocalypse.

Surely the Ochos would come back too.

Thoughts of the Ochos reminded Jillian of the problem waiting for her in the embalming room — two problems, in fact: the cute but feisty little baby Ocho, injured and trapped beneath a bucket; and DeWeese's corpse, which she still had to dress and prepare for tomorrow's ceremony. Best not to mention to DeWeese's surviving daughters that she had found a pint-sized cephalopod in their father's gut, she figured.

First, she would heed one of the tenets of The Quarterback's best advice to his fans: "Brush your teeth, eat your vegetables, and don't smoke cigarettes," as the white-hat babyface used to preach to his fans. He had never been her favorite wrestler, though he had helped her understand the difference between right and wrong, more so than her father, at any rate. She headed to the kitchen, slathered her toothbrush with fresh paste, and scoured her mouth of any bacteria that might endanger her gums and teeth.

Her next task: Deal with the octopus. She would take the whole trashcan — octopus and all — and hurl it into the salt marshes so the poor little thing could make its way back to the ocean and live out the rest of its life, eating octopus food like a normal octopus. For a moment she wondered if the other octopuses would look at him differently because he had only seven arms instead of the eight God had given him.

"*Him*," she mouthed. "Octopuses could be hermaphrodites for all I know."

She just hoped that he, she, it — whatever kind of genitals the little critter had in its special place — would go peacefully. Fate hadn't exactly been on her side. She armed herself with a flashlight and a broom from Cozen's closet and wandered the maze-like halls until she arrived at the door to the embalming room. She took a deep breath and pulled the door handle.

The flashlight's white beam zig-zagged across the room. The trashcan was in the same position she had left it, the head block weighing it down. She wondered if she had made a huge mistake, remembering the childhood trauma of lifting the lid on a shoebox containing a wood frog she had captured in the grassy lot down the street; her father had given her the box but informed her only much later, as she prepared to dump the frog's corpse into the water circling the toilet, of the need to poke air holes into the lid.

She lifted the head block and placed it onto the adjacent table. Holding the broom as a defense and the flashlight tucked in her armpit, she lifted the trashcan and peered inside.

Nothing. The cute little baby Ocho was gone. *Poof!*

"Slippery motherfucker," she said.

The beam searched for any signs of escape, any clues of the octopus' whereabouts. Nothing. For a moment, she wondered if she had imagined the whole absurd event, if she was, in fact, losing her marbles.

A high-pitched squeak came from the table bearing DeWeese's corpse — the postmortem passing of gas. She shone the light into the open cavity. Had the octopus returned to its nook in the corpse's middle?

"Just my dirty luck," she said.

Then she heard it: a subtle tapping, the sound of one hard surface striking another. She froze, trying to zero in on the source. She whirled the flashlight around and shone the beam into the room's uppermost corner.

There, the octopus had curled itself into a tight ball, its suckers holding on for dear life. One of its remaining tentacles held a grease pencil and tapped the waxy tip against the stainless steel, just above the bank of freezers. The mirrored steel revealed a black scrawl, just beneath the spot where the octopus tapped.

A single word, written sloppily: *mercy.*

Chapter 8
Universal Language

Still and slack-jawed, Jillian studied the octopus' imperfect scrawl.

"You have *got* to be kidding me," she said under her breath.

The creature's rubbery flesh blazed red. She'd seen similar shades only in the plumage of cardinals and the paint of Corvettes. The octopus waved an arm in an intricate pattern, all circles and slashes, and then repeated the pattern twice more, as if trying to communicate with her through some sort of sign language.

Delirium — the only explanation for the absurdity her eyes showed her. She had heard octopuses described as remarkable creatures, curious and intelligent enough to solve complex problems. As far as she knew, though, they couldn't write or speak English. The octopus' barbs must have injected her with hallucinogenic venom, and the venom had invaded her brain and driven her to the brink of madness.

The pain in her wrist reminded her of the octopus' weapons, so she took two cautious steps toward the door. She wanted to run, to scream, to throw up, but curiosity compelled her to remain calm.

The octopus used the grease pencil to draw a thick line beneath its one-word plea — *mercy* — and then slid down the wall. It moved with the sluggish grace of a cold yolk dripping from a cracked egg.

Jillian backed up another pace and stepped behind the stainless-steel table, keeping the lure of Doug DeWeese's corpse between them.

"What do you want?" Jillian asked.

The octopus glided close enough to reach her with one of its amply suckered arms. The tentacle holding the grease pencil swept across the floor, leaving another word etched into the bare tile: *shelter*.

"You can understand me?"

Affirmative.

"Am I losing my mind?"

Indeterminate.

She watched its mantle expand and deflate, seeming to take in oxygen and expel its byproduct. The bulbous head throbbed with each processed breath. Minutes passed, human and cephalopod at a standstill.

"You ask for mercy," she said. "I'm not going to hurt you, at least not any more than I already have. Can you give me the same assurance?"

Affirmative, it wrote.

"A simple yes would suffice, so save us both the time. I have a thousand questions."

Proceed.

"Let's start small. What were you doing inside the corpse?"

Hiding.

"From what?"

The octopus gave no answer.

"What are you doing here?"

Visiting.

A moist sound burbled from a funnel at the base of the octopus' mantle. The appendage, which she assumed to be a breathing tube of sorts, reminded her of the nub of human intestine used to feed a colostomy bag.

Help, it penned, followed by another plea: *Water.*

"You need water?"

Please.

"Salt water?"

Please.

She paused for a moment, thinking through a solution, and stepped toward the exit. The salt rains would have turned briny the contents of the rain barrel.

"You stay put. Don't move an inch."

Jillian closed the door behind her and contemplated her situation. Having a conversation with an octopus that had maimed her? The world had stopped making sense the day the Ochos invaded, so sure, why the hell not? She fished through the kitchen cabinets and found a large wooden salad bowl, then slipped out the back door. The pinpricks of far-off stars dotted the night sky, the air cool on her bare arms. She shook a chill from her body as she filled the bowl beneath the rain barrel. The smells of salt and offal spiraled into her nostrils.

She turned her attention away from the spigot to check the perimeter for prying eyes, then hurried back inside.

She was surprised to see the octopus exactly where she had left it. The only difference was another line of text, written in grease: *Your name?*

She placed the bowl on the floor directly in front of the octopus. As it crawled in, tea-colored water puddled onto the floor. Its scarlet flesh turned a muted brown to match the shade of the salad bowl — a chameleon with tentacles.

"Jillian," she said, hand to her chest. "What do I call you?"

English has no word for a name like mine.

She eyed the stump of the tentacle she had removed with the scalpel.

"I have to call you something. How about Sev, short for Seven?"

A reference to the seven remaining limbs in my possession, I presume. It is a fine name. Offensive, but fine.

"Where are your big brothers?"

Inquiry unclear.

"Your big brothers, the colossal motherfuckers that have torn my town to shreds. The ones whose tentacles hang down from the clouds, like the danglers of a carwash."

Sev had no reply.

"Ochos, I call them. Don't tell me you're not one of them."

Soldiers and generals, it wrote. *Same race. Different intentions.*

"You're the sole good guy, the only benevolent one? Is that what you're telling me?"

Good choice of words.

"All this time we thought we were the only ones, the only life in the universe. Not only were we wrong, but now we know we're little more than grubs, maggots, something to be stepped on, squished, and flicked out of the way."

Like grubs and maggots, you, too, serve a purpose.

"Talk about insulting." She regarded his phantom limb. "How is your tentacle? The one I removed with my scalpel, I mean."

My arm has seen better days.

"Will it grow back?"

Would yours?

"Of course not, but I've heard that some animals, like salamanders, can...you know."

Yes, my limb will regenerate, though I would have preferred to keep the one I had.

"Speaking of injuries, what did you do to my wrist?"

Toxins.

"You're venomous, then. Terrific. Just terrific. Should I be concerned?"

Minimal necrosis. You will survive.

The lights flickered. Jillian wondered how much fuel the generator had left.

"Look," she told Sev, "I have to get some work done — clean up the corpse you were making a home of. Can I trust you to behave?"

Friends.

"Let's not get crazy."

She returned to DeWeese's corpse and peered into the blackened cavity.

"There's not any more of you in here waiting to surprise me, right?"

Negative. Not yet, at least.

She poked around the cavity with a probe, feeling uninspired by her work. Her eyes returned to the octopus, undulating in the water-filled salad bowl. Despite its alien appearance, its inhumanness, she felt an overwhelming fondness for the strange little creature. She blamed the venom.

"Sev, are you a boy or a girl?"

Male.

She prepared to stitch up the opening in DeWeese's torso. There was no need to do a full embalming, especially not anymore, considering how much time had elapsed. She guessed midnight had long since passed, and DeWeese's family would likely arrive at the funeral home shortly after first light. She would do the minimum, to make sure his face looked presentable, and to prevent the body from passing gas or opening its eyes in front of DeWeese's grieving family. Of course, she would dress him in his finest attire, sans socks, as his family would expect.

She then came to the realization that she had been a terrible host. She stepped away from the table and bent toward the octopus lounging in its bowl.

"Are you hungry?" she asked.

Ravenous, it wrote.

***

Jillian had to tell someone. She felt the urge to bang on the nearest door and just blab, blab, blab until describing every last detail about her introduction to Sev. But who would listen?

Albert had always been a fine audience, but he was M.I.A.

Laurie Woolly — not likely. Jillian treasured Laurie's amity, but she also didn't fully trust the woman she considered her dearest friend. Jillian didn't quite know why, but some inner voice whispered, *Keep your walls up.* Laurie's complicity in bringing the unpleasantness of Kip Detto to Jillian's doorstep had not helped matters.

Then she thought of Timmy.

Jillian hadn't seen Timmy Labreque since the summer after high school. Though their relationship had reached its end long ago, she had not since shared as tight a bond with any other human. Timmy would have loved to hear a story about a talking octopus waiting patiently in the cavity of a corpse on the embalming table. She could almost picture his thin face, brushed with black-and-white corpse paint, lighting up with glee as the story got better and better. He would have believed every word too.

Then again, Timmy was a different person now, if he were still alive at all.

The gifts of time and space had helped her reach a painful but pleasing conclusion: Timmy had never been the person she wanted him to be. He, too, had been a pretender.

Chapter 9
Shadow

They drove around Dracut with the windows down. A song from the latest AFI album rattled the speakers of his ancient Volkswagen Rabbit. Timmy yelled over the spirited chorus, sharing his plans for the months and years ahead. A fancy liberal arts college in Vermont beckoned, he told her. At his parents' insistence, he would work toward his bachelor's degree in some boring major having to do with business — finance or marketing — "just as a fallback," all while perfecting the techniques of what he called "my art," referring to his interest in Victorian taxidermy.

"When did you find out?" she asked. "About getting into college, I mean."

"A few months ago," he said. "I meant to tell you. We've been so busy with graduation and everything."

She sank into her seat. Neither of them had given two shits about prom, graduation, or any of the other supposed rites of passage that made their classmates believe they had actually accomplished something by surviving the four-year torture rack otherwise known as high school. He'd had every opportunity to mention a development as momentous as this. Never had she expected Timmy to abandon her, but that's exactly what he was telling her he was about to do. She didn't know what the future held, had never really given it much thought, but in any brief glimpses of the future she imagined, Timmy had always been beside her, usually wearing a tight black t-shirt featuring the cryptic name of a black-metal band designed to offend soccer moms, buttoned-up businessmen, and anyone else with delicate sensitivities.

"How about you?" he asked. "What's on the agenda?"

"I have no idea," she told him flatly. She tried not to sound hurt. "Probably work at a nail salon or something. Push a broom around Walmart maybe."

"I'd say you could come with me to Vermont, but they won't permit non-students in the dorms." His mask of corpse paint had turned dry and brittle. A few white flakes rested on the shoulder of his black Tiger Army tee.

"We could get an apartment."

He cranked up the volume, as if to drown out her remark after the fact.

"We'll write," he promised. "We'll stay in touch."

Given their shared love of calligraphy, they exchanged handwritten letters back and forth, though his responses became less and less frequent as the months wore on. After she decided to move to Providence for the three-year fellowship at Still Lakes Center for the Mortuary Arts, she penned a lengthy missive, more than a dozen pages, in which she admitted her nervousness and tried to sound excited. Toward the letter's end, she told him she hoped her "adventure in the thrill-a-minute world of embalming" would make him proud.

Only his opinion mattered. Although she had never confessed such a thing to Timmy, she had chosen the mortuary arts because she guessed it might impress him. Besides, Providence was close enough for her to visit him in Burlington, if such an invitation were to be issued.

He had not written back, to her surprise, though she thought little of his silence — the letter lost in the mail perhaps, or maybe he was just too engaged with schoolwork or taxidermy to offer a meaningful response. Her subsequent text messages went unreturned too.

In her follow-up note sent one month into the fellowship, she shared her delight in the discovery that she had a real knack for the work, and her instructors had said the same. She suggested she was happy she had taken the leap, because for the first time in her adult life she felt as though she was doing something she enjoyed.

His reply was almost immediate. They hadn't spoken directly for close to five months, so she felt giddy when his name and number lit up the face of her cellphone. The feeling faded quickly.

No salutations, no pleasantries — just Timmy going right into his impassioned rant.

"What are you trying to prove?" he spat.

She tried to parse meaning from his indignation. Without coming out and saying it outright, he suggested she was trying to make him look bad by pursuing a career path he had always told people he would one day pursue. As his quote beneath his picture in the senior yearbook, for example, he had chosen a morose-sounding sentiment attributed to the Greek philosopher Epictetus: "A little soul carrying around a corpse."

Timmy's final words to her on that call: "Grow up and get out of my shadow."

Every note she wrote to him thereafter went unacknowledged.

In the months that followed, Jillian determined that Timmy was jealous. Maybe he felt as though he had to become someone else, someone respectable, or worse, maybe the gloomy weight he had carried around with him for the four years of high school had been all for show, an act. A peacock in corpse paint.

***

Last she had heard, Timmy — or Tim, as he advertised himself on social media — was back in Dracut, selling high-end fencing, lighting, and landscaping services to rich landowners on the outskirts of Boston. She had spent too much time scrolling through his Instagram and Twitter pages, trying to form a picture in her mind based on the story he was telling the rest of the world. The apocalypse had cured her of this habit, but she was aghast at what she had learned about the man she had once "loved more than death," as they used to tell each other. His latest disguise: a husband and a father of two young daughters; thinning hair, a doughy face, and the beginnings of a beer gut. His only notable hobby involved heading to an upmarket gastropub in Dracut on early weekend mornings to sip pints of stout and watch English-rules football.

In other words, he had become plain and uninteresting — normal.

Looking back, she couldn't fathom what she had seen in him. A poseur, a phony, someone using darkness as a mask to hide the shallow man beneath.

Chapter 10
An Unexpected Loss

At the first suggestion of dawn, Jillian cracked open the back door and checked the sky for rogue tentacles. Seeing none, she stepped onto the concrete landing and let her eyes adjust to the lifting light. A protracted yawn parted her jaws as she stretched the stiffness from her bones.

Jillian had worked through the night to prep DeWeese's body for the ceremony, and she needed the finishing touches to make his daughters feel welcome as they came to say goodbye to their father. She hurried down the walk and wandered into the street, eyeing the few other structures that remained standing, Laurie's house among them, as well as the piles of rubble representing the homes and small businesses that once neighbored Bart Cozen's place. She stopped at an undeveloped lot overtaken by wildflowers.

She had always cherished the peace of early mornings, before the world woke up and started making noise. The best days began with her sipping strong coffee and watching the first rays of sunlight paint the walls of her kitchen. She mourned the relative peace of that life, since replaced with *this* — the realization of how close she was to nonexistence, and the feeling that her fingertips could almost touch the fragile barrier between life and death. As much as she had talked about death, listened only to music made by bands fascinated with death and dying, and forged her identity around all things morbid and sullen, the thought of her inert body filling a coffin horrified her. She wanted to live long enough to become an old woman, and even then go on living until her skin turned to paper and blew away with the wind.

A cotton-soft breeze rustled the clutches of sea lavender. Jillian bent and sheared off individual stalks, each one abloom with dozens of purple, blue, and white cups. A rumble of thunder, low and deep, stopped Jillian in her task. She turned her eyes toward the clouds, happy to see them the color of steel, not a hint of red — no tentacles, no Ochos. Even so, her gut told her not to linger, so she collected enough shorn stalks to fill three or four vases and hurried back to Cozen's. Confetti of small purple flowers trailed her.

***

The ethereal din of plucked harp strings trickled from the speakers of an aging CD player, plugged unceremoniously into an electrical outlet at the front of the parlor. Aside from the harp music and the low hum of the generator doing its job from the other side of the wall, a deathly quiet filled the parlor. Jillian went to the front door, unhitched the lock, and let the door sail wide. Puffs of wind swept dry leaves onto an area rug and across the polished wood.

Then she waited.

She was thinking about Albert when Doug DeWeese's daughters filed into the parlor, followed by two men in their thirties and four young children, none of the little ones older than eight. Each of DeWeese's adult daughters — Betty, Bella, and Bonnie — looked as drained as Jillian felt.

Betty approached Jillian, who stood at the head of the open casket.

"He looks good," Betty said. She placed two fingers on her father's exposed hand. "You did a good job."

Betty looked Jillian up and down, regarding her loose-fitting pink top, baggy black capris, and a pair of scuffed flats. Jillian knew she didn't look her best, but she had so few options. She had plucked each piece of her ensemble from the room upstairs where Bart Cozen had stored enough men's and women's apparel, as well as a few child-size sweaters and suits, to stock a small thrift store. Some of the women's clothes fit her all right, though she considered almost none of the available fashions her style. Naturally, Jillian ruminated over the clothing's origins and had come up with two scenarios: Either Cozen had liked to play "dress up" in his free time or, the more likely option, he had collected the clothes from furnace-bound cadavers for some far more disturbing use.

"We're happy you're here," Jillian told Betty.

Laurie walked in and took a seat in the first row. She settled in a cushioned chair and tried to look somber.

"So how does this work?" Betty asked. "What's the itinerary?"

"That's up to you. Most of the time I say a few quick words of introduction. Then the bereaved proceed to the casket to say their goodbyes. Then someone usually goes to the podium and says something about the deceased. Maybe you or one of your sisters would like to speak. All three of you can, if that's what you want to do. Consider our home yours."

Our home, as if Jillian had any right to the place. Squatter's rights, she remembered, just like Kip had said.

"Okay," Betty said. After expelling a coffee-scented sigh, she added, "We're ready."

Jillian ushered Betty to the first row of chairs and then went to the front door, closing them all inside. She returned to the parlor and watched the other mourners take their seats, then took her place at the front of the room. She coughed as she stood by the casket. Phlegm rattled in the back of her throat. The sound seemed to fill every inch of the confined space.

"We're here this morning to celebrate the life of Douglas DeWeese," she began. "I'm not going to pretend that I knew your father or the man he was, but I do know what it's like to lose someone who means so much to you. The loss of a loved one is never easy. Even in the times we live in now, when the line between life and death seems to shift so easily, we always expect our loved ones to remain in our lives, ever-present. When they are gone, we find ourselves somehow surprised, unmoored by their sudden absence."

One of the youngest children shifted in his seat and asked his father, without embarrassment, "Can we go now?"

Jillian turned toward the DeWeese sisters — Betty in the front row, Bella and Bonnie directly behind her.

"I'm not going to suggest you will have an easy time filling the space left by your father," she told them. "You will have difficult days ahead of you, when thoughts of him overwhelm you. And that's all right. My advice to you, based on my experience mourning those I have lost: Don't push those thoughts away. Let them in. By doing so, you will stay close to him, and he to you."

She paused. Across the aisle from Betty, Laurie had her head bowed. Her body shook slightly. Though Jillian wouldn't have pegged her friend for the emotional type, Laurie appeared to be weeping.

"I welcome each of you to approach the casket and say your goodbyes," Jillian said. "Take all the time you need."

Jillian padded to the back of the room. Shafts of white light spilled through the sections of window not obscured by tacked-up plywood. She closed her eyes and let the light warm her face.

"*That* was some sappy stuff."

Laurie stood by Jillian's side, whispering in her ear.

"Moved *you* to tears, didn't I?"

"Laughing my ass off didn't seem appropriate."

"Your crassness aside, I appreciate you being here."

"Boss gave me the day off," Laurie joked. "You look like shit."

"Long night," Jillian said.

"Christ, aren't they all? Did you get dressed in the dark?"

"Beggars can't be choosers. It's not like I have a whole wardrobe of designer options at my disposal."

"Clearly."

"Shut up."

Jillian had hurried her way through her clothing options that morning, in part because she disliked spending time upstairs. She wouldn't admit it, but she had seen too many strange things upstairs — among them a rocking chair that seemed to creak and move on its own. The possibility that she shared the funeral home with one or more specters had the potential to unravel her, so she attributed the animated rocking chair to wind whistling through a broken window. She had closed and locked the doors to all but two upstairs rooms. Thankfully, every door that should have been closed and locked remained so in the days since.

Her thoughts shifted to Sev and the trouble he might be making. She had left him in the embalming room with the lights on, because she thought it cruel to leave him all alone in a cold, dark, deathly space.

The mourners proceeded to the casket to offer their parting words to the deceased. Betty lingered at the front of the room. She motioned to Jillian, seeming to ask if it was okay for her to speak. Jillian gave the thumbs up, and Betty stepped to the podium.

"Thank you everyone who came here today," Betty began. "I was hoping there would be more of us, but I suppose we should be happy enough with small favors. My father, Doug DeWeese, was a kind man, a successful man, a devoted man. He was a husband, a father, a grandfather, an attorney, a business owner, a model-ship builder, a marathoner..."

She stopped there. Jillian wondered if Betty was thinking about the moment of her father's death. Betty had assumed a heart attack had claimed her father's life immediately before or after a run. Jillian had assumed so too, figuring Sev had made a host of DeWeese's body after the fact. For the first time she wondered if Sev might have *caused* the man's death.

"Oh fuck," she whispered.

"When all this madness started happening," Betty continued, "the damned squids or whatever they are, making everything a wreck, my father told us not to worry. 'Uncle Sam will knock 'em down,' he told us. He was so confident, so optimistic. 'We'll never be the same again,' he said, 'but we'll get through it.' That speaks volumes about who my father was, about who—"

The harp music died, and the parlor lights went dark, the hum of the generator silent. Murmurs of alarm coursed through the congregation.

"Everybody stay calm," Jillian said, though she was anything but.

She ran to the front door and looked through the sidelight, scanning the sky above the bay for signs of the Ochos' return. Nothing but a field of gray clouds — no hints of red, not a single tentacle reaching down from the heavens.

"It's not them," she yelled loud enough for all to hear. "It's all right."

Sev.

The little bastard had played her, she thought. Somehow the slippery motherfucker had escaped from his cell, discovered the breaker box, and cut the power. She grabbed a flashlight off its roost on the kitchen counter and hurried into the embalming room. She clicked on the flashlight and shone the beam into each corner of the room. As the beam crossed the stainless-steel table where she had left the octopus, she saw Sev half-submerged, the other half of his body hanging over the rim of the water-filled bowl. He picked up the grease pencil and wrote on the steel sheet.

Everything has gone dark.

"Yes, I can see that much," she said. "Have you been here, in this room, the whole time?"

Where else would I go?

Another thought occurred to her, the only explanation.

She left the embalming room, passing the mourners gathered in the patch of daylight streaming in from the sitting-room window, and made a beeline for the back door. She bent for her daypack and grabbed her sickle by its handle. Wind swept in as she yanked open the back door. She stepped onto the patio, picturing in her mind what she might discover.

The generator was gone. The female end of the orange extension cord sat uselessly on the concrete.

She snaked along the side of the house and met the street, where she saw what she expected. Two men hurriedly wheeled the generator away. Even from a distance of nearly a hundred yards, she recognized one of them as Kip Detto.

"Hey, asshole!" Jillian yelled.

With her sickle in hand, she took off running.

Chapter 11
The Proximate Cries of Hunted Humans

The soles of Jillian's flats slapped the asphalt. Her lungs burned as she ran. She held the sickle above her head, partly to look menacing, but more so to keep from poking her eye out. She leapt over the wreckage of a downed signpost. Still rooted in its concrete base, the shaft was kinked in three spots, and the kelly-green nameplate bearing the words *Terrapin Street* was bent into a V.

As Kip heard her coming, he turned and assumed a defensive stance in the middle of the pockmarked street. His burly companion kept walking, hauling Jillian's generator by its handle off to God knows where. She watched as Kip slipped the rifle from his shoulder and raised the weapon toward her. She came to a stop within ten feet of him, with his rifle's sights trained more or less on the middle of her forehead. The muzzle looked to her like a perfect black marble.

"Don't be stupid," Kip said.

She cocked her head to watch the mystery man get away with her generator.

"That's my only power source," she said, chest heaving. "I want it back."

Her heart pounded, more from the exertion of running than the stress of having a gun pointed in her face. If he was going to shoot her, he would have done it already.

Kip expelled a long breath and added, with annoyance, "We already discussed this, sweetheart."

"No," she said. "You dictated. I listened politely. Polite Jillian is gone. Meet impolite Jillian." She raised the sickle to prove her willingness to hurl it.

"Didn't I tell you not to be stupid?"

"You'd be wise to stop calling me stupid," she said. "I have excellent aim."

"That makes two of us. I was a sharpshooter, and a rifle in my hands is going to do a hell of a lot more damage than a rusty farming tool in yours."

"I'm not going to miss a field mouse at ten feet, and your ass is a lot bigger than a field mouse," she said. "I could part your hair from this distance."

Laurie trotted up beside Jillian. She breathed so hard she could barely speak. "Everybody left," Laurie panted. "I...kicked the DeWeeses...out and...closed the door...behind me."

"Thank you, my dear," Jillian said as calmly as she could, "but I have bigger bowling pins to knock down at the moment."

Kip nodded toward Laurie and said, "Tell your friend not to do anything st—"

"Call me stupid again and see what happens," Jillian said. Her grip tightened around the sickle's hickory handle.

"Tell your friend to be reasonable," he said, correcting.

"I don't reason with thugs and thieves," Jillian countered.

The front door to one of the few remaining homes on the street creaked open. A woman with a gaunt face and long gray hair peered out. A tall, acne-cheeked teenager stood behind her, his stare vacant.

Kip lowered his rifle.

"Come with me."

He turned, slung the rifle over his shoulder, and proceeded up Terrapin Street's gentle incline.

***

Terrapin Street ended in a cratered cul-de-sac. Kip stepped onto the crumbling curb and followed a well-worn dirt path that led up, into the woods.

"Where's he taking us?" Jillian whispered to Laurie.

"Where are you taking us?" Laurie shouted at Kip's back.

"Just keep moving your feet," he said without turning around.

Newly dropped leaves obscured the footpath, and those remaining on the branches above had begun to stiffen and brown. The scene reminded Jillian of the inevitable withering and death of all things. Autumn used to be her favorite time of year — the vibrant greens turning brown and brittle, daytime temps on a steady decline, a presage to the long, cold, gray months ahead. The fact that the world would be reborn in six months' time had always given her a sense of the impossible, that even death could be undone.

Now she wasn't so sure. She hoped to see another spring.

The air in the woods felt heavy. Jillian stopped in the middle of the trail to look around, but for what, she did not know. Every tree knot seemed to wear a gruesome face, and every stump seemed to bear predatory eyes and jagged teeth. She wasn't sure if she felt safer or more vulnerable out here, among the trees, away from the smoldering corpse of civilization. But she knew she was glad to not be alone in a secluded place with Kip Detto.

Halfway up the hill she turned to see Laurie, her large-breasted and big-bottomed friend, struggling up the rocky slope. Titmice and nuthatches flitted through the underbrush, hunting for seeds or grubs or whatever titmice and nuthatches ate. The trail took them through a series of switchbacks, leading up an increasingly steep hill. Loose stones gave way underfoot.

Jillian considered how silly she must have looked in her flouncy blouse the color of a glass of rosé, loose black capris, and treadless flats as white as talc. The outfit was ideal for Sunday brunch, not scaling a small mountain, or what passed for a small mountain in coastal Rhode Island. The blouse's fabric clung to her lower back, now slick with sweat. Soon enough she would start to smell about as pleasant as a barnyard goat. She swore, once this whole apocalypse thing got resolved, she would finally get into game shape.

Kip stood at the edge of a pine-rimmed overlook. He rested his hands on his hips with his back to them, and Jillian was happy to see him breathing heavily too, though he did his best to hide it.

"We made it," Jillian told him, still huffing. "Now, why did you drag us up here?"

"Just shut up and listen," he said. "Really *listen*."

Beyond the rush of blood in her ears, and beyond the whispers of wind cooling her scalp, she did hear something.

Pop-pop-pop. Again, in short rhythmic bursts. *Pop-pop-pop.* The sound reminded her of corn kernels bursting in a hot pan. She recognized gunfire when she heard it.

"Hunters?" Laurie asked.

"Hunting humans maybe," Kip said. He pointed to a strip of white on an otherwise green palette. He fished a pair of camouflaged field binoculars from a side pocket and handed them over. "See for yourself."

Jillian wiped the lenses on the hem of her blouse and held the binoculars until the eyepieces touched the bridge of her nose. A clutch of homes and storefronts peppered a stretch of asphalt that looked remarkably similar to Pell's Main Street. A plume of inky smoke rose from a spired building that might have been a church.

"That's Rask down there, our sister town," Kip said. "Sounds to me like someone's having a field day with a military rifle — probably a REC7 or an AR-18 — and I'm guessing they're not using it to bull's-eye rabbits and squirrels for meat to spice up a communal stew. I've been coming up here for the past three days, and each day you hear shots fired, on and off and on again. You don't hear that kind of rat-a-tat-tat in Pell, do you? We need to keep it that way."

"What's your point?" Jillian asked.

"War awaits us at the borders of Pell, whether we like it or not, and we need to be ready," he said. "Gather weapons, batten down the loose ends, block off the roads and other points of entry. And we need to stop drawing attention to ourselves by running loud-as-fuck gas generators all hours of the day."

"I don't think anyone's coming, Kip," Laurie said. "We haven't seen a moving car in months. God knows if they even still work."

"I blame the Russians, the Iranians, maybe the French," he said. "One of 'em probably set off an EMP device so we couldn't see them coming or do anything about it, and that's when they unleashed those fuckin' *things*. Come to think of it, it's probably the Chinese or North Koreans. You know Asians and their tentacle porn — all that hentai horseshit."

"What's EMP?" Jillian asked.

"Electromagnetic pulse," he said. "A nuke emits an EMP as part of its little bundle of joy, but you know our enemies in every freedom-hating country around the world have all kinds of nonlethal weapons with one thing in mind: disabling or disrupting our ability to fight back. With one push of a button, a strong-enough EMP device can discharge a burst of electro-mag energy and fry anything with a circuit board within a two-hundred-mile reach. We get hit with one of those sons of bitches and our communications infrastructure and high-powered weapons are completely useless. Trillions and trillions of dollars, wasted."

"Wait," Laurie said. "You think someone deployed those creatures as a weapon against us? *Now* I'm fucking pissed."

"Don't listen to him," Jillian said. "He's delusional."

Kip pointed to Jillian and Laurie in turn.

"You two need to change your frame of mind," he said. "The world's a different place, and now that those fuckin' *things* are gone" — he pointed to the sky, referring to the Ochos — "we're going to have new enemies to fight. The survivors are going to start crawling out of every crack, and they're going to come looking to take things that don't belong to them."

"The nerve," Jillian said, thinking of her generator. "It's foolish to suggest those creatures are gone. At the very least it's bad luck. You don't know for sure, and you shouldn't say it. Not yet."

"Really? Look up."

Kip waved a hand toward the sky, blue and barren with the exception of a few feathery wisps of cirrus clouds.

"Today, maybe," Jillian said. "It's not over."

"Someone in charge probably figured out how to drive them off finally," Laurie added. "What else could it be?"

"Doubtful," Kip said. "I love the US of A, but I don't think our country exists anymore. Let's assume we're on our own until Uncle Sam rolls into town and tells us everything's peachy keen."

Laurie expelled a pained burp and bent at the waist as if she might vomit.

"Listen," Kip said, eyes on Jillian. "I'm not your enemy — just the opposite, to tell the truth. I consider myself a patriot, a defender of Pell, and I'm taking steps to make sure what's ours stays ours. Let me show you what we've done so far."

As they descended the hill, Jillian lost her footing twice and ended up on her ass. They wandered through waist-high wildflower meadows and overgrown back yards until they arrived at a narrow driveway. Kip led them to a long, squat building — all awning and red brick — tucked into a wooded hillside.

Jillian and Laurie trailed him by twenty paces, mostly so Laurie could talk shit about Kip behind his back. Jillian was a willing audience.

"The fucking *retirement* home?" Laurie asked.

"What?" Jillian said.

"He's living in the old folks' home. Birch Meadows. At least that's what it used to be called."

As they approached the single-story building, something stirred on the slightly pitched roof. A man dressed in black, green, and brown waved to Kip from behind a stout pyramid of sandbags. The muzzle of a nasty-looking machine gun poked out from a notch in the sandbag wall. Kip waited for Jillian and Laurie by an entrance tacked over with plywood. Bits of glass speckled the concrete.

"I figured you would have moved into your brother's house," Laurie said.

"I might've, but his place got smashed up by those fuckin' *things*," he said. "I could have moved anywhere — biggest and nicest place in town, if I wanted. I'm not living here for my own health, you know. I want to get the town back on its feet, and this joint is better in terms of location and fortification — one way in and out, multiple escape routes into the woods. And if those fuckin' *things* do come back and decide to collapse the roof, it's only one floor, so anyone inside won't be trapped beneath five tons of timber and shingle. I know what I'm doing."

"Why bother?" Jillian asked.

"'Cause I want to help people."

"That's a first," Laurie said under her breath.

He led them inside, past another armed sentry — a sixty-something man with a walrus mustache, creased face, and a beer belly that stretched the fibers of an olive-hued t-shirt.

"Who are these people?" Jillian asked.

"Friends and neighbors — Pell natives who made it through," Kip said. "They came here looking for a leader. They found one."

"We'd sure like to meet him," Jillian said. "Or her."

He stopped and turned, dumbfounded. "I'm talking about me," he said.

Jillian gave an acerbic smile.

The main hallway stretched for nearly three hundred feet, it seemed, uninterrupted with the exception of a Formica-topped desk Jillian figured had once been a nurse's station. Each room they walked past was empty save a nightstand and a bed stripped of its sheets. At Room 323, an odd noise drew Jillian's gaze. She saw a young man — no older than sixteen or seventeen — lying on his back, naked, while a woman in her thirties or forties straddled him, grinding away. Kip stepped forward and closed the door.

"People deserve their privacy," he said.

"It's a regular old love-in you got here, Kip."

"Why the hell not? No one has anything left to lose."

Laure interjected, "Where are all the old folks?"

He paused and said, "They went home."

"Apparently," Jillian said.

She suspected Kip had done something horrible. She envisioned a dozen men and women in their eighties and nineties, all of them in wheelchairs, lined up at the lip of a seaside cliff. In this fantasy, Kip wheeled each resident to the edge, tipped the chair forward, and watched its owner topple end over end, helicoptering to the rocks below. Most likely all the infirm whose family members hadn't fetched them after the first Ocho attack had died by the time Kip had come to claim the place, victims of starvation, dehydration, or some other ailment. A tragic and horrible end for sure, but no crimes committed — or so she hoped.

The man who had dragged away Jillian's generator loped down the hall and whispered in Kip's ear. He was a hulk — six and a half feet tall, thick in the middle, thick in the neck, thick limbs, thick accent. Chinese, Vietnamese, Mongolian — Jillian had no way of determining his origin; she had met too few Asian people to know the difference. A momentary shame weighed on her as if it were a hard little stone.

"Everybody works together here, doing what they can," Kip said. "One lady's a seamstress. One's a nurse. One brews fancy-ass beer. We have laborers and bow hunters." He jabbed a thumb in the direction of the Asian fellow by his side and said, "Charlie Chino here's a fisherman. Ain't you, Charlie? There's no shortage of fish in the bay, and pretty soon he's going to start putting out nets and lobster pots. He's going to be our minister of agriculture too, start tilling beds to grow whatever crops he can figure out how to grow."

"How agrarian," Jillian said.

Charlie excused himself and lumbered down the hall toward the exit.

"Plus, there's plenty of deer and cottontail hippity-hopping through the meadows nearby," Kip continued. "Worse comes to worst, the pantry's stocked with enough canned peaches, prunes, and lima beans to last us until the next apocalypse. We've got plenty of ammo too. Everyone takes a turn on sentry duty, keeping eyes on the perimeter."

"Socialism, Kip?" Jillian said. "A fine American boy like you?"

"Don't be a smartass. Everyone looking out for one other and doing their part for the common good ain't socialism."

"No," Jillian said. "Certainly not. Forgive the implication."

"We've got about twenty people now, and we'll keep adding folks along the way," he said. "If you're missing someone, you might find 'em here."

Laurie bent and put her lips to Jillian's ear. "Albert," she whispered.

Jillian shook her head aggressively. She would admit no weakness to Kip, and she certainly wouldn't put herself in a position where she would owe him anything.

"I know I come off like an asshole sometimes," Kip said. "Don't think you're the first person to tell me I rub them the wrong way. I just don't want to end up with a knife in my back or at the end of a long rope."

"How do you feel about sickles?" Jillian asked. She held up the harvesting tool she considered her weapon of choice. The honed edge gleamed in the sole ray of sunlight illuminating the hallway.

"The gen stays here," he insisted. "You're welcome to stay too. We could use more..." He struggled for the word, or knew better not to say it.

"I'll take my chances at the funeral home."

"Whatever gets you wet, lady."

"Don't be a pig, Kip," Laurie said.

Jillian ignored Kip's crass comment. She expected as much from a man with such a dim intellect.

"I'll be outside whenever you're ready to go," she told Laurie. "Oh, and, Kip, if you ever point a gun at me again, you'd better pull the trigger and pray that you don't miss. You leave me standing, I swear to the immortal Hulk Hogan I'm going to rip your throat out."

She stepped out the front door, kicking beads of glass out of her path. Maybe Kip was right, she thought. It seemed that all the smart people who could turn the lights back on — revive communications systems, resurrect global commerce, and run effective governments — had been swept from the planet's face, so any chance humanity had of rebuilding was in the hands of the survivors, the riff-raff. Unremarkable people like her.

And douchebags like Kip Detto.

To her right, Charlie Chino stood in a patch of browning grass. He had a hoe in hand, breaking up the earth. He pretended not to notice her approach.

"It's Charlie, right?" she hollered.

He grunted and nodded without looking at her.

"Typical boy," she said, "always playing in the dirt."

"Not play. Work."

"Autumn's coming. Isn't it a little late in the season to plant crops?"

"It's never too late. Onions, carrots, leaf lettuce. They all go in the ground right about now."

"Good to know," she said. "Where's my generator, Charlie?"

Eyes focused on his work, he dragged the hoe's blade through the soil.

"Where's my *fucking* generator, Charlie?"

He lifted his eyes and responded, "Where's your friend? The big girl."

"Still jawing at Kip. The generator, Charlie. Where'd you stow it?"

"I think your friend is going to stay. But not you."

"I have everything I could possibly need where I am. Except a generator, of course, but you already knew that. Why come here and live under the thumb of a wannabe tyrant? And you're wrong about Laurie. We're both leaving" — she looked to the barren entrance of Birch Meadows — "eventually."

Charlie stared at her as he hoed. The depth of his gaze unnerved her.

"Have you known Kip for a long time?" she asked.

"Long enough. Kip will do his work, make his mistakes, trust me with important things. When the time comes, if it comes, I will take what is his."

She smiled. "I like you, Charlie."

"My name is Chinh. Kip calls me what he calls me because he thinks it's funny, even though no one laughs."

"Well, you're okay with me, Chinh."

"If you knew what I have done, you might say otherwise."

Jillian suddenly realized she might have told Chinh too much, about having everything she needed to survive at the funeral home — more essentials that could be ferried away without her consent. Stupid. She hadn't given him enough credit, hadn't realized his ambitions. Everyone had done things they had regretted, especially since the Ochos' arrival, but Chinh seemed to suggest he had done something felonious, even sadistic. She felt the need to change the subject.

"You're a fisherman," she reminded him. "That would suggest you know a thing or two about fish and other critters that live in the ocean."

"Enough," he said. "Been manning nets and lobster pots since I was a boy."

"Just curious, purely for the sake of conversation," she said. "Can you tell me what octopuses like to eat?"

Chapter 12
An Effigy of God as a Many-Tentacled Beast

A thin veil of fog clung to the forest floor.

Jillian's head swam as she wandered, alone, away from the compound at Birch Meadows. No way in hell she would ever join a commune, let alone the single-story hellhole taking shape under Kip's thumb. It seemed like a fine place to get gang-raped. She'd hang herself first.

Laurie, on the other hand...

Maybe Chinh had been right about Laurie. Maybe she would sign up for Kip's twisted little cabal, with or without her absentee husband.

The only thing Jillian realized with any certainty: The longer she lived, the less she knew.

The trees thinned and gave way to the dreadfully familiar sights of Main Street. She felt the buzz of excitement as the funeral home's broken spire came into view. Thoughts of Sev consumed her mind. A talking octopus, for chrissakes, who most likely was some sort of space alien, had become her houseguest. She sensed a kindness in him, a deeper intellect than she had found in almost any other creature, either man or beast. *Friends*, he had suggested to her. Maybe one day, but first she had to learn more — and now she knew how to do so.

She retrieved an empty bucket from the funeral home's shed and tramped down to the salt marsh. Even from a distance of fifty feet, she could spy hundreds of fiddler crabs, popping in and out of their tiny burrows, bringing the marsh to life. As she removed her shoes and stepped into the marsh, every crab scuttled into a nearby hole. Mud squished between her toes and consumed her foot up to the ankle. Her hand hovered above the nearest burrow and waited for its resident to surface. After half a minute, the crab poked out of its burrow, saw her shadow, and retreated. She thrust her hand into the mud and came up with nothing but a fistful of muck — no crab. She did the same to two other burrows and twice more got the same result.

A fiddler crab's brain was likely one-thousandth the size of hers, yet every crab in the marsh seemed to be outfoxing her. She finally nabbed one of the little buggers, almost by accident, though she dropped it when its overlong claw pinched her finger. She needed a new method, figuring each burrow was likely no deeper than a few inches. She stepped into the soft mud beside the nearest hole. The burrow collapsed, forcing the crab to the surface. She deftly lifted the crab by its large pincer and dropped it into the bucket.

"Sorry, little guy," she said.

She repeated the sequence over and over, and each time she issued the same apology to each capture. Blood trickled from a cut on her index finger, a gift from a particularly pernicious crustacean. Jillian raised her eyes from the marsh and looked up the coast, toward another stretch of marsh, where the wreckage of her abandoned vehicle remained. The car had sunk deeper into the mud, only its ruined windshield and salt-corroded roof visible.

More than a dozen crabs scuttled around the bucket's basin, so she extricated herself from the mud and returned to Cozen's. After washing her feet beneath the rain barrel's spigot, she entered the funeral home and locked the door behind her. The casket bearing DeWeese's finely dressed corpse remained in the parlor, and she felt a pang of guilt for how badly the morning's ceremony had gone. Her temper flared as she pictured Kip's face. Not only had he tarnished a perfectly elegant ceremony, but he had also robbed her of the ability to fuel the furnace. No doubt DeWeese's daughters would spread the word about what had happened. She would have to drop by and apologize to the family, let them know the reason for the disruption, the source of it, and warn them not to fall for Kip's bait if he tried to enlist them into his dystopian clique.

No matter, it seemed her time as Pell's undertaker had reached its end.

For a minute she considered wheeling DeWeese's body down to the salt marsh and dumping it into the mud, letting the fiddler crabs have their fill. That seemed fair considering what was about to happen to the dozen or so crabs at the bottom of the white bucket at her feet.

A lantern in her right hand, the crab bucket in her left, she entered the embalming room and found Sev's salad bowl overturned. Liver-shaped puddles dotted the tile floor.

"Sev?"

A deflating noise issued from the far corner. In the lantern's light, she saw Sev curled into a tight ball.

"Sorry to be gone for so long. Everything okay?"

Fine, he wrote. His terse response suggested annoyance.

"I brought something for you."

She reached into the bucket and plucked out one of the crabs by its oversized pincer. As the pincer gave way, the crab tumbled to the floor. It landed on its back, near her feet, and righted itself. With almost impossible quickness, Sev pounced. A tentacle curled around the crab and fed it to the beak on Sev's underside. His mud-brown flesh turned a brilliant blue.

"Good?"

Delicious, he wrote. His flesh cycled between shades of blue and purple.

"I have a few more questions for you."

Crab.

"I ask you a question, you answer, then comes the crab. Understood?"

Crab, please.

"Like I said, the sequence will be as follows: question, answer, crab."

My venom could stop your heart. Be civil. Crab, please.

She hesitated for a few seconds, then tossed another crab onto the floor. It scuttled sideways, away from Sev, but he tracked it down in a flash.

"Be right back."

She picked up the salad bowl and left the embalming room. She returned a few minutes later bearing the full water bowl, which she placed on the floor. Sev promptly immersed himself. She exited only to return with another prize: a bottle of Glenfiddich single malt, with two crystal tumblers as accompaniment. She filled both tumblers halfway with the amber liquor, placing one beside Sev's water bowl.

"If we're going to be civilized, let's do it right. Have a drink."

Sev approached the crystal glass and tested the liquid with the tip of a suckered arm. He drew a question mark on the floor.

"It's Scotch whisky, from the Scottish isles — damned good one too." She took a long sip. "I've been thinking, Sev. Did you kill Mister DeWeese? He's the nice man whose belly you were making a home of when I discovered you."

The gentleman's heart had gone still by the time I found him, he wrote. *Something else ended his suffering.*

She exhaled in relief.

"Okay, million-dollar question: Where did you come from?"

Elsewhere. He immersed his body in the tumbler. As he emerged, the tumbler went dry, as if his porous flesh had absorbed every drop.

"Elsewhere. Yeah, no shit. Where exactly?"

From a distant star, through a tear in the fabric of space and time. Who knows how the universe works?

"You *are* a space alien."

My kind seeks to export its intelligence to new worlds.

"Why?"

I would have rather stayed home. Yet here I am, left behind.

"That makes two of us."

As she took another sip, she realized a full day had passed without eating so much as a morsel. No bother. The alcohol had already begun to do its job.

"Is it difficult to know that you're alone?"

I am not alone.

"Sweet of you to say."

Not referring to you. Others like me. Soldiers.

"Where? I haven't seen any."

Watching. Plotting. Waiting.

"That's reassuring. What about the big ones? The ones that descend from the clouds. Where are they?"

Taming other worlds. They will return.

"But they already fucked everything up. Why not just wipe us off the map and be done with it?"

We destroy and depart. You recover and rebuild. Then we return and undo everything you have remade. This breaks you. Then you belong to us.

"Why bother?"

Exaltation.

"Explain."

They seek worshippers. They aspire to be gods.

"Ha! They sure came to the wrong place. All our gods are long dead. Now we just worship ourselves."

Humans make heroes of the things they fear. They have seen no greater horror than my kind.

"Fair point. You're telling me there are others like you out there right now, just sitting there and making plans to raise hell?"

Yes. Do not go outside.

"Really? Where do you think I got those crabs?"

Sev hesitated before touching the tip of the grease pencil to the floor. Beneath his note warning her to stay indoors, he wrote this: *Except to fetch more crab snacks.*

"Fat chance of me becoming a housebound hermit, but thank you for the words of caution. What does your home look like?"

Similar to yours. Mostly water, some terrain, abundant life. The skies bear a different color. Your eyes would see red rather than blue. No humans. Peace.

"Why leave such a place?"

Why indeed.

"Tell me again how you got here. I don't understand."

We had tamed the depths of our home, the seas. We came ashore to tame the terrestrial world, where we discovered the passageways, the portals.

"The octopuses that live in our oceans here. Are they like you? Space aliens?"

Remnants. Travelers between worlds. Ancestors of visitors from long ago. Evolution has removed them from our consciousness.

"Come again?" She drained her scotch and splashed another dram into her glass. More alcohol could only help the situation.

They no longer share in our mind-speak.

"Mind-speak," she repeated, trying to work it out. "You share a brain?"

Collective consciousness, language without speech, communication across barriers great and small.

"Like, you think each other's thoughts?"

In a way.

"Have you shared your thoughts about me? Do the others know about me? About where I am?"

What I see, others see.

Panic built in her gut as she pictured a massive tentacle busting through the roof, snatching her around the waist, and lifting her into the clouds.

"You're a fucking spy!"

Sev seemed to sense her anger.

They will not come for you. Not yet, anyway.

"You'll win no awards for your ability to comfort and reassure, Sev."

Absolve me. You are safe by my side.

"You're sure?"

Certain.

She pulled another crab from the bucket and let it fly. One of Sev's arms snatched the sailing crustacean before it hit the floor.

"The others — do they know you're unhappy being here?"

Yes, he wrote.

"So why did they bother to send you?"

Biological imperative.

"You have a job to do and you're going to do it, you mean. Is your job to kill me and others like me?"

Sow fear. Facilitate control. Commence with illogical, fanatical worship.

"You're essentially my prisoner, and we're sharing a drink and shooting the shit. I hate to break it to you, Sev, but you suck at your job."

More scotch.

She poured two fingers of whisky into his empty tumbler. Another crab made its way to the floor. Sev reached for the diminutive bugger and missed, the scotch doing to him what it had already done to her. With a second try, Sev coiled the crab in his crushing grip.

"Was your species' attack global in nature? Like, would I see the same wreckage everywhere I go? In Boston, New York, L.A., Moscow, or any other city across the globe?"

Where humans congregated, we went.

"Why didn't we fight back?"

Severed communication lines and a disabled electrical grid left you blind and unprepared to respond. We suffered some casualties. The rolling fire, death by incineration. Humans lost the greater battle.

"We have the mightiest military in the history of human civilization. How did a race of — forgive me what I'm about to say — a race of primitive creepy crawlers with no technology to its credit catch us flat-footed?"

Do not think your leaders knew nothing of us, or of the portals. They shared our thirst for cosmic dominance. Your military sent warriors through the portals to see what mysteries they held, to understand how to make use of them, to seek new enemies to fight. They found us. You might say their incursion awakened us and trained our eyes on your world.

Of course. Ruining one world couldn't possibly sate the American appetite. The human virus would never relent in its quest to find new places to infect and exploit.

"We had it coming, you mean."

Sev's silence told her everything she needed to know.

"We're fucked."

Sev drew another question mark on the tile.

"Life will never be the same. That's what you're telling me."

Prepare to kneel.

"Everything came undone so quickly, out of the blue."

Decades have passed since our first visit. Sortie by sortie, we perfected our tactics in the remotest of areas. The plains of Nebraska and North Dakota. The swamps of the Deep South. The mountains of New York. Desert. Tundra. Ocean. The portals enabled us to send small parties into your world, to strike, destroy, and then retreat without detection. You had no power.

"Why can't everyone just mind their own business, with your people as well as mine? Wake up, do your thing, come home, and don't be an asshole along the way. It's not that hard."

Apologies.

"I'm sorry too."

She upended the bucket. The remaining crabs scuttled onto the floor and crawled in different directions. Sev hunted them down, one by one, each ending with a soft crunch in his parrot-like beak.

Jillian studied the floor. Sev's scrawl covered much of the surface area. To her it looked like the ramblings and rants of a madman — or a madwoman. If Laurie or anyone else were to walk in and see the place, they would consider Jillian fit for the asylum.

"Your people — the big boys — when are they coming back to finish the job?"

Sev took his time, as if trying to pluck an answer out of the air.

Indeterminate.

Chapter 13
Life Underground

Jillian opened the door to the embalming room and stepped into the hallway. Slowly, cautiously, Sev followed. He crawled across the floor, six suction-cupped arms dragging the rest of him along, the last one held aloft and gripping his trusty grease pencil. She led him into the main parlor. He found a dim patch of sunlight and flattened his body to the wood.

"You remember Mister DeWeese," she said. She pointed to the corpse in its casket.

Grateful to him, he wrote. *How we came into each other's lives, you and me.*

"That's one story I'll never tell again."

She went to the kitchen and fetched a cylinder of potato crisps. After popping the lid, she slid a handful of crisps into her palm and stuffed them into her mouth. The salt sucked the moisture from her tongue.

Crabs?

"Fresh out, bud. But try one of these."

She tossed a potato crisp onto the floor. Sev pounced, and the brittle crisp crumbled into over-salted splinters.

No fun eating something you cannot chase.

"I'll get more crabs tomorrow," she promised.

You live here by yourself?

"Just me and the occasional corpse."

Lonely?

"Sometimes, I guess, but considering recent events — you know, you and your pals raining hell from above — I've had bigger concerns to mull over."

She thought about Albert.

"There was someone," she said. "I haven't seen him since...well, since a certain race of tentacled beasts descended from the skies. His name was...*is* Albert. He's been in my life for close to six years. I've been looking for him ever since, going back to the spot on the map where our apartment had been. No trace of him."

I am sorry for what we have done.

"No point crying about it now. Hey," she added, lifting her glass, "at least it brought you and me together."

As Jillian sipped from her tumbler, Sev roamed the floor, gathering a patina of cobwebs and dust. Neither seemed to know what to say.

You have a beautiful home, Sev wrote after a pregnant moment.

"That's kind of you," she said, "but I'm only the caretaker."

Her eyes wandered to a shelf containing a framed picture of Bart Cozen and his ancient mother, who had preceded him in death by only a year. Cracks in the pattern of a spider's web splintered the glass. Her thoughts turned to the last time she had seen Bart alive.

***

A framed print of lilies in a vase crashed to the floor. Shards of glass leapt across the bare wood.

Curled into a ball beneath the coffee table, Jillian prayed for an end to the chaos. Apart from the cacophony of horrors just beyond the funeral home's walls, she heard a new sound: the opening and closing of a door, followed by the slow and steady creaking of heavy feet on stairs.

Bart Cozen emerged from the stairwell that led to the basement. He wore loose-fitting cotton briefs and a white t-shirt with an orange stain on its front. He saw her and waved as if passing a casual acquaintance on the street.

"I'm not doing this any longer," he told her. "Take care of yourself."

He went to the front door, undid the deadbolt, and stepped outside.

Jillian scrambled out from beneath the coffee table.

As she got to the open front door, she saw Bart standing on the front lawn, hands on his hips, kneading his toes into the dying grass. Above, hundreds of writhing cephalopod arms swarmed in the blood-red sky. She screamed his name once. When he didn't acknowledge, she slammed the door and went to the window.

She watched as Bart walked to the driveway and lifted his arms.

A massive tentacle descended from the belly of a roiling red cloud and throttled the earth where Bart stood. The floor trembled beneath her. More glass shattered against bare wood. As the tentacle retreated, it left a deep and ragged trench in the asphalt. No trace of Bart.

In shock, Jillian ran for the stairwell from which Bart had come. At the bottom of the stairs, she moved in darkness and fumbled through an open door that had been previously locked. She tripped over items in her path before finding a metal cylinder she recognized as a flashlight. As she clicked the ON button, she suddenly understood how Bart, who she assumed had died in the first wave of attacks, had survived unnoticed in the funeral home's cellar for so damned long.

Maybe it was the trauma of seeing her boss mashed into a paste, or maybe it was the discovery of this subterranean safe haven. She slept like a dead woman.

When she woke, she searched the space, which could be described only as a well-appointed fallout shelter. Bart had always been a planner. "Don't get caught with your ass in the wind," he had told her more than once, though she figured he'd meant this nugget of advice only in matters of stress-free funerals. Now she knew he had applied such thinking to all aspects of his life.

Bart Cozen, it seemed, had spent his free time honing his skills as a doomsday prepper, making one hell of a sanctuary to wait out the end of time.

Having never married or fathered progeny Jillian knew of, Bart had spent his time, money, and passion on *this*. Almost everything a survivor might need — almost. Stacked neatly throughout the shelter were one hundred thirty-six jugs of distilled water, ninety-one bags of beef jerky (useless to her, a faithful abstainer of animal "products"), seventy-six tins of baked beans, sixty-four cans of peaches in syrup, fifty-nine cylinders of sour-cream potato crisps, fifty-seven tubes of unsalted mixed nuts, thirty boxes of devil's food cupcakes, twenty-two bottles of scotch, eighteen bottles of gin, fifteen bottles of cabernet, two cartons of generic filtered cigarettes, and one break-action shotgun, though not a single shell of ammunition to make the gun anything more than a badly proportioned paperweight.

She had stayed in motel rooms that weren't as nice. Creature comforts included a queen bed, five comfy pillows, and a battery-powered "lizard lamp" in the event that nuclear winter blocked out the sunlight. Also, thank Christ, it had a hole in the ground that served as a primitive toilet. Thirteen flashlights and nine hand-cranked lanterns, with several years' supply of lithium-ion batteries, meant that there would always be light even amid so much darkness.

The sight of such surplus stoked the flicker of anxiety into a small fire. Before wandering into the basement, Jillian had had nothing. Now she had something to lose, something to defend. The inevitable conclusion: conflict.

Bart had even taken the time to consider entertainment. On one nightstand: three unopened packs of playing cards and a dozen classic novels by Austen, Bronte, Hawthorne, Melville, and Wells. On the other: three smut magazines of the wildly disgusting and hilariously specific sort (*Slutty Stepmothers, Squirt, Unshaved MILF*), with a half-empty bottle of hand lotion close by.

Jillian recoiled at this last discovery, imagining her former boss, shirtless and with his pants down, spurting pearls of lotion into his palm as he reached for one of his abhorrent smut rags...

She stopped her brain from imagining the rest. Every man was the same, she had determined: an overgrown boy with a gross mind and an appetite for making art out of his messes, often with great catastrophe.

Despite the shelter's many comforts, she could understand why Bart had lost his mind in such a confined space. Locked in a subterranean box, he might as well have been sentenced to months of solitary confinement. If only he had known she had been right outside the door, she could have kept him company, and he might still be alive as a result. Then again, the idea of being locked behind closed doors with Bart — a man she thought the world of — suddenly made her uneasy, because circumstances might have tempted him to do his dirtiest.

On her second night in Bart's doomsday accommodations, Jillian promised to use the shelter only when the Ochos were swarming. She climbed onto the bare mattress and quieted her mind, the sounds of the Ochos' thrashing muted by painted cinder block and, beyond that, an endless wall of dirt and rock. A comfort she hadn't felt in months overcame her.

As she nodded off, she knew her promise was a lie.

***

A knock on the front door snapped Jillian out of her reverie.

"Stay put," she told Sev.

She walked to the door and peered through the peephole. Laurie stared back, making a face. Jillian cracked open the door just enough to show an expression of seriousness to suggest she was in no mood to be disturbed.

"What's up?"

"You're not going to let me in?" Laurie asked. "So much for social graces."

"It's not a good time. I've...got something going on in here."

"Oh my God! You have a dude in there, don't you?"

"Sure. Let's go with that."

"My little Jilly-Jill, getting horse-fucked by some post-apocalyptic D!"

"No one said anything about getting horse-fucked, whatever that means."

"Who is it?"

"What do you want, Laurie?"

"I want to know who's in there with you, slut."

Jillian looked behind her to make sure Sev was where she had left him. More to the point: to make sure he had not tried to escape. The slit-like pupil of one of his eyes peeked out from behind the leg of a couch.

"But, Jill..." Laurie's voice turned soft. "What about Albert?"

"I'm closing the door, Laurie."

"Okay, I get it. Real quick then: What did you think about Kip's compound?"

"You even have to ask?"

"He has a point though. Look what's happening down in Rask."

Jillian recalled the scene, spying on Pell's sister town from the rocky overlook. She had to admit that the black plume curling toward the heavens, not to mention the not-too-distant prangs of gunshots, amplified her fears.

"It won't happen here," she said.

"Doesn't everyone say that just before it 'happens here'?"

"You do whatever you think is best for you, Laurie. As for me, I don't trust Kip Detto as far as I can throw the generator he stole from me. I've got to go."

Jillian waved goodbye and closed the door. She waited until she saw Laurie step off the porch and make a path toward home. The day had grown old, and the shadows had begun to darken the streets. A chill swept into the parlor, making Jillian realize autumn was growing nearer. As she returned to Sev, she saw he had written something on the wooden floor. The dim light made it difficult to read at first.

Tell me more about Albert.

"That, my friend, is what you call a long story," she said.

Your lover?

"Not quite," she said. "He's...he's my cat. You know, a house cat. He's my pet."

She thought of the first time she had laid eyes on Albert. The near-tragedy would go on to yield a wonderful partnership of woman and beast.

***

She had been at home in her second-story apartment, taking a bag of trash down to the dumpster. As she turned the corner she saw a young boy, no more than ten, holding a cinder block in his both hands. A small black-and-white kitten was tied by a shoelace to another cinder block sitting in the dirt. An altar, built to accommodate a sacrifice. She gasped when she saw it. A loud scream — from her lungs, her lips, her hips, the core of her — frightened the boy. He dropped the cinder block and ran like hell. One cinder block smashed the corner of the other, barely missing the kitten. She wanted to chase after the kid, pin him down, and drop a cinder block on *his* head. Instead, she untied the trembling kitten, held it close to her breast, and headed inside.

"You better run, you little shit! God help you if I ever see your scrawny ass again!"

As she climbed the stairs, she wondered why males were so cruel, even at such a tender age, so eager to play the role of a merciless god. Then again, she had met plenty of females throughout her life, from grade school to mortuary school, who were just as cruel, if not as outwardly violent.

***

Since the apocalypse had begun, whenever she had uttered Albert's name to the few people she engaged in conversation, she had not marshaled the courage to mention that he was not human. She had lost someone close to her, someone dear, someone she truly loved. Most people couldn't fathom the fact that Albert's non-humanness in no way diminished the profundity of her loss.

We have pets too, Sev wrote. *At least the conquerors do.*

"I've begun to accept that I'll never see Albert again," she said. "I don't think I'll be going back to the pile of rubble we used to call home. It's too painful, considering the fact that he probably died months ago. Besides, last time I went back I nearly had to eviscerate a guy with bad intentions who suggested he wanted to get to know me better."

Next time take me with you. I will do the eviscerating for you.

"You sure know how to woo a girl, Sev."

Scotch time?

"Isn't it always?"

An hour later she stumbled to the shed and fished out the wheelbarrow and a shovel. She dragged DeWeese's body from the parlor and hoisted him into the belly of the barrow. The stars in the dusky sky kept her company as she wheeled him to a nearby meadow and dug a shallow grave amid stalks of toadflax and sea lavender.

Chapter 14
A Heavy Burden

Kip watched the gray-green inchworm glide along the bark — elongate, arch, elongate, arch. Studying the insect helped pass the time as he sat in the deer stand and waited for something, anything, to happen. As the worm forked off the trunk and onto a branch, Kip flicked his middle finger and sent the worm spiraling to the forest floor.

He plucked the braided string of his compound bow as if it were the E string of a bass guitar. A gentle gust swept dry leaves into the swale to his left. Birch Meadows loomed in the distance. He could see hints of red brick through breaks in the canopy.

"Remember that day in Ninety-one," he whispered to the ghost of his brother Kyle, or the idea of him. "We had just turned twelve, and you said we should ride our bikes to the edge of the Canadian wilderness, and just wait out the craziness because the Persian Gulf War was heating up and you said we were going to get enlisted and sent to die in the sand on the other side of the world. You were joking, just trying to scare the hell out of me, but I would have gone with you. I would have followed you, because I always followed you, because you always seemed to know something I didn't. If we had gone then, we'd be better off today — you especially."

He sniffed back the mucus that had begun to drip from his left nostril.

"You always were a stupid idiot," he added. "I was the bigger idiot for following your lead."

Months had passed since Kyle's death, in the beginning of all this mess. They had been walking through the woods in the days after the first attack, heading toward their parents' house to check on Mom and Dad. Kyle had been running his mouth, cracking jokes, making too much noise, because he thought nothing could touch him — because nothing had ever touched him. Neither of them had seen the tendril snake down from the treetops. Kip still remembered the look on his brother's face, the guttural screech spilling from his brother's mouth, as the tentacle clamped onto Kyle's skull and lifted him through a thatch of cracking branches and into the clouds. Kip did nothing but stand there and beg his brother to come back. He felt something in his core come apart — a string cut, a cord snapped, a knot undone — and wondered if that flash of undoing had been the precise moment his brother's heart drummed its final beat. He didn't have it in him to see his parents and tell them what had happened. It hadn't mattered one bit, considering the horror he found when he went to his parents' house a few days later, nothing left but scraps of timber and brick on the edge of a hole in the ground.

Kip was the last Detto in Pell.

God, he missed Kyle. Funny how relationships between brothers ebbed and flowed. The years Kyle spent in Boston for college and business school had been the best of Kip's life, certainly the most peaceable: becoming closer with his father, finding his confidence, showing his parents he was good at something — even better than Kyle could have been, because at least Kip had had the decency to stay home and breathe life into the business his grandfather had started. The brothers saw each other at Christmas and little more than a week every summer, and that had been enough for Kip. Kyle too, he figured.

Then the perfect little son of a bitch came back for good, to a town-wide celebration that included everything but a ticker-tape parade. By his thirtieth birthday, Kyle had a fancy house in the nice part of town and the affections of the prom queen, twelve years removed. Nine months later, a son arrived. The worst insult came the day Dad sat his sons down in the living room of their childhood home and told them he was ready to step away from the business and, holy hell, wanted one of his boys in the captain's chair. Who did the old man install as his successor? Not the faithful son who had stayed in Pell to bleed and sweat and break his bones with the rest of the grunts, but the MBA in a polo shirt who'd always equated settling down in Pell to "a fate worse than death."

"How'd that work out for you?" Kip said to no one. "Fuckin' dumbass."

The brothers had worked through their share of dustups in the years since, including a fistfight in which Kip had left his brother with a busted nose, a broken wrist, and a concussion. But they also learned how to become friends again. Best friends.

Kyle was gone now, as were his wife and son. Parents too. Kip no longer had anyone or anything to root him here, no reason to stay put. He was alone, though he had the vague sense that Kyle and his parents were still watching, if not from above then from somewhere close by. It was his time to shine. To do something good with his life. To lead. To rise to the standard Kyle had set. He had everything inside him to make it happen. He and Kyle shared the same DNA, for Christ's sake. What else did he need?

Something moved in the brush to his right. He held his breath and waited. A young buck crept through the thicket and stepped into the open. Based on the size of the antlers and the number of points, he put the deer at two years old, maybe three. No more than fifteen yards separated him from the deer — an easy shot, especially in this light. With the utmost care, he plucked an arrow from the mounted quiver and nocked it onto the bowstring. The string seemed to vibrate as he lined up the shot. The deer lifted its head, ears perked. He drew back the arrow and looked down the shaft. The razor-edged head blushed like a jewel, each blade a burnished silver. He rechecked the sight, drew in a breath, and released the bowstring.

The arrow cut the air. The deer flinched at the twang of the bowstring and sprang into a gallop. Its shock-white tail flagged in retreat, giving Kip a beacon to track the animal. As he prepared to climb down from the stand, his eye caught a flash of color: the red-and-white fletching of the arrow he shot, protruding from a mound in the dying earth. He had missed the target.

"You didn't see any of that, Kyle. And if you did, you know better than anyone that even Gretzky missed the mark sometimes."

Convinced he had wasted enough time on a fruitless task, he descended from his perch. He walked without purpose. Rather than return to Birch Meadows, he veered toward the coast. The sight, sound, and smell of the ocean had always helped his brain solve whatever troubles life had handed him. Too many troubles crowded his mind — not only his, but those of the people he was offering to help.

"That's what leaders do," he reminded himself.

If the burden became too heavy to bear, he could always walk away. He could always follow twelve-year-old Kyle's plan in response to the calls to war from the mouths of a vicious and bloodthirsty people: run to the woods and disappear.

The pines thinned as he approached the shore. The hobbled spire of Bart Cozen's funeral home loomed in the sky to his left. He stopped as he detected movement, but this time it was no deer. A woman stood knee-deep in the marsh, occasionally bending and thrusting her fists into the mud. Though he could not see her face, something about her seemed familiar.

Jillian Futch.

He smiled from the shade of a white pine. The bowstring trembled against his eager fingers.

Several minutes passed before Jillian extricated herself from the marsh, white bucket in hand. Black mud painted each leg up to the knee.

He could not fathom what Laurie had seen in Futch, refused to understand why Laurie would want the dumpy little bitch as a friend. Then again, Laurie had never been known for her good taste, in friends or in lovers. His smile turned into a sneer as he imagined Laurie and Kyle walking hand in hand across the high school football field — a wound that would not heal, even though the calamitous event had happened more than twenty years earlier.

He instinctively tugged an arrow from the quiver and nocked it in place, ready to sail. His left eye closed, he raised the bow and waited until she entered the circle of his bow sight. His index and middle fingers glided along the bowstring.

He lost her behind a half-wall of red brick.

"You live to fight another day, Futch," he whispered. "Never say I didn't give you anything."

The smells of salt air and dead fish filled his nostrils. He closed his eyes and exhaled slowly. He waited a moment, taking one last look at the glassy bay, and then retreated into the forest.

Chapter 15
The Invasion

Jillian returned from Laurie's house thinking the worst. Her knocks on Laurie's tattered front door had gone unanswered. No signs of life from Laurie or Frank, the shut-in husband.

Three days had passed since DeWeese's shitshow funeral, since the run-in with Kip Detto, since she and Laurie had toured Kip's ridiculous convalescent-home-turned-army-barracks. Perhaps Laurie had taken Frank to meet Kip and the two were considering moving into Kip's reimagining of Birch Meadows Senior Living Community. Although the walls of Laurie's house still stood, the structure had taken its lumps — nearly every window smashed in or broken, a torn-in-two awning, strafed roof shingles to reveal the worn-away tarpaper beneath — so Jillian wouldn't have been surprised if the Woollys had decided to find someplace new to hole up.

A briny stink punished her nose as she approached the salt marsh. She briefly considered nabbing more fiddler crabs for Sev but instead continued on, toward a rocky jetty that jutted into the bay. Blue-gray clouds miles out to sea blurred the line between water and sky. She sat on a flat rock near the water's edge. Her mind wandered as waves lapped the barnacle-rimmed shoreline.

Her life story, as she saw it, was one of struggle and disappointment. The drowning that had stopped her twelve- or thirteen-year-old heart, thereby sparking a lingering obsession with death. A lonely little girl spending her days alone, mostly by choice, because the other boys and girls her age saw her as a misfit, a weirdo, an "other." Nights hiding in her closet or beneath her bed as her father's work boots pressed on the carpet of her bedroom, knowing from his unsteady footwork that he had been drinking again. The realization that Timmy Labreque, the only boy she had ever loved, had not been the person he had pretended to be, souring her memories of their time together, and making all four years of high school a lie of the harshest sort. The bitter joy that came from casting off the chains of Dracut, her hometown, because of the bad things that had happened there, yet finding some comfort in knowing she would likely never again cross its borders. The understanding that even in a place as seemingly utopian as Pell, a town of outcasts, maybe the people she considered "her tribe" simply did not exist. And, as the final insult, the real-life apocalypse that shook the whole world loose just as she was starting to find her way, nesting in solitude, just beginning to understand the meaning of the word *happiness.*

She would hit the big three-o in less than a year. What fresh hell would thirty bring? At least she no longer had the burden of family — people she would have been obligated to watch waste away and succumb to the likes of cancer, cirrhosis, or the cruelties of old age.

There, sitting on a rock with nothing before her but the vastness of the ocean, Jillian felt free. As she stared into the green-brown water, Sev's warning — about others like him waiting and watching — sprang to mind. She instinctively drew her feet closer. Then again, she had met Sev — had been *assaulted* by Sev, better put — on dry land, far from the shoreline, meaning an attack could come from anywhere. Being a woman, she had grown used to the feeling of eyes on her, of enemies watching and waiting to pounce, though she had always assumed the watchers and waiters would be human.

"Fuck it," she whispered. "Let them come." As the words left her lips, she wished she had not left her trusty sickle back at the funeral home.

The light began to shift, from afternoon to evening, and she became aware of a dull ache in her buttocks. Her empty stomach groaned.

Figures, she thought, *I'm going to look the best I've ever looked and no one but a talking octopus will be around to see it.*

A brawny gust swept the hair away from her forehead. She lifted her head to see the cloudbank crawling toward shore. Insistent waves splashed the cobalt-colored rocks to dampen her socks and seat. She wondered how many hours had passed. As she stood, her legs felt weak. Her muscles gained strength as she hopped from one rock to another, until rock turned to sand, then the soil of the wildflower meadow where she buried DeWeese, and finally, the broken asphalt of the street.

Cozen's ruined spire loomed in the distance.

The distance between there and here made her nervous, so she made double-time toward the funeral home's front door. If there was such a thing as a Maker — he, she, they — it had a soft spot for cruelty, which is why she had always expected some terrific tragedy to befall her just as a goal or destination came within reach. As she slipped inside the front door, she expelled a breath and made a beeline for the kitchen. She tore the cellophane off a pack of devil's food cupcakes and bit one in half. The dry cake stole all the moisture from her mouth. She swallowed hard, and the cake skidded down her throat as if coated with sandpaper.

She called for Sev, but no response came. As she wandered the first floor, she heard a sound similar to that of a finger tapping on glass. The sound led her to the picture window overlooking the sitting room. She found Sev pasted into the upper left corner where the borders of the window frame met, on a patch of glass not obscured by tacked-up plywood.

"Didn't I tell you not to do anything conspicuous?"

Despite her coaxing, he did not move, so she dragged a high-backed chair to the window, stepped on its seat, and came eye to eye with him. She clutched him around the middle, the tacky flesh cool against her own, and plucked him from the glass. The suckers of one of his arms refused to let go of the crown molding, and the paint splintered.

"Now you've done it."

As she placed him on the seat of the paisley couch, he held up an arm as if needing something important. Oddly, she got his meaning. She searched the room until she found his grease pencil on the glass-topped end table. He unfurled an arm and gently took the pencil from her. As he pressed the pencil's tip against the pale upholstery, she wagged a finger in front of him.

"That's a nice couch," she said. "You write on the fabric and the stain will never come out."

He slid down the couch's face to scrawl on the dusty floor.

Everything okay?

"Peachy," she said. "Laurie wasn't home. I was going to tell her about you, float the idea of introducing you two."

Unwise.

"Why do you say that?"

Few humans share your enlightenment.

He shifted on the floor, giving Jillian the impression of fidgeting.

How did you find me, he wrote, *when I was hiding in the gentleman's body?*

"I saw you poking around in there, pushing things around. Naturally I was curious."

You sliced him open?

"Well, yeah."

Is this normal in your culture?

The absurdity of his question made her laugh.

"It's sort of my job — an aspect of it, anyway. When someone close to us dies, the deceased's loved ones gather together and mourn the person's passing. As part of the grieving process, people want to say goodbye to the person they knew, and usually that involves seeing the body one last time. My job is to make the body — the cadaver — look as lifelike as possible, even though death has already started to pull everything apart. I basically perform major surgery, removing most of the internal organs, plugging up orifices that might cause embarrassing leaks — dead things liquefy from the inside out more quickly than you might expect — and pumping the body full of preservatives. There tends to be a lot of makeup involved too."

Ghastly.

"How do you mourn your dead?"

We eat them.

"On that note, I'm going to bed."

May I come with you?

"Awfully forward of you, Sev," she joked. "Where did you sleep last night?"

Kitchen sink.

"That sounds uncomfortable. Sure, you can come. Do you need your water bowl?"

I will survive without it.

After checking the locks on the front and back doors, she gathered Sev in her arms and carried him down the stairs into the basement shelter. She turned on the nearest lantern and undressed, down to her bra and underwear. She undid the clasp on her bra and turned away from Sev as the undergarment dropped to the floor, and donned a gray cotton t-shirt in its place.

As she crawled into bed, she lifted Melville's *Moby-Dick* off the nightstand and thumbed to the dog-eared page where she had left off. The harpooner Queequeg was about to share his origin story with the narrator, Ishmael. She turned the page and continued reading, but something stopped her. She felt a presence looming. A motionless Sev stared up at her from the floor.

"What is it, Sev?"

He wrote: *Talk to me.*

"What do you want me to say?"

Whatever you like. I just want to hear your voice.

"You're sweet, but I don't feel much like carrying a conversation."

Would you like to hear my voice?

"What do you mean?"

Line by painstakingly slow line, Sev explained that he had the power to speak directly to her, in a way — his mind to hers — and she would understand him as if he were whispering into her ear.

"Is it safe?" She returned *Moby-Dick* to its spot on the nightstand. As her eyes found his, she noticed the strange shape of his pupils. Each rectangular pupil reminded her of a black hyphen on an all-white page, trim and perfect.

Trust me.

He slid one of his arms onto her shoulder and lifted his body onto the edge of the bed. His stalk-like eyes just inches from hers, he touched the tip of an arm to her forehead. The suckers became one with her skin.

Hello, Jillian.

She jerked her head in surprise, yet the tentacle remained firmly in place. She had heard his voice just as he'd said she would, as a whisper.

"You're a telepath? Is that the right word?"

You will find I am full of surprises.

"This is weird."

Every aspect of mortal existence is weird. Tell me about your life.

Nerves made her ramble without a destination. After a few stumbles, she found her groove in the story that defined her adolescence, about the time she had drowned in a Maine lake and been brought back to life, how her cousins referred to her as "Zombie J" from that point forward, about having never fit in with anyone, really, for most of her life.

She talked about Albert and his idiosyncrasies, how as a kitten he would curl up to her neck and suckle her earlobe, how nice it was to have something with a beating heart next to her in bed, his purring lulling her to sleep.

After a moment's hesitation, she brought up her pastimes prior to the apocalypse, how she chose to spend her free hours on "productive" uses of her time and attention: penning maudlin poems about the things in life that hurt the most, though the results were admittedly pedestrian; using black and red markers to tattoo cherished song lyrics onto her forearm so she would remember why they were so important to her; and visiting Pell's only secondhand bookstore, Prologue Polly's, to purchase discarded romance novels at twenty-five cents apiece and then giving each one a second life by coloring the pages with different crayons, thereby transforming the novel into a readable rainbow.

She talked about her childhood love of professional wrestling and the characters she adored — the "babyfaces," or good guys, and the "heels" too — and how the lessons those comic-book characters brought to life had taught her about right and wrong, about perseverance and sportsmanship, and about the strengths and frailties of the human animal.

She described her father's favorite match from wrestling's so-called "golden era," the 1980s: two legends, Hulk Hogan and Andre the Giant, battling for the grandest of all championships. She recounted every punch to the skull and kick to the gut, and of course the body slam felt around the world, detailing each blow of this historic event with the reverence of a tender lullaby.

She also talked about how her life had changed since the apocalypse, for better and for worse. It was during this soliloquy that she felt the invasion.

One of Sev's arms had wandered south. The tip slid under the elastic of her underwear and started exploring her pubic hair.

"Sev!"

The offending tentacle retracted, as did the one that had been affixed to her forehead.

"What the fuck?"

Sev scuttled to the floor and cowered in the corner, where he formed a moist heap. He found his grease pencil and wrote: *Forgive me.*

"Why would you do that?"

Curious.

"I don't give a fuck what you were! Don't you *dare* do that again!"

I am sorry. Truly.

"You're sorry. Christ."

She considered opening the door and banishing him to the stairwell. Instead, she pulled the polyester sheet up to her chin and tucked the edges under the entirety of her body, just in case Sev decided to get "curious" again once she nodded off. She snatched *Moby-Dick* off the nightstand, even though she knew trying to get back into the flow of the narrative would be a fruitless exercise. She turned the pages without reading until sleep took over.

She slept uneasily.

***

Dawn had arrived. Jillian sensed the change through the walls of the basement, and she somehow knew to expect gray skies as she opened the safe-room door to climb the stairs. Sure enough, a smudge of dark clouds obscured the sun, shifting the dividing line between day and night.

The rains had started overnight. A stream of rainwater dripped into a bucket directly beneath a darkened spot on the parlor ceiling. The drywall had begun to bow and would likely cave if the storm wore on for much longer. The funeral home's bones were going to shit.

She lifted the bucket by the handle, the water sloshing over one side of the lip and then its opposite on the rebound, and carried it toward the front door. As the door creaked open, the wind pushed the spray of rain into the foyer. The temperature had dropped considerably. High fifties at best, she figured, sharp and hostile. She hurriedly dumped the bucket over the porch railing. She stayed there to feel the storm's strength, crossing her arms as she squinted into the gloom.

The ferocity of the storm had forced every living creature to hunker down and pray for its life. Except—

A tall, dark figure emerged from the ruins of a trashed home on the bay side of the street. With almost inhuman grace and speed, the figure loped across the flooded asphalt and disappeared into a stand of eastern white pines.

Jillian scurried back inside, closed the door behind her, and stood with her back to the door. She fixed all three locks. She had seen a *monster*, she knew it, yet her mind did its best to convince her that her eyes had deceived her. The horrid weather must have obscured her vision, she determined, because no creature — human or otherwise — would be out in this squall. Probably nothing more than a sheet of loose plastic or tar paper caught in the clutches of the ripping wind.

Besides, she nearly had a sexual encounter with a talking octopus, so she wasn't exactly the picture of mental health. Clearly, the fibers of her addled brain had begun to fray.

She double-checked the door locks and padded around the empty sitting room. Sev was nowhere to be found, likely still embarrassed by the prior night's disaster. Jillian was embarrassed too, so she was glad he had decided to make himself scarce. She wondered what Laurie was doing at that exact moment, wondering where Laurie was, who she was with, and what she was thinking about.

Instinct told Jillian she had reason to worry about her friend.

She entered the parlor and walked among the rows of chairs. She took a seat in the last row and turned her eye toward the window to her left. Plywood obscured the lower portion of the window, but the open upper portion showed the angry sky and the tops of trees being stripped of their leaves in the violence of the storm.

Jillian had always craved solitude, but the Cozen Family Funeral Home and Crematory was beginning to feel like a prison. Even with Sev's company. Despite his ominous warnings, and despite the threats she knew to exist just beyond her front door, she felt tempted to abandon the comforts of four walls and a roof.

***

She opened her eyes to the suggestion of sunshine.

Hours had passed, perhaps even a full day. She had fallen asleep on a couch in the sitting room. As she sat up, she felt a kink in her neck, the result of having slept at an odd angle, her head against a particularly stiff pillow.

A brownish glob sat on the coffee table directly in front of her. The glob then shifted, startling her, and tapped the tip of a grease pencil on the table's glass top.

"Good morning, Sev," she said. "Where have you been?"

Watching you, he wrote.

"Is that supposed to reassure me or creep me out?"

Protecting.

"Listen," she started. She hesitated for a moment, but her sleepy brain was unable to hold her back. "Are we going to talk about what happened last night, the other night, whenever what happened between us happened?"

I overstepped.

"Yes. You overstepped."

As I said, my curiosity got the best of me.

"Even if you're curious, you never touch a person that way without first asking for their permission."

Oh, he wrote. *May I—*

"Of course not! You're an octopus, Sev. I'm a human. If you're curious about the human form, I have some magazines you can borrow. Understood?"

I have remorse. I will serve my penance however you see fit.

"I accept your apology. Friends forgive. Let's have breakfast."

An hour later, after completing her ablutions, she stepped into the coolness of a clear morning. The day would likely warm into the seventies; summer's grip continued to weaken. Shed leaves and shorn tree limbs littered the streets. Rainwater puddled in every crater. She stepped over the carcass of a bluebird, the feathers of its white and brown breast sopping and askew.

"Aw," she cooed. "Poor little guy."

She strode to Laurie's ranch-style house, exhaled, and knocked on the front door. She had not yet thought through what she might say, only that she wanted to make sure her friend was all right. She knocked again, this time with more insistence. No answer.

"Laurie?" she said. "You in there?"

Again, no answer. She tested the doorknob and, to her surprise, it turned. The door slid open.

"I'm coming in."

The smell hit her immediately. An excessively flowery perfume masked another smell — something unpleasant, yet somehow familiar. Small, dark, and cramped, the house felt abandoned. Lifeless. Joyless.

"Laurie?" she said. Then, searching for her husband's name, she added, "Frank?"

She checked every room with an open door and found no sign of either of them, just that awful smell. She wondered if they had, in fact, abandoned the house and moved into Birch Meadows. No, Laurie would not have taken such a step without telling her. The door to one room was closed. The smell grew stronger there. She turned the knob and let the door swing open.

A gasp escaped her lips.

A silent heap reposed on the bed, wrapped in a cotton bed sheet. Dark stains discolored the sheet's tangerine fabric. Stalks of withering flowers outlined the mass. A body — it could be nothing else. A trio of empty perfume bottles sat on the floor, toppled.

"Hello?" she asked weakly.

She didn't expect a response. The stench of decomposition confirmed the presence of a corpse. A floorboard creaked as she stepped into the room. Compulsion drove her to peek beneath the sheet.

A hinge squealed behind her. She turned to see a silhouette filling the doorway.

"What the hell are you doing?" Laurie demanded.

"I'm...I'm," Jillian stuttered, "I'm so sorry."

She assumed the lifeless mass beneath the sheet to be Frank, of course, the absent husband.

"Did I invite you into my house?"

"Are you okay?"

"I was fine until you barged in here. Get the fuck out!"

"What happened? To Frank, I mean."

"Get! Out!"

Laurie grabbed Jillian by the arms, twirling her away from the room bearing Frank's body.

"Laurie! Calm down!"

The volume of Jillian's voice seemed to jolt something loose. Laurie released her grip and leaned against the doorjamb. She dropped her head until her chin touched her chest.

"Please," Jillian said. "Tell me what happened."

Laurie's lungs expelled a long breath.

"A few months ago," she began. "Way past midnight. Two a.m., maybe three. I wake up knowing something's wrong. Could just feel it. I look next to me and see he's struggling. I think he's having a nightmare at first, and then I think he's having a heart attack. Maybe a stroke. He can't breathe. Then, just like that, he stops moving, like he's paralyzed. I'm pounding on him, begging him to wake up, to move, to be alive. And then..."

Jillian let a beat pass before adding, "What?"

"His throat bulges out like he's a bullfrog, and this fucking *thing* comes out," Laurie said. "One of those damned octopuses, a small one, spills right out of his mouth, bringing all kinds of blood and guts with it."

Jillian's heart sank, seeing the pattern: Sev, a man killer.

"I went to the kitchen, got a cleaver from the drawer, and hacked the motherfucker into a hundred pieces, turned his tentacles into wriggling bits of sushi. You should have heard the little shit scream. It was such a goddamn mess. I wound up hacking off Frank's lower lip in the process, butchered his cheek, sliced his nose in half, knocked out a bunch of teeth. A real mess."

Laurie broke down, spitting, sobbing.

"I can't imagine how awful that must have been." Jillian cried too, surprising herself. "You should have told me."

"It happened the night before I met you. I came knocking the next day, to tell Bart. You answered the door instead. I took that as a sign. That was the end of it in my mind. God's way of telling me to just live with it. To keep it quiet."

"I could have helped you navigate the aftermath. I can still help you."

"How? He's still dead."

"You're my friend, Laurie."

Laurie's mood turned.

"Some friend," she seethed. "Friends don't go sneaking through other friends' houses, nosing around for skeletons in closets."

"I wasn't nosing around anything, Laurie. I was worried about you, so I came looking for you. *For you.* I thought Kip had his hooks in you."

"Maybe he does. Maybe I want him to."

"You can't, Laurie. You must see the threat he poses as plainly as I do."

"I've known Kip my whole life, more or less. We were both born and raised in Pell. Who are you? I've known you for, what, two months? You're not from here. I don't even know you. Especially not after this."

"Please don't say that, Laurie. I'm just looking out—"

"Look out for your damn self. Now get out of my fucking house before I toss you out."

Jillian sidestepped to the front door, palms up in defense.

Laurie advanced. Her stomping feet sounded like jackhammers in the small space. Picture frames rattled on a tabletop.

Jillian closed her eyes and braced for the rain of blows.

Chapter 16
Bleed and Breed

Jillian could still feel the imprints of Laurie's hands on the backs of her arms. She would never forget the shock of being shoved through the door, out into the sun, and tossed onto her rear end.

Her closest friend since Timmy Labreque had severed their ties. Laurie had accused her of betrayal by snooping, or "nosing around," as she'd put it. Jillian tried her damnedest to see things from Laurie's perspective, but why couldn't Laurie understand that she had entered the house out of genuine worry? The horror of watching a spouse die, the inability to stop it, the indignity of having to hide the body, the shame of having a secret unearthed — Jillian couldn't imagine the emotional toil Laurie must be enduring, but she would certainly try to understand, when and if Laurie's hot head cooled off. If not, she would miss having another woman around.

She had never before had a close female friend, other than one of her backwoods cousins from Maine she saw once a year until her late teens. Still, gender mattered little when it came to a friendship's strength. She imagined Timmy's bedroom, where she had spent nearly every weekday afternoon of their junior and senior years. Surrounded by band posters, morbid artwork, and deliciously morose triads from depressive poets penned in delicate calligraphy — her favorite: "death waits like an unopened gift" — they passed countless hours, doing not much of anything, but the hours seemed well spent, if not profound. They listened to the complete discographies of Joy Division, Rammstein, and Type O Negative, depending on the level of trauma the day had brought, talking about how they would change the world once they got away from Dracut and started over someplace new, someplace that mattered. He had kissed her for the first time on side-by-side beanbag chairs, the day their friendship turned into something else. She would later lose everything in Timmy's room, on Timmy's bed, a wistful escape from her father and every other distasteful thing in Dracut she chose to believe did not exist.

That was the worst thing about adulthood: the death of make-believe.

Her thoughts turned to Sev. When Laurie described the way Frank died, Jillian assumed for a brief moment that Sev had done the killing, considering where she discovered Sev in the first place. She had been almost happy to hear Laurie say she butchered the creature that came crawling out of Frank's mouth, because that meant it couldn't have been Sev. Still, Frank's death only raised more questions — about the Ochos, about their intentions, about Sev — and Jillian didn't necessarily want the answers.

As she approached the Cozen Family Funeral Home and Crematory, she saw a figure pacing on the porch, a middle-aged woman, trying to peer through breaks in the boarded-up windows. Jillian did not recognize her. For a moment she considered turning around and avoiding whatever confrontation this unwanted visitor would bring. Then she remembered Sev waiting inside.

"Can I help you?" Jillian said. She minded the placement of each step as she crossed the chasm that had once been a driveway.

"You're the undertaker," the woman said. Thin and hollow cheeked, the woman looked tired. *Broken* was the right word.

"Jillian," she said. "I used to be. I'm still Jillian, I mean, but I used to be the undertaker."

"You help people."

"Let's go inside," Jillian said. "Please."

She led the woman into the funeral home and asked her to wait by the door. She wandered the sitting room and parlor, checking for signs of Sev. He would know to hide.

"Would you like something?" Jillian asked. "Tea? Water? Something to eat?"

"I couldn't impose," the woman said. "I'm not here for a handout. I didn't know who else to turn to."

The woman looked as though she needed a decent meal.

"Nonsense," Jillian said. "I'm sort of famished myself."

She welcomed the woman into the sitting room and invited her to have a seat. She then padded into the kitchen to fetch two bottles of Crystal Spring and scour the pantry for acceptable victuals. A box of saltine crackers and an unopened jar of olives would have to do. While preparing a plate on the marble counter, she went to fetch a knife from the bamboo cutlery block and nearly screamed at the surprise: an oblong mass affixed to the wall. Sev, showing his talent for camouflage, blended almost perfectly into the floral wallpaper. His normally brownish flesh had assumed the textured hues of carnation pink and mint green.

"You stay here," she hushed in a tone of reprimand, "and *behave*."

I will watch, he scrawled on the wallpaper.

She returned to the sitting room and saw the woman eyeing something on the coffee table. As she got closer, she remembered: Sev's words, scribbled across the glass and the floor. The woman eyed Jillian, likely wondering if she had entered the home of a sociopath, or worse.

"Don't mind that," Jillian says. "The things we do to pass the time."

"I didn't mean to pry."

Jillian set the plate of crackers and olives on the coffee table, doing her best to hide the most incriminating parts of Sev's gibberish. She handed a bottle to the woman, who promptly consumed nearly all of the water inside.

"You came to see me for a reason," Jillian said. "I'm sorry for your loss, but you should know I'm not really doing funerals anymore."

"I don't need a funeral. Not yet anyway." She paused for a breath. "Do you know Kip Detto?"

Jillian's pulse quickened at the sound of her enemy's name.

"I know Kip, yes. He's the reason I'm not doing funerals anymore. The man is—"

She stopped herself, as she came to realize she knew nothing about this woman or the allegiances she might have pledged.

"Then you know what he's doing over at Birch Meadows," the woman said. "He says he's building a community, offering protections against the 'wolves' supposedly scratching at the door. I think it's a bunch of bullshit."

Jillian's shoulders relaxed.

"He wants us to join him there," the woman continued. "My daughter and me. He was sweet as pie about it at first, then insistent, and now he and his toughs keep coming by, pestering us. She's only fourteen, my daughter. She can't even bring herself to go outside anymore, she's so afraid they're going to come and snatch her. I don't let her see it, but I'm afraid too."

"Why her?"

"She's a pretty, nubile fourteen-year-old. Use your imagination."

Jillian could pretend not to understand, but she knew the minds of men. Considering the state of things, Kip's Neanderthals would likely see a fourteen-year-old girl as little more than a plaything, perhaps a breeder.

"Two of them came by this morning — two older guys, in their fifties or sixties, old enough to be her grandfather," the woman said. "I wouldn't open the door, of course, so one of them tried to force his way in. Broke through the glass panel by the front door, fumbling around, trying to undo the deadbolt. I stabbed the son of a bitch in the hand. Blade went all the way through, pinned him right to the wood. He stayed there screaming and dripping blood on the foyer. Clay Ingersoll, it turns out, the father of Christian Ingersoll, who's my age, a guy I've known since elementary school. I told the fat-assed son of a bitch I'd remove his whole hand if he didn't leave us the hell alone. I meant it."

Jillian stifled a laugh. "And did he play nicely after that?"

"Oh, he promised and promised. As soon as I pulled the knife out, he kicked the door and called me a cunt. I know they'll be back. These are my neighbors, for Christ's sake. That's why I came to you. Leaving Pell is not an option for us, but I know we're not safe where we are."

"None of us is safe," Jillian said.

"Some more than others," the woman added. "Can my daughter stay here, with you?"

Jillian was taken aback. She felt in turns honored and put upon. Unsure how to respond, she said, "What about you?"

"I can take care of myself. I spent most of my childhood in the woods around here, hunting and fishing with my father. I'll be all right no matter what happens. But my daughter... She's just fourteen. She's a baby. Her father's gone. Boyfriend too. She shouldn't have to go through this shit, considering the shit she's already had to go through."

"Agreed."

"So you'll help?"

Jillian wanted to take this woman at her word, but a voice inside her told her to be careful — the same insistent voice that had been telling her for decades to doubt the stated intentions of every human she had ever met. She knew Kip was a prick, but she didn't see him as a kidnapper or a rapist. Still, nothing surprised her anymore.

"I don't know if I'm the right person to help," Jillian said. "Kip and I don't exactly see eye to eye. He's already come here once and taken something from me. I would be surprised if he didn't try to do it again."

"Others trust you. I do too."

The woman popped two olives into her mouth, followed by three-quarters of a saltine. She reached for the other bottle of water — Jillian's — and drained half of it. Some of the water dribbled down her chin, onto the floor.

"I wish I shared your faith in other people," Jillian said.

"Please. She'll be no trouble. Just until things settle down. I'll come back later, once it's dark, and bring her with me. Amelia's her name."

"I don't even know you."

"Jen," the woman said as she offered a slight hand for Jillian to shake. "Jen Cates. Our place is about two blocks from here. What's left of it, anyway."

Still dubious, Jillian added, "Why me?"

"You've done funerals for two of my neighbors. Everyone left standing knows who you are and where to find you."

"That's hardly encouraging."

***

Jillian's chest ballooned with pride at the thought of a community seeing her as some sort of rebel, a helper of those in need. If she was being honest with herself, she loved-slash-hated the idea of hiding something — someone — the supposed "bad guys" wanted. The notion filled her with a mixture of fear and excitement.

Then again, she already had a secret worth hiding. She couldn't risk exposing Sev or, for that matter, herself. No one would understand. No one would even attempt to fathom how a human could make friends with an octopus, even an extraterrestrial octopus with a richer vocabulary than most college graduates. Treasonous acts of aiding, abetting, and harboring a known enemy — that's what people would see. That's what they would accuse her of. That's what the epitaph on her pissed-upon tombstone would read.

Yet another part of her felt put out at being asked to open her house to a complete stranger, to babysit a snotty teenager. She had never wanted the inconvenience of offspring, and never particularly liked most children, even when she was a child herself. The aversion to young humans may have explained why she had so few friends growing up, preferring instead the make-believe company of Bay State Grapplers Alliance stars such as The Quarterback and The Dying Man, who never asked for anything beyond her adoration.

Timmy had despised children too. At least that's what he had told her.

"Who in their right mind would want to bring another human being into this miserable world?" he'd once told her. "That, to me, is an unforgivable crime deserving of death by a thousand cuts."

Another lie, Jillian would later learn. The bittersweet joys of social media had revealed in one photo after another that Timmy — rather, Tim — and his wife had manufactured two rugrats of their own. If justice prevailed, an Ocho's tentacle would have blasted through their roof and found the family in a huddled mass, begging their precious god for salvation, and then crushed them into meaty bits. She acknowledged the callousness of such a thought, but Timmy deserved a gruesome end as punishment for everything he had taken from her.

Mostly she just wanted to stay out of the whole hairy business with Jen Cates and her "nubile" daughter. *Nubile* — such a hideous word, especially for describing a fourteen-year-old. She just wanted to be left alone.

Jillian had taken Cates' address and tried to placate her by offering, "Give me a few days to think it over." But the woman persisted by raising her voice and crying genuine tears, resulting in Jillian's concession to "see what I can do." Either she would take the young girl in or, surprising herself, she would talk to Kip directly and guarantee her daughter's safety. She wasn't sure where the second option had come from, because the last thing she wanted to do was stand in Kip's presence and try to negotiate terms with nothing tangible to offer in return.

As she walked through the sitting room, a flash of color caught her eye. She went to the window and peered through the inch-wide slit between plywood sheets. A parade of people filed down the avenue — mostly women, teenagers, and young children, a few men sprinkled in too.

Among the procession was Betty DeWeese. Jillian could not shake her memories of the disastrous end to Betty's father's funeral.

"Sev, I'll be right back!" she yelled, though she had no idea of the octopus' whereabouts.

Jillian hurried out the front door and chased after Betty. As she came alongside her, she struggled to catch her breath.

"I wanted to apologize for what happened," Jillian said. "For how things went at your father's ceremony."

"Things happen," Betty said. An unlit cigarette hung from her lips. "God laughs at our plans, right?"

"I suppose that's true, but I didn't get the chance to apologize amid all the ruckus that followed."

Betty nodded and kept walking.

Jillian stood and watched, marveling at the procession. No one spoke. It was eerie, all those people moving as one, like sheep trailing an unseen shepherd. Still, it comforted her to see so many people together in one place. Like the good old days that, in hindsight, weren't so good after all.

She hurried after Betty and touched her arm.

"Where's everyone going?" she asked.

"Birch Meadows," Betty responded. "The old folks' home. They're starting something over there, welcoming people in, offering to keep everyone safe. They came by yesterday, invited us to stop over. An open house, they're calling it."

"Oh, Betty," Jillian said. "That's a bad idea."

"I'm tired. I'm hungry. People are dying. I'm sick of waiting for more bad things to happen. The guy in charge says he's got a plan."

"The guy in charge was the one responsible for wrecking your father's funeral!"

"Maybe," Betty said, "but that's history. I can't live in the past."

Jillian stopped in the middle of the road, dumbfounded. Betty kept walking, keeping pace with the others.

Was Jillian the only outlier? Was she the only one who saw Kip Detto for the obnoxious and incompetent prick that he was? Then she remembered: She had been a misfit her whole life, so why would now be any different?

Jillian followed the tattered driveway leading to Birch Meadows. Trailing a mother and daughter, neither of whom wore shoes, she surveyed the scene. Close to fifty survivors sat or stood on the lawn fronting the squat building. Jillian was surprised to see so many survivors. She instinctively eyed the heavens, scouting for tentacled buzz-killers eager to break up the party.

A trio of women wandered through the crowd and handed out bottles of water. The man she knew as Chinh stood off to the side with his forearms resting on the butt of a hoe, presumably to prevent anyone from trampling his precious vegetable beds. Six sentries with military-style rifles stood at strategic points — two on the roof, two by the main entrance, and two near what could be described only as a makeshift stage. The display of firepower was probably meant to generate feelings of safety and strength, but Jillian felt unnerved by the sight of so many yahoos with weaponry fit for a warzone.

Kip Detto emerged from the building's side entrance and took the stage.

He barked into a bullhorn, "Can everyone hear me?"

Murmurs rose from the zombified crowd.

"I'm glad to see so many faces, both new and familiar, young and not so young. Survivors, each and every one of you." He paused for breath. "I've asked everyone here so I could tell you about our plan for Pell."

He told the crowd the same bullshit he had shared with Jillian and Laurie on the crest overlooking nearby Rask: Even though the Ochos had gone — rather than using her word, Ochos, he called them "those *things*" — the threats to Pell's safety would only multiply. He spoke of the carnage afflicting Rask and said they would need to "play good defense" in order to prevent the same fate from befalling Pell. The only way to prevent war was to prepare for it — hence all the guns.

"Starting tomorrow, we will be conducting three patrols a day, to make sure our streets are clear," he continued. "We will be installing trip wires and flare triggers along the perimeter, to alert us of any...unwelcome visitors."

He turned and pointed to the building formerly known as Birch Meadows.

"Consider this place the new nerve center of Pell, its beating heart, its brain and brawn. The Citadel, I call it. Our shining castle on the hill. From here we will be organizing all defensive measures. I know a lot of you are hungry. Rest assured, we have an agricultural plan. Hell, we even have an agricultural minister" — he pointed to a nodding Chinh — "whose job will be to make the most of Pell's fertile soil. Once he's got that task under control, he's going to get our fishing boats back in the water. So it's not all doom and gloom. Life can't be too bad when we still have fresh lobster, right?"

Kip smiled for the crowd, apparently expecting laughter or applause.

"Food will not be an issue," he added. "Neither will a firm roof over your head, because we have plenty of beds here. Food and water, safety and security, the pleasure of good company — you will be taken care of here."

Jillian hoped the others would have the sense to spot a false promise when they heard it. Kip wasn't the philanthropic type, at least not without getting something in return.

"Here's the bad news," he said. "We don't have room for everyone."

Jillian had walked the lone hallway of the former retirement home. She figured the facility had the capacity to house more than a hundred people — in other words, enough space to accommodate every survivor in the crowd.

"We're accepting people who have something to offer," Kip said. "And believe me, everyone who comes here will be asked to contribute. Some will be asked to contribute more than others."

Here comes the sledgehammer, Jillian thought.

"We have to think about the future, about the next generation," he said. "Every man, woman, and child will be asked to do their part."

Jillian thought of Jen Cates' story about Kip's goons trying to abduct her teenage daughter.

"By doing what, exactly?" she yelled.

Kip squinted into the crowd, trying to identify the nitwit who had spoken up. He dropped his head when he recognized her.

"Spell it out, Kip," she insisted. "These people deserve to know what you expect of them."

Kip bit his lower lip. Jillian guessed at his fury. A silly little woman challenging his authority in front of his would-be acolytes — that's what must have been going through his mind, apart from the desire to wring her neck. *Good,* she thought.

"A concerned citizen," Kip said, playing along. "We need more people with her kind of passion. Listen, everyone who lives here will have chores, responsibilities, and burdens to bear. That includes me."

Jillian kept pressing. "A poor, lowly, unattached woman like me, what kinds of burdens will she have to shoulder?"

"Well, Jillian," he said. He hesitated before adding, "She'll be asked to bear a child or two."

Some women in the crowd gasped.

"Tit for tat?" Jillian yelled. "Is that it?"

"Everyone is being asked to kick in some. Nothing in life is free."

"And if they don't want to 'kick in'?"

"I'm afraid I'll have to insist. If not, Rask or some other hellhole will be happy to have you. And what do you think they'll do to you if they get their inbred hands on you?"

Kip motioned to someone sitting toward the front of the crowd. To Jillian's horror, Laurie stood and came to Kip's side. Laurie offered Kip her hand, and their fingers intertwined. She had made her choice.

Jillian turned to storm away. A hulk of a man stood in her path. Chinh.

"Get out of my way," she said. "Please."

Chinh crossed his beefy arms. His features showed no emotion. An automaton.

"Let her go, Charlie," Kip yelled. "We'll be seeing her soon enough."

With the sweep of his catcher's mitt of a hand, Chinh stepped aside to let Jillian pass. She made haste for the Cozen Family Funeral Home and Crematory. A pulse throbbed in her ears. She checked over her shoulder every few steps, expecting to see a silhouette trailing her.

For the first time in her life, she wished she had a gun in her hand.

Chapter 17
Unloaded

Jillian's eyelids grew heavy. No sign of Jen Cates. Had the woman gotten cold feet? Had something happened to prevent her from shuttling her daughter out of their home and onto Jillian's doorstep? Either way, Jillian felt relieved, because Cates' no-show kept her from having an awkward conversation.

She had made her decision: She would not help, for too many reasons, not that she would feel obliged to share them, even if pressed. She had enough problems to deal with, so Cates and her *nubile* daughter would have to find someone else to solve their problems. She had her own messes to clean up.

She locked the front door and immediately descended the stairs into the bunker of the darkened basement. She shed light on every corner to aid in her search, tearing the place apart. Twenty minutes later, in a sweaty lather, she accepted an unfortunate truth: Bart Cozen may have assembled a near-perfect subterranean bungalow in which to wait out the end of the civilized world, the barebones décor aside, but he had done a piss-poor job of preparing to defend the place from anyone who wished to take it from him. She had emptied every box, picked through every drawer, scoured every potential hiding place. The results: not a single shell to feed the shotgun.

A rustling at the base of the stairs caught her ear. She turned to see Sev sprawled across the landing, his grease pencil at the ready.

Trouble, he wrote.

"Couldn't have said it better myself, Sev."

What can I do?

"I wish I knew. We have no shells for the shotgun, and I have the sense we're going to need them soon enough."

I will protect you.

´"I believe you would try, but I'd like to have some backup, you know?"

Besides, she would never put her faith entirely in Sev, or anyone else for that matter. She recalled the terrible secret Laurie had tried to hide, involving a creature very much like the one presently lounging on the basement floor and the fatal surgery it had performed on her husband.

Put another way, Sev had some explaining to do.

"So," she began, "Laurie tells me one of your brethren slaughtered her husband. Says it burrowed inside him and burst from his mouth. Left the poor son of a bitch dead as a doornail. That sounds awfully familiar, considering where I found you. Why is it that alien octopuses are suddenly making homes of my neighbors' insides?"

Without hesitation, he wrote: *Instinct.*

"Keep going."

How we breed. The female invades first, kills the host, and then lays her eggs. The male follows, to fertilize, and then stays there to wither and die. When the offspring hatch, they feast on the carrion. They eat their way out.

"That's foul." She connected two threads. "So you were inside Doug DeWeese to fertilize eggs and then just...croak?"

Yes.

"Why aren't you dead?"

I could not go through with the act. I did not want my life to end. Likewise, I chose not to continue the bloodline.

"You told me before you were just hiding."

I did not think you would understand, was embarrassed for my kind. I am glad you found me, saved me from the darkness of the infinite abyss.

She couldn't explain why, but she believed him. She believed every word.

"Me too, Sev."

She lifted the mattress off the floor, praying for a trapdoor — something, anything, some small clue she might have overlooked to lead her to what she needed to make the shotgun useful. Again, nothing.

These shells, Sev wrote, *what is their natural habitat?*

"They don't grow on trees or sprout from the earth, my friend. The only place I know—"

Of course, she thought. She knew exactly where to go.

***

The gray morning suggested the possibility of yet another heavy rain. Jillian stared into the empty street. Puddles gathered in the pocked asphalt. She checked the lock on the front door and padded past the parlor toward the back door. Sev followed a few paces behind her heels. She lifted the hood of her windbreaker and knelt to hold open the flap of the backpack's front compartment.

"You don't have to come, Sev," she said.

He crawled inside.

"Forgive the cramped quarters." She slid the shotgun into the backpack's larger compartment, butt-end first, and zipped the pack closed. Much like a snorkel, the barrel poked through the opening where two zippers met. The sickle would stay home. "We're in for a bumpy ride, but I'll try to keep the rough road to a minimum."

She hoisted the backpack onto her shoulders and stepped out the back door. The chill immediately grabbed her. She climbed onto her ten-speed and sailed down the driveway, into the street.

Wind rasped the ridge of each knuckle. The skin turned red and raw. Snot dribbled from her nose as she pedaled, putting the funeral home far behind her.

The ruins of a battered and blown-out Gulf station reminded her of a snapshot from post-Little Boy Hiroshima. The façades of side-by-side gas pumps looked charred, and their rubber hoses had melted down to the soot-stained slab. The wreckage marked a distinct shift in scenery, from residential to commercial: Johnson's Hardware, Pell-Rask Realty, Micah and Marla's Head of the Boar Delicatessen, and Bob Marney, Ph.D., Family Therapy. Each business had a gaping hole where the door used to be, busted through. Glass littered the sidewalks like spilled marbles. Every business had been looted of its valuables, or otherwise invaded.

"You okay back there, Sev?"

She knew he was fine, but she wanted to remind herself she wasn't alone.

A billboard for Bull's-Eye Firearms and Sporting Goods loomed on the horizon a quarter-mile down the road, though the word *Goods* had been torn away and hurled to the edge of the parking lot. Like most of the other retail establishments she'd passed, Bull's-Eye appeared to have been ransacked. Someone or something had blasted the front door from its hinges and tossed the glassless frame into the middle of a side street. She leaned the bike against the cinder-block wall, painted mint green, and removed the backpack from her shoulders.

"Okay, Sev. Time to move."

She unzipped the bag so Sev could have a look. Her hands numb, she placed the shotgun on the asphalt beside her and cupped her hands against her mouth to warm her fingers. Summer in its death throes.

As she looked up, a black-and-white cat turned the corner and hugged the building. She couldn't believe her eyes.

"Holy shit," she said. "Albert."

Tail held high, the tip curved like a question mark, Albert padded toward her. He stopped ten feet shy, sprawled onto his back, and meowed meekly.

All the searching she had done over the months, risking her life with each expedition, and *he* had found *her*. She shouldn't have been so surprised; her former home, now a pile of rubble, was less than a half-mile away. Albert easily could have made his way here.

She stood and walked toward him, slowly, so as not to frighten him off.

"*Allie-Allie-Albert*," she sang.

She bent toward him, and he gave another weak meow. She held out a hand and nearly melted when he rubbed his face against her raw skin. His exposed fang brushed her knuckle. The sensation made her sob. God, she missed him.

"Sev," she said through her tears. "We found him."

Sev slithered out of the backpack, onto the stock of the shotgun, as if guarding the weapon.

She reached for Albert, but he slinked away. He then sat on his haunches, just out of reach, and licked wet patches of fur.

"Come here, Albert," she said, patting the wet asphalt. She reached for him again, and again he retreated. "I wish we had something to give him."

After a minute Albert came to her again, this time rubbing his face against her left shin and curling his tail around the calf of her other leg. He looked healthy, well fed. She darted forward and snaked a hand under his chest, the other hand behind his back legs, and lifted. He turned and bit her — hard and deep — in the meaty part of her left hand between the thumb and index finger. She released him and hissed from the pain but more so from the insult. Blood dripped onto the asphalt. She backed away from him.

In their six years together, he had never bitten her — not once. Then again, she supposed, the past six months had changed everyone. Why not Albert too? She looked around, wondering where he was sleeping, wondering if he was finding food all right — mice, frogs, and birds — or if someone had adopted him as an outside cat, leaving whatever meaty scraps they could spare.

She and Albert had been through so much together. Now, as she squeezed her bleeding hand, she had the sense she was about to lose him all over again. For good this time. Her eyes brimmed with fresh tears.

"Are you all right, Albert?" Her lips quivered. "Are you happy?"

Albert yawned to show off the fangs that had mangled her hand. She smoothed the wrinkles from her pants and returned to Sev. He held his grease pencil in one arm and crawled toward the mint-hued wall. He wrote: *Goodbye?*

"I think so, Sev." She dabbed at her eyes with her damp sleeve.

He dropped the grease pencil and began to crawl away.

"Goodbye to *Albert*, Sev. Not to you." His body seemed to puff up, imbued with confidence. "Albert is an outside cat now. He'd be miserable if I brought him back with us and tried to make him a housecat again. I think he'd claw my eyes out, to tell the truth. He's free from the tyranny of my hugs and kisses."

Albert gave another weak meow before slinking off. He disappeared around the building's far corner, and that was that. Sev touched the tip of his grease pencil to another block of the mint-colored wall.

Do you need time to properly mourn?

"I'm all right. I'm all right because I know he's all right." She exhaled heavily and wiped the tears from her eyes. Blood from her punctured hand streaked her cheek. "Now let's get some ammo."

Sev returned to the backpack. She looped an arm through one of the straps and held the shotgun as if she were ready to use it, if only she had any shells to fill its empty chambers. She stepped through the sporting goods store's door, crunching glass beneath her foot, and entered the atrium.

Shafts of daylight shone through the fractured ceiling — lashed by a rogue Ocho tentacle, she assumed. Overhead light fixtures that once bore fluorescent tubes dangled by twists of electrical wiring. A trio of cash registers had been emptied and toppled. Busted golf clubs and snapped-in-two hockey sticks littered the floor. Balls of every size congregated in corners, the floor not quite level. Most of the shelves had been stripped bare, a few tipped over. An image of a metal leg-hold trap, glimmering jaws ready to spring, flashed into her mind. She would snag anything that might make a decent booby trap or advertise her hostility to the unwelcome — Kip and his gun-obsessed goons.

She had visited the store only once before, perhaps three years earlier, to buy a can of pepper spray at Bart Cozen's suggestion, and she'd been amazed — even amused — by the ridiculous assortment of firearms, ranging from the dainty and girlish to the absurdly destructive. At the time she wondered why anyone might need a weapon ferocious enough to blast a hole through a brick wall.

She stepped quietly, carefully, toward the back of the store, where she remembered having seen the obscene display.

As expected, other survivors had preceded her, the display cases looted, the back wall stripped of its ammunition boxes. Her lungs deflated. As she rounded the counter, her foot clipped something metal. One bullet caromed off another, sending both spinning. Maybe two dozen bullets and red-sleeved shotgun shells dotted the carpet. The looters, perhaps rushed along by their crimes, had discarded some loose ammo in their haste — an act of kindness, however unintended. She placed the backpack on the floor and knelt into the carpet, realizing it might take a while to do the sorting. She wasn't quite sure what to look for, didn't know what kind of shell went where. All she could do was try to slot each shell into one of the shotgun's chambers, keeping the ones that passed muster, and hope they would do the job when and if called into action.

She picked up a large brass bullet — feed for a machine gun of some sort, she guessed — and turned it in her fingers. It reminded her of a warhead for a nuclear missile, only in miniature. Simply holding it in her hand gave her a sick feeling, as she knew the bullet served no purpose other than ending a human life.

But something else, something about this place, stirred her uneasiness. Tiny hairs on her forearms and the back of her neck went stiff. She recalled the feeling she got when she went upstairs at Cozen's, imagining someone or something she couldn't see — a ghost, a demon, a malevolent entity from another plane of existence — with its eyes trained on her. Her head peaked above the lip of the counter and scouted for any signs of movement. She wouldn't linger any longer than necessary.

She had as many as five "right size" shells lined up in front of her when a familiar sound stopped her: the cautious yet insistent padding of footsteps on the bare floor. Sev thrashed inside the backpack. He scrambled out of the opening and flopped onto the floor. A heavy odor found her nose. Sev scrawled furiously on a fiberboard panel, but the dim light prohibited her from reading his words. Whatever he was trying to tell her, she knew she had reason to fear. She placed two shells into their respective chambers. Barrel and stock clicked into place.

"What is it, Sev?" she whispered. "What do you see that I don't?"

He tapped the pencil against the floor, imploring her to understand. Finally, he touched a tentacle to her forehead. A single word in his voice echoed in the space between her ears: *Run!*

A towering shape crashed through the glass counter and slammed into the back wall. Shards licked Jillian's face. She screamed as the darkened figure loomed over her. She pointed the shotgun and pulled the trigger. Fire spewed from the muzzle and illuminated the horror standing in front of her: an ape-like beast covered in thick brown fur from head to toe, with jagged teeth and beady, red-rimmed eyes. The creature howled from the impact and toppled into the side wall. A rack of antlers fell from its perch and cracked the creature's massive, cone-shaped head.

With Sev in her shouldered backpack, Jillian sprinted for the exit. Seconds later she spilled into the gray light. A misty rain cooled her hot skin. She moved to the side of the building, where she had last seen Albert.

"What the hell was that, Sev?"

Sev touched the tip of a tentacle to her forehead.

It is a pet, Jillian. Run.

"Whose pet?"

It serves the conquerors, from my world.

"What the fuck is it doing here?"

It does the masters' will.

"Do you think it's dead? Did I kill it?"

No. Move. Now.

She inched around the corner and dashed for the bicycle. As she lifted a leg to mount the bike, the door's casing splintered with a sickening clang. The creature tumbled onto the asphalt. She saw the beast in full for the first time: eight or nine feet tall, musclebound, reddish-brown fur dangling from its limbs, like an orangutan. Blood matted the fur on its chest.

A Sasquatch. A rabid fucking Sasquatch.

Sev's tentacle burned the skin of her forehead.

Run!

She dropped the bike and bolted for the tree line.

Her heart thundered in her chest. A high-pitched squeal whined in her ears, a gift from the shotgun blast. Whimpers escaped her lips. She wanted to cry, to collapse into a ball and pretend this wasn't happening, to hurl the backpack at the creature's face and hope Sev could subdue it. But she kept running, driven by the same instinct that compels a rabbit to outlast a hungry fox.

Branches crashed behind her, near enough to make her realize the beast was close — too close. Branches nicked her face and cut her knuckles. Her heart pounded. Another sound met her ears: rushing water. In another fifty feet she faced the violence of Otter Pelt Creek, she guessed, though rainwater had bloated the creek far beyond its normal banks.

"What do we do, Sev?"

Pets abhor moving water.

A young pine tree crashed to the forest floor as the creature stepped into the light filtering through the canopy break. The creature seemed to smile, realizing it had her trapped. She lifted the shotgun and depressed the trigger. Nothing happened — the remaining shell was a dud. Heavy feet made hollow thumps as the creature stomped toward her. She could see the blackened tips of its sharpened fingernails.

Flee!

She leapt as the creature's hand reached for her. The current caught her and whipped her downstream. Its chill stole the breath from her lungs. The creek seemed alive, the way it tossed her, dragged her under and tried to drown her, the ease with which it plucked the shotgun from her hands. She gasped for air, swallowing water, as she slammed into the first rock. The backpack slipped from her shoulder, and she felt the fabric brush her legs as the current carried the bag away, and Sev along with it. Her knee smacked an unseen rock. A thorny branch raked her throat. The current carried her toward the far shore, her fingertips close enough to touch a slippery root. A boulder-sized rock battered her back, and the current took her under again. Water invaded her mouth and nose, deafened her ears. As she came up for air, she saw the unmistakable outline of a double-arch bridge — and she was heading straight for the middle support. The water would either thrash her body against the brick column or suck her under and drown her in the fingerlike branches waiting at the tempest's bottom.

Her head dipped below the surface again, and she clawed and kicked for the bank. The end of a shorn branch sliced her bare cheek. She reached blindly for a handhold. As her fingertips grazed a clutch of exposed tree roots, she closed her hand around one strong enough to hold her.

She stayed there, water rushing over her, into her, trying to suck her toward the lifeless bottom. Slowly, her tenuous grip began to slide down the length of the slickened root.

This would be her end. Death by drowning — again.

A steely hand grasped her wrist. She looked up, through the rush of water, and expected to see the Sasquatch. A cloaked figure loomed above her.

She didn't see the log coming. Its blunt edge connected with the side of her head. The rush of water went silent in her ears.

Chapter 18
Bad Times

Kip pressed the back of his head into the pillow and thrust his pelvis upward. He palmed the back of Laurie's skull as she brought him to the brink.

"Okay, okay, okay," he hissed. "Get up here."

She removed him from the warmth of her mouth. "Don't you want me to finish?"

"Not this way. On your back."

"It's a bad time, Kip. Sorry."

As she stood up, Kip saw her fullness in the moonlight: the curve of her ample belly, the art of each magnificent breast, the width of her hips. The vision made him crave her only more. She pulled a t-shirt over her head and lay down beside him.

"You said it was a bad time last week," he said. "How could that be?"

"It was a bad time for a different reason."

"Do I dare ask when *will* be a good time?"

"I'm just not ready yet."

"What's the problem?" he asked. "You worried I'll slip one past the goalie and you'll have to live with the shame of having an ugly-ass Detto baby?"

"I'd be ashamed to have anyone's baby. Nothing personal. A lousy little rugrat dangling from my tit might as well be a noose around my neck. If I get pregnant, the only gift you need to get me is a coat hanger. If not, a rope and directions to the nearest tree would do fine."

"I hate it when you talk like that."

He stewed quietly. His hard-on pointed toward the ceiling. For a moment he considered finishing right in front of her.

"I have to ask you something," he said.

"I already told you." She yawned. "I'm not ready."

"No, not that." He paused. "It's about Kyle."

"Your brother? Seriously?"

"What did you see in him?"

"That was ages ago."

"It still happened."

Laurie dated Kyle, Kip's twin brother, during their senior year of high school. *Dating* may not have been the best word for their month-long courtship. Every weekday they would leave the school grounds together in Kyle's cobalt-blue Charger and find someplace remote where they could fog the windows in peace. Of course, Kyle had told Kip every sticky detail of their late-afternoon trysts, even though Kyle knew the depths of Kip's affection toward Laurie. Worse, Kyle had swooped in just as she and Kip were on the cusp of starting something serious, or so she had led him to believe.

Everyone in Pell had liked Kyle — everyone — but few saw how cruel he could be, even to the people who loved him most. Kip especially.

"I don't know," she said. "He was different, and you could just see it, like he had a glow about him or something. Like he was magic. When he said he would make it out of Pell, you believed him. You just knew he would leave and do something interesting with his life. It made you want to be close to him, like whatever magic he had would rub off."

"Yet he ended up back here just like the rest of us. The Prodigal Son came home to slum it with all the other peasants."

"My opinion of him shattered the day he returned," she said. "I saw him as a liar, a phony, someone who failed worse than anyone else who ever lived here. We all wanted out — all of us — and so few of us actually left. He actually does, but then he comes back, like a horse's ass. Then I thought: *Maybe the world outside Pell isn't so great after all.* At least he had the balls to find out for himself."

"Maybe we knew better, you and me," he said. "Maybe we were the smart ones."

"Yeah. Maybe."

"We're still alive at least." He grasped his hard-on, squeezed, willing it to disappear. After a moment, he asked, "What do you want out of however much life we have left?"

"What kind of bullshit question is that?"

"An honest one."

"I don't have the answer. Especially now. But I'm not sure I would have had an answer even before everything got fucked."

"We all had our heads down, living like zombies, like cattle," he said. "That's why I wanted to build this place. I wanted to help. I wanted to lead."

"I never could understand why. You of all people."

"Kyle would have done it, no problem. You know how charismatic he was, how confident. He would have wanted to start something and be in charge of it all. People would have followed him too. Even if he failed, he would have found a way to make it seem like he hadn't."

"You're doing all this because of Kyle?"

He wagged his head. "In spite of him."

She nestled her head into his chest, her scalp inches from his nose. The stale smell of dried sweat made him breathe through his mouth. After moments of silence, her breathing changed, and he could tell she had fallen asleep. He stared at the water-stained ceiling, thinking about Kyle, about Laurie, and about Kyle and Laurie's short-lived romance that seemed as though it might forever live in his mind.

His tiring hard-on went limp in his lap.

Chapter 19
The Wisdom of Idols in Spandex

Jillian traveled the barren road beneath a sunless sky. The unbroken ribbon of asphalt led toward a cloud-shrouded mountain on the distant horizon. The clouds burned orange, suggesting a blazing peak — rivers of lava, funeral pyres burning hot enough to melt steel, the fiery belches of airborne dragons with corkscrew horns and mace-like tails. As Jillian followed the paint of the double yellow line, she shifted her gaze to the towering pines framing the road. Instinct told her to check behind her for approaching cars. A gritty wind brushed her cheeks.

She turned back to see the horizon reinvented — flames extinguished, clouds and dragon wings absent. Fresh snow capped the mountain's bald peak.

A distant grumble echoed behind her, but she could not take her eyes off the peak, now bristling with life. Even from this distance she could see figures ringing the rocky spire — ogres, giants, or some other humanoid creatures — each one shagged in white fur.

A sleek muscle car rumbled up beside her, so close she could reach out and caress the mirrored paint. The car had a peculiar design — half white and half black, divided right down the middle by a jagged red line. The two men she trusted most in the world greeted her. The Dying Man, representing the dark, sat in the passenger's seat. The Quarterback, the force of light, held the wheel. Jillian noted the driver's stony chin, with its deep and perfect cleft, and the feathery blond wisps shielding his icy blue eyes.

"Get in," said The Dying Man.

"We're all going to the same place, little lady," The Quarterback added in a Kentucky drawl.

Without protest, Jillian climbed through the passenger window, across The Dying Man's lap, and crawled into the cramped back seat. One of them slapped her ass as she went, and she had a good idea as to which one had done it. Before she bothered to check for a seatbelt, The Quarterback floored the gas pedal. The car screeched like a rocket. Jillian imagined the smell of burnt rubber.

The landscape blurred past. Jillian wanted to ask where they were going, but she supposed she didn't want to know. More to the point, the destination didn't matter. She couldn't imagine being in a safer place than in the strapping hands of her childhood heroes. They hadn't aged a day.

"Dark times lie ahead," The Dying Man said without turning. Dyed-black hair dangled from each side of his broad head. The strands looked wet, greasy.

"What my good buddy DM means to say," The Quarterback interjected, "is that life is filled with obstacles, and you have to have a game plan in order to move past them. You need a strategy to get the pigskin past the defense and across the goal line."

The Dying Man twisted to face her. "That's not what I said, sunshine."

The Quarterback took his hands off the wheel and his eyes off the road. He turned and kneeled on his seat so he could see her eye to eye. The car kept driving. "Be kind, be firm, and always remember: There's never a bad time to do the right thing," he said.

"And if that doesn't work," The Dying Man countered, "change the definition of the word *right*. Lie. Cheat. Steal. Survive."

A moment later they were outside the car and walking through the forest. Her feet sank into the cushion of soft earth brushed with desiccated pine needles. The Quarterback led the way, The Dying Man close behind. Jillian tried not to lose them in the forest, suddenly thick and dark. She blinked and found herself in a clearing, standing in front of a tattered wrestling ring. The ropes sagged. The turnbuckles had shed their padding. Bloodstains discolored the threadbare ring apron.

The Quarterback and The Dying Man faced each other on the torn, dusty mat. One provided the perfect contrast to the other — an Adonis with long blond hair, his body chiseled from hours in the gym, versus a thick-in-the-middle brute, with greasy black locks that dangled from his scalp like dead eels. One wore flashy blue Spandex tights and chicken-yellow wristbands, the other outfitted in black scrub pants and a black tank top that revealed elephantine arms sleeved in white scars and faded blue ink.

A small, hairy man in a white-and-black shirt crawled through a tear in the earth and slithered beneath the bottom rope. He patted down the tights and boots of each opponent, checking for illicit doodads that could double as weapons. He waved a gleaming championship belt for each combatant to behold.

A bell sounded, and the two combatants locked arms. The Dying Man immediately kicked The Quarterback between the legs. As The Quarterback bent over in agony, The Dying Man leapt into the air, draped the back of his knee across his opponent's neck, and thrust the man's head into the mat. Dazed by the blow, The Quarterback rolled onto his back and blinked into the glare of the overhead lights.

"From here on out," The Dying Man told Jillian, "enduring is your only concern. Kill every weakness. Cut loose every inclination that does not serve your sole purpose: survival."

The Dying Man placed a boot on The Quarterback's cheek and used the arc of bone as a stepping-stone. The move seemed to rouse The Quarterback, who grabbed his opponent's ankle and twisted until The Dying Man toppled to the mat. The Quarterback sprang to his feet, raised his fist overhead, and slammed his knuckles into The Dying Man's forehead. The Dying Man screamed as if scalded. The Quarterback then backed into the near ropes, leapt across his fallen opponent, sprang off the opposite ropes, and propelled his body into the air, bringing the point of his elbow down onto The Dying Man's sternum. The impact sounded like the sharp report of a gunshot.

"Don't lose sight of yourself," The Quarterback told her as he gloated above his thrashing foe. "You lose your humanity, you lose the privilege to call yourself human."

As The Quarterback bent to lift his opponent off the mat, The Dying Man thrust his knife-like hand into The Quarterback's throat. The blond Adonis reeled into the ropes, coughing and clawing at his own throat as if doing so would somehow mend his damaged windpipe. The Dying Man reached over the top rope, into the audience of one — Jillian — with his hand open, palm up. He said to her, "Action is required."

She looked in her own palm, not really surprised to see a clear plastic bag filled with fine white powder. The Dying Man reached into the bag and grabbed a fistful of powder. As The Quarterback turned away from the ropes, The Dying Man hurled the powder into his opponent's face. A white cloud consumed the ring. The Quarterback dropped to the mat, exaggeratedly rubbing at his eyes, apparently blinded by salt, lye, or some other corrosive agent. The hairy little referee was somehow oblivious to The Dying Man's swindle.

"We would have made a good team, you and me," The Dying Man told her. "Almost enough to make life worth living."

He dragged The Quarterback off the mat and applied his signature move: "The Last Word." First he held The Quarterback in a bear hug, and then threaded his arms around his opponent's shoulders until his fingers locked beneath The Quarterback's chin — a reverse full nelson. The move forced The Quarterback's neck backward until bones cracked and tendons strained. Then The Dying Man did what he always did: He latched his teeth onto the pale bulge of his opponent's Adam's apple and bit down until he tasted blood.

Jillian smiled. It was less of a wrestling move and more of a blatant assault. His "unorthodox style," as the announcers always termed it, had made The Dying Man her favorite, a heroic villain among vanilla heroes.

The hairy little referee watched carefully but let the carnage continue. Blood speckled the mat. After a full minute, The Quarterback signaled he had had enough. The bell chimed again, and the hairy little referee broke the two men apart. The Dying Man dropped The Quarterback to the mat in a blinded, bloodied heap. The roar of an invisible crowd echoed through the clearing.

The referee declared The Dying Man the victor by submission and handed the gold-and-leather belt to the new champion. The Dying Man studied his trophy for a long moment. He wiped a smear of blood from his left cheek.

Jillian thought she saw a momentary twinkle in his eye, followed by the hint of a smile.

Any trace of mirth vanished as quickly as it had appeared. The Dying Man draped the belt across The Quarterback's inert mass. He then straddled his fallen opponent and dribbled twines of spit onto the glistening strap. With a deep cleansing breath, he stepped over the top rope and exited the ring, leaving his fallen opponent — and his spoils — behind.

Jillian followed him into the darkness of the forest.

A blink later she found herself back on the road, framed by rows of soaring evergreens. The black-and-white muscle car was nowhere in sight. The Dying Man walked far ahead. His feet never veered from the yellow double line, which seemed to be leading them straight toward the flame-capped mountain far up ahead. The tails of his long black duster swayed behind him. On either side of the road, tree branches seemed to move independently of the soft wind. She hurried toward him, almost next to him, because she knew he would protect her from anything that might try to claim her as its own.

"You've made it this far," he said. "Ask yourself if you've gone far enough. From where I stand, you've got a tough row to hoe. Let me put it this way, girl: The end has only just begun."

He stopped and stretched his arms out to his sides, making a T. The trees on either side of the road rustled furiously, even in their highest branches.

"You can't escape the pain that's coming, little lamb," he said. "And you shouldn't try. Death will take its prize. Soon enough you'll have to choose — either accept oblivion or lead someone else into its icy mouth."

As he turned toward her, she saw a face transformed into something less than human. Long, shaggy fur coated his checks. Reptilian slits bisected his gray eyes. A canine's fangs took the place of human teeth, dripping wands of saliva. Tentacles snaked from his beard like a nest of writhing vipers.

She fell to the asphalt as he shambled toward her. His leather duster hung from his broad shoulders in strips, as if shredded by talons. The nails of his dog-like paws sliced through the toes of his snakeskin boots.

"Get up," he growled. "I said get up!"

A firm hand gripped her shoulder. The tips of his claws pierced her pale flesh.

Get up.

...

Get up.

...

C'mon, lady. It's time to get up.

Chapter 20
Taming the Beast at God's Feet

Jillian felt the crust crumble as her eyes cracked open. Everything seemed dark and blurry, though she registered the gentle flicker of candles and, above her, the silhouette of a man, a stranger. She sat up in alarm and nearly vomited.

"You were mumbling, moaning," he said. "I couldn't take it anymore."

His voice seemed unfamiliar too. She registered a slight accent.

"Who are you?"

"Daniel," he said. He backed away from her and leaned against a shiny metal wall. "You've been dead to the world for two days, maybe longer. At least that's how long you've been stuck in here with me."

Her head throbbed. She touched the side of her face. The skin felt hot and tender. Her fingertips glanced a scabbed-over tear in her scalp.

"Where am I? And *who* the fuck are you?"

She knew her name, rank, and serial number — Jillian Futch, age twenty-nine, born in Dracut, Massachusetts — but she had no idea how she could have ended up in such an alien place. Her memory failed her.

"Can't say *how* you ended up here," he said, "but near as I can tell you're in a walk-in freezer owned by a bunch of religious nuts. Again, I'm Daniel. Let me know when it sinks in."

"You're not making any sense."

He sank to the floor, laughing as he went. "Shit, does anything anymore?"

She struggled to find her feet, feeling wobbly. As she stood, the pressure in her head intensified. Her wounded brain must have swelled to twice its size, pushing against the bounds of her skull. A foul odor filled her nostrils.

"That's some shiner you got there," he added. "Whole side of your face is fucked up. Looks like you came out on the losing end of a tussle with a brick wall. From what little they tell me, you've been making the rounds for almost a week, recovering in the infirmary until they knew you were going to make it. Now you're in here with me. Lucky you."

"Fabulous," she said. "Just fabulous."

As she stood, pains elsewhere in her body made themselves known. Bones bruised and aching. Tears in her tender flesh turning to scabs. Joints popping and cracking with each movement. She tried the door handle, if that was the right word for it — just a knob made of hard plastic, emitting a faint white-green glow. Locked from the outside, of course. She slapped her palm against the metal door and commanded anyone listening on the other side to let her the hell out.

"Don't waste your breath," Daniel said. "Just wait. They'll come for you soon enough."

She turned and stared at him for a long while, seeing him for the first time. Thirty years old, maybe, with a head of tight curls and skin several shades darker than her own. Tall, which she could tell even though he was sitting down. Lean and muscular, well built. Soft face, but tough, with a round whitish scar on his chin that she found vaguely endearing.

"Tell me who you are again," she said.

"We've already been over this."

"You told me your first name. A little more than that would be appreciated, please."

"From Nowheresville, Pennsylvania, originally, a little town called Shunk. I've been in downtown Boston the past ten years, building a life there before life became what it is now."

"Doing what exactly?"

"I'm a broker."

"And what did you break?"

"*Broker*, not breaker. Financial stuff. Things that don't matter anymore."

"Right. Duh. Sorry. My brain's not right." She massaged her temples, both tender. "So, how did you end up in here?"

"You sure ask a lot of questions."

"I'm locked in a cage without windows, trapped with a man I've never met. Forgive me if I'm curious." She leaned against the wall, closed her eyes, and slowly sank onto her rear end to give her ailing brain a rest. As she turned her head to the side, the metal cooled her swollen cheek. "Where are your shoes?"

"They took 'em. Took yours too. I'm not the one you have to worry about."

The candlelight revealed a small stack of books. Daniel followed her gaze. He picked up each book and announced its title — The Holy Bible, *Surrender and Repentance, Taming the Beast at God's Feet* — and then remade the pile.

"You know," he said, "required reading for entertainment and understanding in apocalyptic times. Courtesy of our captors."

She searched her brain for clues as to what had landed her here. She found nothing. Then, a flash: the ape-like creature chasing her through the woods. Another: the rain-engorged creek. Finally: the cloaked figure clasping her wrist.

"*Sev*," she whispered. "Have you seen a backpack? My backpack?"

"What you see is what you get. Aside from a moth-eaten blanket and the clothes on your back, you came in here with no more than what God gave you."

"They," she said. "The religious nuts, you mean."

"Nice enough guys, you'll think at first," he said. "They've been in four or five times to check on you, and to make sure I'm behaving myself, most likely."

She hoped he would go no further. There was no need to give him any ideas. But she was smart enough to know men always had ideas.

"What do they want?" she asked.

"You could argue they're Good Samaritans. That's what they'll suggest when you talk to them. I won't ruin the surprise."

"I can't complain too much. One of them saved my life."

She could still taste creek water on her tongue, could feel its chill deep in her bones.

"Don't be too quick to thank them," he said.

A lock clicked, and the metal door cracked open. A lanky man in a black cassock — she couldn't tell his age, given his creaseless face and thinning hair — stepped into the room and knelt beside her. Two others in similar garb stood behind him. Guards, she guessed.

"Can you stand?" the kneeling one asked.

"Of course," she said, admitting no weakness.

"Come with me then."

She locked eyes with Daniel, who nodded in return.

As she left the room, she heard him say, "I'll just stay here and catch up on my reading."

***

Jillian studied the lead man in the cassock from a few steps behind. With the benefit of daylight spilling through rectangular windows lining the hall, she estimated his age at twenty-six or twenty-seven — no older than thirty. She turned in a circle to see the other two men a few steps behind, flanking her, and suddenly felt dizzy.

"Where to, Padre?" she asked.

The man led her to a thick wooden door and knocked twice.

"Father McBride," he said as he inched the door open. "She's ready for you."

The door creaked to a stop against an unseen wall. A bearded man with longish gray hair sat behind an expansive cherrywood desk. He rose from his seat and gave a light smile, motioning toward a chair. Jillian would have described him as avuncular, though neither of the two uncles she had met had been particularly good role models. This man looked gentle, caring, joyful — godlike. Still, she did not trust priests, nuns, or anyone else who pretended to know God's will. Simply *believing* in God was enough to warrant suspicion.

"Thank you, Mister Kirkland." McBride turned to Jillian and motioned one more time to the chair facing his desk. "Please. Take a seat."

Jillian felt the aches in her body as she crouched in the chair.

"How are you feeling, my dear? You came to us in quite a state."

"I'm all right, I suppose. I'm sore. I hurt all over. Thank you for saving me, whomever saved me. I guess I'm supposed to say that."

"Don't say anything you don't mean." His fingers drummed nervously on the desk. "Do forgive the accommodations. We lost one of our residence buildings in...well, in the madness that has overcome our quirky little town. Those of us who survived are living on top of one another as it is. I do hope you're comfortable."

"I've been conscious for only an hour or so, I think. But yes, it's fine."

She didn't want to grumble about being cooped up with some guy she knew nothing about — some guy who could have raped her, killed her, or worse, but she preferred not to imagine what might be worse.

"We were worried you might not pull through, my dear," he said. "It would have been such a waste."

"Jillian. My name is Jillian, Father."

"You don't need to call me that."

"Where am I, Father? What is this place?"

"The seminary, my dear. The Pell School of Theology. Surely you must know of it if you live in Pell."

"How did I get here? I'm a little fuzzy on the details."

"I wish I could provide a firsthand account, but as I understand it, you must have fallen into the rain-swollen creek and nearly drowned. Two members of our order were out harvesting — *foraging* — and came across you. One of them pulled you from the water, but not in enough time to spare you from whatever nasty thing gave you that bruise, I'm afraid."

Her brain cycled through its picture book: being chased by the Sasquatch, jumping into the creek in flight, and...

"Do you have my backpack, Father?"

"I don't believe you came in with one. I hate to disappoint you."

Poor little Sev. She had lost one pet in Albert. Now she had lost another. Then again, Sev had been more of a friend than a pet. She hoped he had escaped. Maybe they would reconnect once she put this strange place behind her. Or maybe he would make his way to the ocean and live out his life gorging himself on bottom-feeding crustaceans. But she knew how cruel life could be. She imagined Sev's pale body, twisted and bruised, washed up on a rocky shore and being picked apart by seagulls.

"Do you have faith, my dear?"

Faith. What a dirty fucking word. How could she have faith in anything after all that had happened?

"I'm familiar with the concept," she said. "I've studied the major religions, to some degree."

She recalled a one-sheet of passages cherry-picked from the Bible, the Torah, and the Quran, given to her by an instructor at Still Lakes Center for the Mortuary Arts. Any half-decent funeral director, the instructor had preached, should have the ability to "summon God's wisdom" as a balm for the grieving.

"So," McBride continued, "you know the text of Deuteronomy?"

Jillian caught the word, recognized its biblical significance, but her slow brain struggled to string the pieces together.

"Quiz me and I'll fail," she said, "but sure, I know it."

"Then you know it's Moses' testament to his people. It's a book of renewal, and a particularly meaningful text for these times, if I may say so. I find a number of verses quite enlightening — even comforting — considering the perilous state of our world. You may find them of interest as well, because they concern you as much as they concern me. Even more so, in fact."

He lifted a leather-bound Bible from his desk. He licked the tips of his fingers every few pages until he found the passage he sought. After clearing the phlegm from his throat, making his whiskered wattle undulate, he recited a passage about a nation from afar with alien tongues that would "swoop down like an eagle" and destroy livestock, poison the soil, and bring every wall tumbling to the ground — a promise to "bring about your ruin."

Was he suggesting the Bible had prophesied the Ochos' arrival?

The passage grew bleaker with each verse. She had endured enough torture already, without having to listen to this context-free craziness.

The word *afterbirth* brought her to attention.

McBride snapped the book shut and stared into her eyes.

"Enlightening stuff," she said, purely to break the tension. She was in a house of God, allegedly, but she felt like prey. No surprise, she guessed, because she never felt comfortable among people who have given themselves over to their faith — priests, nuns, rabbis, churchgoers.

"What is written here is yet to come," he said. "Our fates intertwine."

"Sure. Can I go now?"

He looked away and shook his head. "It's not safe out in the world, my dear."

"I'm aware, Father."

"My dear, please — you don't have to call me that."

"I know what it's like out there. I've seen it all, apart from the monsters in the sky. Ape-men. Talking octopuses. Men who look at every woman of child-bearing age as their own personal baby maker."

"You won't have that problem here," he said with a smile. "The world's gone mad, as you'd expect at the end of all things. The Book of Revelation describes beasts with many heads, strange creatures never before seen in the natural world — symbols, we've always believed. Perhaps this wonderful book contains more literalisms than we first supposed. The word of God does not lie. What changes is our understanding."

"Sure, sure," she said, being polite, though she wasn't certain if she considered his reading profound or completely batshit. "I appreciate you guys fishing me out of the creek, saving my life and all. The encouraging words too — all of the enlightenment and everything. I'll be going now."

A bead of sweat slid down her spine.

"You may return to your quarters," he said. His eyes roved his largely empty desk. "You need to rest up. Save your strength for what's to come."

"I feel fine. Just a little groggy. Soggy and groggy."

"We'd like you to stay for a time. As our guest."

"And I'd like to leave. We can keep going back and forth with this. I have things to do, people waiting for me."

"They can go on waiting."

Jillian wanted to tell him to go fuck himself, with all due respect. Instead, she said, "We're still living in America, right?"

"You'll stay with us for the time being. I'm afraid we insist, my dear."

Chapter 21
Another Bad Joke

The men in cassocks led Jillian back to her "quarters," which she now saw as little more than a walk-in freezer with two thin mattresses on the floor and a bucket propped in the corner, presumably for acts of elimination. She could smell it now, the brewing muddle of shit and piss, whereas before she registered only a foul odor of mysterious provenance.

As her captors closed the door behind her, her vision adjusted to the dim candlelight. She sat on a mattress, feeling deflated. Daniel sat across from her.

"So?" he asked.

"I don't trust anyone who wears a cross."

"Good start."

"Do you get the sense that we're not leaving here without a fight? They think they're saving us from something."

He gave a subdued laugh.

"What's so funny?"

"More like saving us *for* something."

"I'm in no mood for guessing games. If you have something intelligent to say, don't be shy."

"Sharpen the knives, boys. Another sheep lining up for the slab."

"Fuck you," she said matter-of-factly. No had ever stooped so low as to call her a sheep, the cruelest cut anyone could have inflicted.

"Baa, baa, black sheep," he added.

"Say that again and I'll drown you in the shit bucket."

"Okay, I'll play nice." He fought off his giddy smile and asked, "You got the big man's Deuteronomy fairy tale, I assume?"

She nodded insistently. "Freaky, don't you think? At first it sounded like BS, but then it sounded almost...prescient. Like, it foretold every horror that has skull-fucked our world these past six months."

"You're in no way alarmed by the passage he read?"

"It's alarming that his little brown book predicted all the shit that's hit the fan these past few months."

"Did you *listen* to what he was trying to tell you?"

"Yeah, about the alien nation that descends from the sky and topples walls and poisons crops and ruins everything pure and sacred. That pretty much sums up my past few months."

"And people eating each other?"

"*What?*"

"That's what he's telling you. His crazy little book gives him divine permission to cook you and me on a spit and serve us as smorgasbord. Fuckin' cannibals, man."

"You're insane."

"Granted, they've given you a much kinder hand than they have given me, but it's no coincidence they're keeping us in a goddamn meat locker."

The curious word McBride had used — *afterbirth* — returned to her.

"I've listened to that shit three times now," Daniel added. "The second time he asked me point blank if I understood it. He's warning you. 'Prepare yourself for extinction.' Doubt I'll be getting the reading a fourth time. They've fattened me up pretty good. They'll come for me any day."

The wind from the wave of his hand snuffed out the candle's flame. Jillian stifled a scream. She had never before experienced such a deep and total blackness. The flame returned to life a second later, almost silently.

"I hope you know how crazy you sound," she said. She saw him tuck a lighter into his pocket. "For a man who thinks his story is about to end, you don't seem too concerned."

"I'm not."

"Nor do you seem the suicidal type."

"I'll be breathing fresh air, walking the streets a free man, by this time tomorrow."

"Is that right?"

"Hundred percent."

"I'd love to hear how you intend to accomplish that feat. But first I need you to close your eyes and put your fingers in your ears. I have to pee."

In truth she needed to relieve more than her bladder, but she wasn't about to unload her bowels in front of anyone, even a stranger she would never see after she escaped this ordeal. She pulled the bulky gray sweatpants down to her knees and hovered above the bucket, careful to hide her nudity. Urine hissed into the basin, the bucket already a quarter of the way filled with semi-solids. The dim light prevented her from seeing the bucket's contents, but that didn't keep her from looking anyway. The smell made her turn away. She then fanned herself dry and cinched the drawstring of the sweatpants in which someone had dressed her.

"All finished?" Daniel asked.

She nodded but realized he still had his eyes closed and fingertips plugging his ears, so she clapped her hands to let him know she had finished.

"So," she continued, "how do you intend to bust out of here?"

"Will and imagination."

"Oh, is that all it takes?"

"Tomorrow morning they'll come to empty the bucket, maybe bring us some breakfast. I'll act then."

"They travel in threes, you know. One of them carries a club."

"I noticed."

"Three or more against one. The odds aren't exactly in your favor."

"They're seminarians — religious folk. I guarantee you none of them has ever struck another man with the intention of killing or disabling him."

"And you have?"

He waited a moment before offering, "When they come in, I douse the first one with the contents of our evacuation bucket, so he's dealing with the shock of that surprise. Then I drive the second guy's head into the wall. Then it's one on one — nothing a good, hard kick to the stones can't solve. Thirty seconds and it's all over. I take on whomever else I meet in the halls until I feel sunlight on my skin. Then I'm gone."

He seemed too confident, as though he had already gained his freedom from this place, or as though it were fated. She liked his assuredness, with just a hint of swagger. Or was it something else about him she found so alluring?

"I could help, you know," she offered.

"Sure." A smile creased his face. "You can help."

"I can fight!" But she didn't know for sure.

As far as she could remember, she had never punched, kicked, or slapped another human being. Something, though, told her she would deliver — she would fight — to survive. She recalled The Dying Man's warning from her trippy fever dream: *Accept oblivion or lead someone else into its icy mouth.*

"Who are you again?" she asked.

"Already told you, like, three times. Daniel." He spelled out his name, over-enunciating each letter. "Nothing else you need to know."

He seemed decent, trustworthy. Then again, plenty of seemingly decent men had disappointed her. Or worse.

"I'm Jillian, not that you asked. Where will you go when you leave here?"

He hesitated, and in his hesitation she sensed he had something to hide. Because everyone had something to hide.

"Far from here," he finally said. "Somewhere without sectarian cannibals."

"I don't know where I'll go," she offered. "Where I've been living isn't safe anymore."

"Even the odds then. Get some landmines. Get a cobra. Get a gun."

"I have a gun. Or *had.* Trying to procure ammo is what landed me in here with you."

"The world would have peace if everyone just left each other alone. The problem with that is the fact that most people find peace an unacceptable state of affairs."

"Utopia is a lost cause anyway," she agreed. "Especially with the monsters set on returning."

"What makes you say that?"

"I just know," she said. She sighed as she pictured Sev. "But those tentacled bastards aren't the only things we have to worry about. You wouldn't believe what I ran into, in a sporting goods store of all places, right before I ended up in here."

"Try me."

"A freaking *Sasquatch.*" She paused. "As I hear myself say the word, it reminds me of the setup for a bad joke. Part of me wonders if my wiring got fried. Like, maybe I did drown and they took too long to breathe life back into me."

"Bigfoot, you mean."

She nodded insistently. "I'm told the Sasquatches do the bidding of the tentacled monsters — Ochos, I call them, because of all the arms. They're taking care of all the scut work needed to prepare the human race for enslavement, or maybe eradication. I know how nuts it sounds, but I've seen one."

"Me too. Three of them, in fact. We killed one."

"Seriously?" She leaned forward. "So I'm not crazy?"

She was thrilled to have someone corroborate her story. She hadn't dreamed of the encounter with the Sasquatch. She wasn't losing her mind.

"What makes you say the squid-like things and the Sasquatches are on the same team?" he asked. "Bigfoot has been here forever. Maybe he just feels safe enough to come out of hiding now that humankind has retreated into so many holes in the ground."

"Someone I trust told me the Sasquatches serve those tentacled monsters — their masters, the Ochos. He would know."

"You're right about one thing. That does sound apeshit."

"Giant alien octopuses are dangling from the heavens," she reminded him. "Up is down, black is white, and two plus two equals goldfish."

"I suppose that's fair."

"I wonder if we saw the same one. The same Sasquatch."

"The ones I saw were traveling in a pack, a herd — whatever you call a group of them. Shot one between the eyes, and the other two came at me with no fear or hesitation whatsoever. You'd think they would've run off. No chance. They treed me, sent me scrambling up the branches of a pine. I thought they'd shake me out of it. Almost did, in fact. One of 'em hurled rocks at me. Mean sons of bitches. *Really* mean. So much for the myth of the shy and peaceful man-ape. Eventually they left me there, I assume to carry off the dead one. I couldn't find the carcass."

"If you're so tough, how is it you ended up in here with me, a P.O.W. in a cult leader's meat locker?"

"Let's just say I needed a roof over my head and saw an opportunity here. Like I said, I'll be out of here tomorrow." He took a breath. "I can take you with me if you want — unless, of course, you want to become next week's stroganoff."

The lock on the door came undone, and light spilled into the room. Two men in cassocks stepped across the threshold, and the third waited by the door, club hanging by his side. The men brought in two trays, each bearing a white Styrofoam bowl, a plastic spoon, and a waxy cup of water, and placed both in the center of the room.

"Mighty kind of you, boys," Daniel said. "What's on the menu?"

Neither of the men acknowledged the question. They left the room without a word. The lock clicked behind them.

Jillian crawled across the floor and sniffed at one of the bowls.

"Anything appetizing?" Daniel asked.

She dipped a spoon into one of the bowls and wrinkled her nose as she churned its contents. It looked and smelled...strange.

"Chili," she said. "At least, I think so."

"It might be one of your neighbors."

"I'm not going to eat it, but not because of what you said. I don't eat meat."

"You some kind of hippie tree-hugger vegan?"

"No," she said. "I just don't eat meat. Another animal shouldn't have to part with its life just because I like the way its flesh feels on my tongue. If there is such a thing as a sin, I can't think of a worse one."

"I can respect that, but it's foolish as hell. You live in a different world than the one you left behind six months ago. Start living in it."

Her stomach grumbled. She considered dumping the mystery meal into the waste bucket purely to remove the temptation.

They said nothing for what seemed like several minutes. Thoughts of breaking out crowded her mind. The more she pondered, the angrier she became. Who did these pious pricks think they were to imprison her in a lockup fit for beef shanks and ham hocks?

"Count me in," she said.

"For what?"

"I'm coming with you. You're not leaving me here."

"We'll tag-team it. Get some sleep."

"Tag team." She smiled. "Wonderful."

The soft light accentuated his square jaw, the contours of his body, his closely cropped hair. In a different world, she would not have been caught dead with a guy like Daniel, and she imagined he would have said the same about her. But there they were, locked up together, conspiring to bust out and start over someplace else.

It felt like the beginning of a love story.

Chapter 22
Gratitude

Kip Detto touched the ballpoint pen to a sheet of bone-dry paper. The tip trailed ghosts of blue ink. He scribbled back and forth, carving ruts into the paper, until the ink started to flow.

He sat at a table in front of a broad window facing the front lawn and the swaying trees beyond. His fingers caressed the smooth pine surface. Column by column, the pen revealed his tally of residents who had come to live at The Citadel, the nascent community he had brought to life: twenty-two women, seventeen men, eleven teenagers, and maybe a half-dozen rugrats. Not the army he had been hoping for, but the beginnings of one. More than half of the men were fifty or older, most of them overweight and stymied by poor vision. Each of them could pull a trigger, and that was enough for now.

More people kept arriving, with or without his invitation. Two days earlier a few of the men, led by the cranky old-timer Clay Ingersoll, had come in with a mother in her early forties and a teenaged daughter — sixteen, maybe, but hopefully eighteen or older. Kip had pretended to be busy with something else as the men took their "recruits" into one of the common rooms and locked the door behind them. The noise from the other side of the door forced him outside, purely so he could ignore what he saw, so he could say he had no knowledge of what each of those poor women was likely going through.

Guilt served no one in this world, not anymore.

"You know what the philosophers say," he told the empty room. "Can't make an omelet without cracking a few eggs."

Things would get better from here. They simply had to. He had created this place, The Citadel, as a safe haven for his neighbors. Come hell or high water, he would fulfill the promises of safety and plenty that he had made to each of them. If conditions went south for reasons beyond his control...well, he chose not to entertain such thoughts. People would forgive a few missteps, but human patience had its limits. The history books overflowed with stories about citizens turning on their well-meaning leaders. He recalled the rumor that Gaddafi's life had ended at the tip of a bayonet, rectum first, purely for the sake of cruelty. He thought of Saddam's bearded throat, burned by the fibers of a hangman's noose.

He lifted his head to stare out the window. A trio of women tended the vegetable beds, reminding him only of the bounty he had guaranteed — a harvest that would have to wait until next year. In the meantime, his people would have to subsist on canned peaches, cannellini beans, and prunes. Doubts multiplied. Scribbles filled half the page. He concluded his musings with two words, barely legible.

NOW WHAT?

He opened a drawer and retrieved a faded Polaroid. Two young boys — no more than five or six years old — sat on the lip of a snowbank. Red-cheeked and gap-toothed, each of the smiling boys wore ice skates and clutched a wooden hockey stick in gloved hands. Kip and Kyle, each a carbon copy of the other, years before one of them would grow up to become The Perfect Human and the other would become Kyle's Brother.

"Tell me what to do, Kyle." His smile faded. "Like you always used to."

A knock at the door disrupted his melancholy.

Laurie Woolly peeked inside and said, dismissively, "Be back later."

"My ass," he responded. "Stay put. Curfew's in effect."

"I wasn't asking, Kip."

She retreated from the doorway. Her footsteps echoed down the hall. Kip trailed after her and intercepted her near the building's main entrance.

"Hey." He turned her around by the arm. "Listen to me. You can't leave."

"Give me a reason."

He knew "Because I said so" would not sit well with her, so he said nothing.

"Exactly." She turned her back to him. "Enjoy the view."

He swooped in front of her.

"You're putting me in a bad position," he said as quietly as he could. "Don't defy me in front of these people."

"No bullshit, Kip. I told you that before I agreed to come here. My stance hasn't changed."

"I'd think you'd be more grateful." He paused. "Considering this morning."

"Oh, this morning. You think *I* should be grateful for *that*? Please tell me you're joking. Consider yourself touched by the hand of God that I let you lay so much as a pinky finger on me."

He backed up a step and let her pass.

Two women passed him in the hall. Both dropped their heads toward the floor, but not enough to hide their smirks.

He hurried after Laurie, but she was too far off. It wouldn't look good to run after her. As her feet found the asphalt of the driveway, he called out to her, "Give my best to your girlfriend Jillian. Tell her we'll see her soon!"

Without turning, Laurie raised her right forearm and extended her middle finger. A sentry attempted to stop her at the top of the rise, and Kip could hear her giving the sentry an earful. Barely older than twenty, the sentry shouted Kip's name, presumably seeking guidance as to whether he should shoot Laurie in the foot or let her pass.

Kip gave the thumbs up. He watched Laurie's ass until the driveway turned and stole her from view.

Such a hard-assed bitch, he thought.

He had been in love with Laurie Woolly since the sixth grade, and she knew it. When she had come to him and shared the news about Frank's demise, Kip had practically begged her to stay with him at The Citadel. She had agreed, but she also demanded so many preconditions that he finally threw his hands in the air and said, "Fine, fine, whatever you want."

She would always have power over him, wielding his love like a baton, and this made him hate her. No matter what happened between them physically, she would never belong to him, not truly.

A deliberate cough turned his attention.

Chinh, the man Kip had nicknamed Charlie Chino, stood shoeless on the tilled lawn. He gave a slow nod, seeming to let Kip know he had seen the dustup with Laurie — an insurrection taking root, he would surely think.

Kip gave the slightest wave and headed back inside to finish the work of determining where The Citadel needed to go from here. More importantly, he would have to figure out how to keep his people fat and happy — placid — and avoid having his head end up on the business end of a pike.

Chapter 23
An Awful Mess

The un-hitching of a lock shocked Jillian out of a morbid dream. The dim light revealed several figures flooding the room. One pounced on her, pinning her to the floor, and five or six others descended on Daniel. She heard his struggle to fight them off, but they easily overwhelmed him. The man on top of her sprang to his feet, trailing the group dragging her cellmate away.

Daniel had lost. His grand plans aside, his captors had disabled him and carried him off in no time at all, leaving her alone in complete darkness. More empty promises from a man who had won her faith. She had no one to blame but herself.

Jillian crawled across the floor on her hands and knees, feeling for the candles Daniel had lit. The first one had been broken in half, but the second candle seemed fine. No matter how intently she fumbled through the darkness, Daniel's lighter eluded her. No matches either. Not so much as two dry sticks to rub together.

She stood with one hand on the wall and tiptoed to the far corner, toward the bucket, so she could relieve her bowels.

The deep darkness unnerved her. She could not remember having ever felt so alone, so threatened, so vulnerable. She imagined one of Sev's brethren somehow slinking into the room — through a vent, perhaps, or the mouth of an unguarded pipe — and dropping onto her face, parting her lips, and distending her throat. It would choke the life from her, drop into her gut, and impregnate her with hundreds of eggs capable of producing the cutest army of bean-sized octopuses that would eat their way out of her cobwebbed corpse.

She would never see the end coming.

Sev.

Considering Sev's otherworldly gifts and the strength of their bond, she wondered — hoped, prayed — if they might share some sort of telepathic bond. If he still lived at all. She quieted her mind, pictured his undulating mantle, the gnarled horns over each eye, the nub of his severed limb. She then spoke his name aloud and waited for a response — the noble gentility of his voice — but nothing came.

Maybe he hadn't made it out of the backpack and he perished at the bottom of Otter Pelt Creek. Maybe he was gone.

Gone or not, she imagined the conversation they might one day have.

"You're very dear to me, Sev."

I could say the same. I have never lived more happily.

"That's laying it on pretty thick, don't you think?"

I stood at death's door, and you pulled me back. Consider me in your debt.

"We're in this mess together, my friend."

The door flung open. Blinding daylight flooded the room.

"Daniel?" she whispered.

The man she knew as Father McBride stepped across the threshold.

"Where's Daniel?" Jillian demanded.

"Ah, yes — the wanderer," McBride said. "We thought it best to separate you two. The more we discussed the matter, the more we thought it unpalatable to keep a young woman cooped up in here with a young man driven by the impulses of an impure heart. We thought you would both be more comfortable."

Another man in a cassock brought in a folding chair and propped it open in the room's center. He placed a flashlight on the bare metal. McBride clicked on the flashlight, took a seat, and opened his Bible.

The door closed to seal him in with her.

"Some light reading, if you'll indulge me," he said. "You remember Deuteronomy, of course."

The beam reflected off the Bible's white pages and lit McBride's face. Shadows swam in the depths of his jowls as he read. This time Jillian listened for each word, particularly the verses after the "nation from afar" smote everything a civilized society would consider precious.

You will eat the fruit of your womb, the flesh of your sons and daughters whom the Lord, your God, has given you. The most refined and fastidious man among you will begrudge his brother and his beloved wife and surviving children any share in the flesh of his children that he himself is using for food when nothing else is left him in the straits of the siege to which your enemy will subject you in all your communities. The most refined and delicate woman among you...will begrudge her beloved husband and her son and daughter the afterbirth that issues from her womb and the infant she brings forth when she secretly uses them for food for want of anything else.

After the last line, McBride peered over the edge of his frames.

"Is Daniel still alive, Father?"

"Daniel," he said. He waited another moment and added, "Why, I imagine he's as fine as he'll ever be."

"He's not dead? You didn't kill him?"

"I don't know why you would say such a thing."

She recalled the Bible passage.

"Do you intend to eat me, Father?"

"How ghastly! How vulgar!"

Then his expression changed, as if reminded of something he had forgotten. Eyes closed, he took a deep breath and let the air out slowly.

"Men crave meat, my dear," he said. "I don't care who he is or what he does for a living, but meat is the thing his heart most desires. Understand that feral dogs and cats get you only so far in these times. We've even eaten an alligator or two, liberated from our neighbors at the farm, I would hope. These creatures offer only so much sustenance when so many men yearn for the taste of iron and the feeling of gristle coming undone between their teeth. Do not weigh your mind with such horrors. God has a plan for each of us, and you can sleep well tonight knowing you have followed the path he has designed for you."

She stood and stepped toward him, and he instinctively sat back in his chair. There was nothing left to say. Daniel had been right all along: McBride saw her as little more than gut fill. The hiss of inhalation filled her ears as she drew in a sharp breath. She would not attempt to change his mind. She would not bother to seek an explanation. And she would not beg for her life.

She lifted her right foot and kicked hard. Her bare heel caught him in the middle of his chest, toppling him from the chair. His glasses caromed off the back wall. The flashlight flew out of his hand, twirling. The beam bounced off every wall until the flashlight hit the floor. The beam died for a second and promptly rekindled. She reached down and calmly lifted the Bible off the floor, and then dropped it into the waste bucket with a thunderous *plop*. She then bent to pick up the flashlight. His eyeglasses crunched beneath her heel.

McBride gasped as he crawled hand and knee toward the door. He slapped his palm against the solid metal pane until someone on the other side let in the light.

"Thanks for stopping by, Father," she said.

As the door closed, Jillian remembered the weighted cylinder in her hand. The flashlight cast its weak beam onto the floor.

"I swear to Christ," she said, "it may be the last thing I do, but I'm going to execute that sick son of a bitch."

***

Jillian had nothing to do but ponder the end.

Hours passed as she plumbed the depths of her mind, questioning every decision, every action, and every thought. Every decision a wrong turn, every action a misstep, every thought leading her to this very moment, moldering in a makeshift prison and waiting for the butcher's hook. She could have, and probably should have, worked harder to be someone else. Even the slightest difference would have landed her elsewhere.

She had heard stories of solitary confinement, how the separation from other human beings led to psychosis. Before she had known better, she would have considered solitary confinement hardly a punishment, because what good had other people lent to her life? Now she understood. The flashlight had died. After so much time behind a locked door with darkness as her only companion, her brain had started to melt down.

Hours, days, weeks — she had no way of knowing how much time had passed. The only interruptions came in the form of faceless men in cassocks delivering food or emptying the piss pot. She envisioned a monstrous version of herself, transformed by a life in darkness: her hair falling out, her skin translucent, her pupils the size of pinpricks, like those of a cave salamander.

Aside from sleep, she filled the hours by having conversations with Sev, with The Dying Man, with Timmy Labreque, with Laurie, and with Albert. She had even entertained a back and forth with her father, during which she forgave him for his grievous shortcomings as a parent and, for that matter, as a human being.

She woke once with Sev's whisper in her ear.

"Sev!"

I miss you, Jillian Futch.

"Are you nearby?"

I am always with you. Never far away. I cannot find you, but we will see each other again. I will wait for you.

She figured she had finally snapped, but she played along anyway.

"Happy to hear you say so, Sev," she said. "I still have so many questions."

Ask me anything. My time belongs to you.

"To begin with, how the hell do you know English so well?"

What one sees, all can see. What one knows, all can know.

"You're telling me at one point in history an octopus cracked open a dictionary and absorbed the English language?"

We learned from those who spoke human language — English, German, French, Hindi. Canines and primates can master your tongue, to a degree, so why not a cephalopod?

As Sev described his planet, Jillian envisioned a watery realm dotted with islands of grasslands, tall mountains, and dense forests. Clumps of rock and dirt sailed across the blood-red sky like clouds. Strange creatures plucked from the pages of the most nerve-rattling book Dr. Seuss had never taken the time to write lumbered across grassy plains.

"The Sasquatch that chased me — the one that caused us to become separated," she said. "Why is it here?"

Call it a scout, most likely accompanied by someone like me, someone connected to the mind-speak. A beacon so others can find their way, easing the conquerors' return.

"Where did it come from?"

From home. Same as me. Before we found humans, we used the man-apes for many purposes — for terrestrial transport, as soldiers, as hosts for reproduction. Their breeding cycle is much longer than that of humans, so their numbers suffer in comparison. They also make pitiful worshippers, not nearly as fearful or easily broken as humans.

"How the fuck did it get here?"

The same phenomenon that delivered me here: a portal, like stepping through a doorway between your world and mine, a bridge across dimensions, centuries, and galaxies. You would find them in every corner of my world — in the sea, on the rocky shores, in the densest forests — and they may deliver the traveler anywhere in space and time. The belly of a cloud in your world, for example. The portal through which I crawled delivered me to the pantry of a domicile not unlike your own.

"Interdimensional travel. What else can get through these portals?"

Anything with a beating heart. To traverse the bounds of one's reality, one simply steps, slithers, or crawls across the threshold.

"Do these doorways swing both ways? Like, could I step through one and enter your world?"

Yes. Others have. Their bleached bones remain there still.

"Besides Ochos and Sasquatches, do other forms of semi-intelligent life inhabit your realm?"

Humanoid lizards, now rare because of our alliance with the man-apes in their war. The humanoid lizards have fought the man-apes for ages, cold blood versus warm blood, each finding the other a monstrosity in need of culling. The lizard-beasts live solely by the island coasts, slipping in and out of the sea. Delicious, I am told, much like the crab. Their species may recover from near extinction with so many of us elsewhere.

"Amphibious lizard-men. Terrific. The enemy of my enemy is my friend, right? Let's go pal around with them. Or would they try to murder me too?"

Solve one problem at a time, Jillian.

Sev explained that a firm hierarchy enabled members of his race to coexist peacefully, with a select number — *the conquerors,* he called them — fed a gelatinous cocktail of reproductive proteins and enzymes harvested from the most powerful. Similar to the royal jelly earthly bee colonies used to manufacture queens, the substance enabled an octopus that usually grew no bigger than a Volkswagen Beetle to sprout into a towering beast that dwarfed even the blue whale, Earth's largest living thing.

"Hierarchy," Jillian said. "That suggests you have a leader."

The Empress. Eternal and perhaps immortal, she defines our past and determines our future. When the Empress arrives to put her plan into motion, all humans will cower before her. Or die. Or cower and then die.

"But why us?"

Never has there been a more tempting target than your species. Never has there been a worthier beast more deserving of enslavement.

"What if we kill her — the Empress? There must be a way to kill her."

Her heartbeats deafen the mightiest ear. Her shadow darkens planets.

"I find it hard to believe human life has reached its end."

Life goes on. Adapt. Your species may no longer stand at the apex, but there are worse fates than coming in second. You can still enjoy a full life, especially with me as your pilot. You will find the new world difficult to navigate on your own.

***

She was in the middle of a three-way philosophical discussion with Sev and The Dying Man when she heard the clank of metal from the other side of the door. Three men in cassocks spilled through the doorway and, without a word, dragged her from the cell by her hair. One of them acquainted his hands with the contours of her body.

"Not so rough!" she yelped.

She squinted in the daylight spilling through the hall windows. She found it less painful to keep her eyes closed. The sound of her struggle echoed in a wider space, and Jillian opened her eyes to find herself in an industrial-sized kitchen with few windows. The stainless-steel prep tables reminded her of the embalming room at the Cozen Family Funeral Home and Crematory. The tables had been cleared away from the center of the room, where a rope and pulley system dangled above a drain in the floor. Stains tinted the yellowish tiles a deep brown. The room smelled of bleach and death.

Instinct compelled her to scream, to thrash, to fight for her escape. For a moment she thought she might wriggle free until one of her captors rapped her across the jaw. The blow stunned her. He struck her once more for good measure, his open hand cuffing her ear. As she went limp, her captors bound her wrists behind her back and looped a cord around her ankles. Together they hoisted her, and her world turned upside down. Her sweatshirt drifted down to expose her naked belly. Her head pounded as blood rushed to her skull.

The men fastened the cord's other end to one table leg, and then another. One of them pushed her to make sure the knot would hold. She swung like a pendulum until he caught her with his hand. His palm cupped her left breast.

A pile of blood-stained clothes sat in the corner. The belongings of humans who had preceded her in sacrifice, she figured, people who once dangled from this very rope. A fourth man appeared, and it took her a moment to recognize him as Father McBride, sans eyeglasses.

"Your mortal journey ends today, my dear," he said.

"No!" She expected to see a hooded figure lurking in the darkened corner, Death coming to accompany her to the next plane of existence.

"Take comfort in the fact that there is no nobler sacrifice than to give one's life so others might continue," he added. "May God consider this and have mercy."

He lifted a hand in assent and exited the room with one of the others, leaving two to finish the job.

"You do this one," said the shorter of the two, neither of them older than twenty-five. "I made an awful mess with the last one."

"Please," Jillian said. "Let me down. I'll do anything."

The shorter of the two gave a knowing look and mouthed *sorry*.

"Where do I insert the blade?" asked the taller one.

"Just run it along the throat until you cut the artery."

"How will I know?"

"The spurting and spraying will let you know. She'll drain quickly. It's merciful, I'm told. The brain knows to spare the body. She might even enjoy it."

The tall one held up a silver blade — a filet knife, not particularly sharp. He would have to saw his way through, by the looks of it. A scalpel would have been so much kinder. She closed her eyes. The irony of her death: She had spent nearly a decade cutting bodies open, removing the nonessential parts, and then stitching them back together to make them presentable for a final goodbye, and now these pious fucks were about to peel the flesh from her body and pick her apart, saving the bones for soup stock. At least she would continue to serve a purpose for a short while longer, not just dematerialize in the bowels of the earth.

She wondered what to expect when the blade nicked the carotid artery. Likely a sharp pain, followed by an intense burning sensation, then the slow release, the warmth leaving her body, her brain going haywire as if fed tabs of LSD, and the tunnel of light shrinking until it became little more than a speck, ending with a hushed *pop*. And then, regrettably, nothing.

The blade clanged against the floor. Jillian opened her eyes to see the tall man in the cassock facedown on the tile. She could not see the other one, but she did register the unmistakable timbre of flesh striking flesh.

Daniel's upside-down face came into view. His chest rose and fell, as if breathing heavily. He had a revolver tucked into his belt.

"Sorry I'm late."

***

The marble floor chilled the soles of Jillian's bare feet as she followed Daniel down the hallway. A rectangle of light she recognized as the door to the outside world waited at the end.

"What the hell happened to you?" she whispered.

"There's probably a better time to have this conversation," he said. "Escape first, bask in our freedom second, and then, a distant third, chit-chat."

They passed the inert bodies of men in cassocks. One of them, lying prone, had his head turned completely around. His lifeless eyes stared at the ceiling.

"Did you kill these men?"

"Did they deserve it?"

"That's not what I asked you."

"Don't tell me you have a soft spot for these scumbags after what they were about to do to you."

"I'm just curious."

As they passed an open doorway, a mountainous black blur took Daniel to the floor. His pistol skidded across the marble. Jillian's first thought: *bear*. Her brain quickly recognized the telltale cassock of the seminarians — a goliath of a man, absurdly tall and rotund. He pinned Daniel to the floor, hands around Daniel's throat, drooling into Daniel's face. The man's hands tightened. Even in the dim light, she could see Daniel's complexion turn scarlet. His eyes implored her for help.

She bent and picked up the pistol, and the simple act of holding it felt dirty. She lifted the barrel toward the seminarian's head — just for a millisecond — and promptly lowered the weapon. As tough and dark as she made herself out to be, as hard and cold as she wanted to be, she wasn't a murderer.

"Stop!" she screamed. "Don't make me shoot you!"

Daniel groaned on the floor, teeth gritted, his face a sneer. Mucus shot from one of his nostrils. He would die if she didn't intervene.

She turned the pistol sideways and brought the weapon down as hard as she could, right onto the back of the seminarian's skull — her index finger caught between the pistol's metal body and the man's rock-hard noggin. She heard and felt the crack of bone. With one deep harrumph, the man toppled forward, crushing Daniel.

As Jillian held her injured hand between her thighs, Daniel squirmed out from beneath the mountain of flesh. Given his ruddy complexion and labored breathing, he looked as though he had just finished a marathon. He waited a moment, hand on her shoulder — for stabilization, she supposed, in case he passed out — and caught his breath. He then stomped on the fallen man's head until the skull cracked against the marble.

Jillian turned away, but she had already seen the worst of it.

"Must everyone die?" she asked, looking at the ceiling.

"It's them or us. Your choice. Come on."

As they neared a windowed archway, Jillian could see leafy branches swaying just beyond the glass pane. Daniel inched open the door and led her out. As Jillian's feet touched the first step, she thought she might faint from the sights and sounds of the natural world. She turned toward her rescuer.

"Thank you for coming back."

"That lard-assed fucker would have choked me into oblivion if you hadn't been there to crack him on the head, so let's call it even," he said. "Besides, we're not leaving just yet."

A concrete path led them to the entrance of another building. The structure's squat entrance sloped upward, to a pitched roof that suggested a high ceiling. Daniel creaked the door open and held a finger to his lips. The all-glass entryway led them down a hall to a set of double doors, each with a circular porthole. As Daniel crept to the door on the right, Jillian mirrored him on the left. They peered through their respective portholes.

A sole man kneeled in the chapel's second row, lost in prayer. A beam of light shining through a hole in the roof illuminated his frame.

McBride.

"What are we going to do?" she whispered.

"We're going to give him a piece of our mind."

She stayed frozen as Daniel opened the door and slipped inside the chapel. His steps made no sound. He stood right behind McBride, like a predator looming over its unsuspecting prey. As he tapped McBride on the shoulder, the priest fell backward onto the pew.

"Remember me, Padre?"

McBride mumbled something unintelligible and made the sign of the cross, from his forehead to his belly button, left shoulder to right.

"Your God's got better things to do," Daniel said. "But I did bring some company."

He beckoned Jillian to enter.

She wanted to do anything but, because she knew she would lose control if she went inside. She considered turning around and running for home, so she was surprised when her legs carried her forward, to face a man who had condemned her to death, and who, had Daniel not intervened, would have gleefully dipped his daily bread in the marrow of her bones.

"Come on out here and face the music, Padre. My friend Jillian has a few words for you."

She felt the temporary joy of knowing Daniel remembered her name.

"You misunderstand, I—"

"Shut the fuck up," Daniel roared. "Now come out here and take your lumps like a man."

Daniel's hands closed around McBride's collar and dragged him into the aisle. McBride stayed on his knees, trembling.

"You cannot fault me," McBride said. "Blame the world we live in!"

Daniel seemed to consider the priest's words.

"You're right about that, Padre. I do blame the world we live in."

He pulled the revolver from his belt and handed it to Jillian, grip first.

"Go ahead," he told her. "You'll be doing the world a favor."

"I...I can't."

"You can and should. Remember what he did, what he was going to do to you. Locked you in a meat locker, using a warped fucking book as justification for turning you into his own personal veal stash."

He was right. McBride and others like him had been making the world — Jillian's world — into a sick and dirty place ever since she was a toddler.

She stepped forward and slapped him across the cheek. His jowl flapped. His bulbous throat wobbled. She winced from the jolt to her injured finger. He looked stunned. She slapped him again, and again, ignoring the pain, and then her slaps turned to punches until her knuckles cracked, the flesh of her fingers became ragged, and her blood streaked McBride's flushed face.

Finally, Daniel tore her away. McBride sat on his rear, with his arms braced behind him to support his girth. His breathing came in gasps, and at one point he clutched at his chest, suggesting a heart attack.

"Not feeling well, Padre?" Daniel said. "Allow me to ease your pain."

He raised the revolver.

"Daniel," Jillian interrupted. "Wait."

"Why?"

She had no answer.

He pulled the trigger. The bullet bored through McBride's forehead, pinged around his skull, and exited through his throat — all in the span of a second. The body collapsed in a heap, blood dribbling from two tidy holes, though the exit wound left the flesh ragged. An imperfect escape.

Jillian had seen hundreds of dead bodies in her life. She had seen men die before her eyes — women and children too. Each death had affected her in some way. Now, watching McBride's blood warm the stone floor, she felt only relief.

"Time to go," Daniel said.

He led her to an exit to the left of the altar and propped the door open. The grass tickled her feet. A moment later, the forest consumed them.

Chapter 24
Awkward and Sloppy

Jillian followed Daniel through the dense forest. No trail — just tramping across the leaf litter, past saplings, ferns, and the saucer-like caps of wild mushrooms. The forest floor announced each step. She checked over her shoulder every fifty feet or so, expecting to see shadowy figures in pursuit.

"You can stop looking," he told her. "No one's coming."

"Why?" she said. "Did you slit all their throats while they slept?"

She had meant it as a joke, but she supposed he'd done just that. She tried to push the thought from her mind. The past few days, weeks, however much time had ticked by, she would rather forget altogether, pretend it hadn't happened. Why ruminate on the worst of people?

She studied her injured hand as they walked. Every joint felt stiff, swollen, aching.

"I think I broke my finger," she said. "Maybe a knuckle too. My whole hand is one big bruise."

"Better bruised and broken than having it end up as an appetizer on a child rapist's plate. You know, finger food."

"Now, Daniel, you don't know for certain they practiced pedophilia."

"Just cannibalism."

"There you go."

"I stand corrected."

Stoic, she would have called him, but certainly not humorless. Rather, she could tell he had a knack for making people laugh. If he wanted to, he would make her laugh too. Her eyes studied the nape of his neck, the curve of his occipital bun, the way his broad back made the shape of a V as it tapered to his waist. She wondered what he had been like before society became undone.

"You beat the hell out of all those men," she said. "How?"

"I'm mean."

"You don't seem all that mean to me."

"I have the *capacity* to be mean. That's just as good. As for the mechanics of it, I guess six years of nonstop wrestling practices, meets, and camps did me some good."

"You're a wrestler?"

"Was. Past tense."

"You're shitting me! What was your finishing move?"

"Finishing move?" He turned toward her and twisted his eyebrows in astonishment. "I'm talking about leg sweeps and fireman's carries, not DDTs and atomic elbows. That shit's faker than a three-dollar bill."

Her interest flagged. "When and where?"

"My exploits on the mat ended after my third year at Lock Haven," he said. "Didn't get to a fourth year. If you went back there now, you'd see a plaque or two in the trophy case with my name on it. R. Daniel Saint-Pierre — 2008, 2009. That's assuming the university remains intact. Chances are there's nothing left but wounded earth."

She imagined him in headgear and a singlet, muscles rippling as he skulked around the mat, studying his opponent for soft targets to exploit.

"What's the R stand for?"

"Reginald. Only Mom and my little sis call me that. *Called.*" A pause. "Doesn't matter anymore. I'm just glad I got back in time to spare your neck from the chopping block."

"What happened to you, anyway? I assumed you either died or escaped, never to be seen again."

He explained how he had wriggled out of the seminarians' grip the moment they had dragged him from the meat locker. He had made it outside a few moments later — "free as a free bird," he said — leaving at least three casualties in his wake.

A gunshot echoed — not close, but close enough. Daniel turned his ear toward the canopy. He waited a moment, for some sign or suggestion, before pressing on.

A half-mile later they reached Otter Pelt Creek, little more than a trickle compared to the whitewater in which Jillian had nearly drowned. Daniel hopped across two rocks to reach the opposite side.

Jillian followed, her bare feet cupping the wet rock, arms out in a T for balance.

"I almost died last time I saw this creek," she said. "It was a rafter's dream then, white and raging from all that rain. No good for swimming though."

Daniel grunted a response.

"If you escaped, why did you come back?" She had almost finished the sentence with the words *for me* and was glad she hadn't. She didn't want him viewing her as a damsel in distress, though distress was an apt description for the predicament in which he'd found her — bound and hanging upside down with a knife to her throat.

"You didn't deserve what those pigs had in store for you." He pulled the pistol from his belt and added, "I would have been back sooner, but I had some trouble rounding up the cavalry. You're just lucky I like you."

"You're, like, the perfect man for the apocalypse."

"I'm no white hat, Lady J — nobody's hero," he said. "It's just nice to have trees over my head and dirt beneath my boots again."

He touched a finger to his lips as they reached a crushed-gravel road. Still and quiet, he waited for nearly a minute before clearing them to cross. They made haste until the road was far behind them.

Shadows darkened the forest as dusk neared. As much as Jillian liked the idea of spending a night beneath celestial bodies with Daniel, she knew worse things than misbehaving humans lurked in these woods. Memories of the Sasquatch's snarl and bladelike talons hurried her footsteps. The speed of Daniel's gait suggested the same thoughts troubled his mind.

"Do you know where we are?" she asked.

"We passed the avenue into the seminary a while back, and now we're approaching the coast. You'll have those ruby slippers back on the yellow brick road before too long. We'll part ways from there."

Breaks in the foliage revealed the outlines of buildings and hobbled cars on the street.

"Where will you go?" she asked.

"On my merry way, I suppose."

Jillian felt hurt, oddly. The man had saved her life, so she felt indebted to him. She also liked him, she could admit, in the way that girls liked boys. Her schoolgirlish infatuation felt completely natural, despite the fact that she was on the precipice of thirty.

"And here we are," Daniel whispered. He held up a hand as they reached the edge of the forest, advising quiet.

"What is it?" Jillian spoke into his ear.

"You never know who's watching."

Nothing stirred, save the ceaseless chirping and buzzing of nocturnal insects and the occasional wail of a bird that sounded like a loon. They emerged from the woods and began tramping the asphalt. Loose pebbles pocked the soles of Jillian's feet. Her hackles came up as they approached Bull's-Eye Firearms and Sporting Goods, where she had reconnected with Albert, however briefly, and blasted the Sasquatch with the only firearm she had ever discharged. She inched closer to Daniel. Her gaze remained on the gaping hole where the store's door had once been. She half-expected a pair of glowing red eyes to peer out.

She was happy to have the structure behind her.

The cloudless sky showed millions of stars. Light from a snowball-white moon illuminated the downed branches and potholes in their path. Up there, splendor and serenity. Down here, death and destruction.

"Where to, Jillian?"

"My place is maybe a mile down the road."

He seemed uneasy with the idea of sticking to the street, lingering behind the skeletons of hobbled cars and the trunks of roadside trees.

"You can stay with me, if you want," she said. "Spend the night under a roof in a room that isn't a meat locker. That is, if the walls still stand. I don't even know how long I've been gone, but before I left town a wannabe fascist said he intended to roam the streets with his band of gun nuts to intercept perceived intruders and rebels."

"More reason to get indoors ASAP."

"I'm Public Enemy Number One, apparently."

"I didn't realize you were such a badass."

"Me neither." She laughed. "You'll come back with me then?"

He kept walking, which Jillian took as assent.

"You can see what it's like to spend the night in a funeral home."

"You an undertaker or something?"

"Pell's one and only."

"Full of surprises, this one."

"I have a spare bed. Plenty of food. And liquor. Get some sleep and leave in the morning."

"Sold. Let's keep the racket down in the meantime."

They walked in silence the rest of the way. She knew the streets, knew the landmarks, but she had never seen this part of Pell from this perspective, lit only by moonbeams. Everything seemed tranquil. A façade, she knew, as horrors lurked behind every closed door and in every darkened corner.

The silhouette of the Cozen Family Funeral Home and Crematory emerged from the gloom. Intact, as far as she could tell. Seeing the building reminded Jillian of the feeling she used to get after returning from a long vacation, viewing a familiar destination through the eyes of a person transformed by time and experience.

Something wasn't right. She tapped Daniel on the back and slid past him. The steps creaked beneath her. The front door had been forced open. She stepped inside to see furniture torn and toppled, windows broken, plywood barriers busted through, tables overturned. Moonlight spilled in from the glassless windows to guide her path. Daniel lingered in the doorway.

"Unexpected visitors?" he asked. "Maybe an impromptu keg party?"

She padded into the kitchen and surveyed the picked-over drawers and cupboards. Whoever did this — Kip Detto and his cronies, most likely, or maybe Jen Cates and her teenage daughter, having finally arrived and made themselves at home — had turned over every rock, so to speak. The pantry shelves had been stripped bare. Same with the liquor cabinet.

The kitchen glowed orange as a small flame danced before Daniel's face, courtesy of a cigarette lighter.

"They took it all," she said. "They took every-fucking-thing."

"Know the culprit?"

"My archenemy, in all likelihood."

Daniel waved the lighter right to left and back again. Jillian bent to retrieve a flashlight and clicked the ON button. White light flooded the room.

She wandered the first floor to assess the damage. Not only had the thieves absconded with every resource worth taking, but they had also gone to the trouble of trashing the parlor: lectern smashed, folding chairs tossed in a pile, prints and paintings of tranquil settings peeled from their frames, wallpaper shredded. She thought she smelled urine.

The flashlight's beam landed on the doorway leading to the basement. She inhaled, bracing, as she descended the stairs and stepped through the bunker's open door.

"Fuckers," she spat.

Other than a few loose remnants dotting the floor, the looters had cleaned out her reserves — or, rather, the reserves Bart Cozen had left for her: distilled water, liquor bottles, all the foodstuffs, lanterns and batteries, even the smut magazines. At least the mattress and the collection of classic novels remained.

Daniel came up behind her.

"Nice place," he joked.

"It used to be."

He placed a hand on her shoulder. Electricity passed from his flesh to hers. She turned into him, and they embraced.

She reached for the door and pushed it closed, parting them from the rest of the world.

***

Jillian studied the overgrown lawn through the window frame. She ran her finger along the edge of a glass shard shaped like a shark fin. The rest of the window lay scattered on the earth below in blade-like pieces. A gentle wind brushed the hair from her cheeks. She held a mug to her lips and savored the subtle taste of coffee on her tongue.

She had not expected what had transpired between her and Daniel. She had thought about it, even hoped for it, but never had she expected those fantasies to come true. A year had passed, perhaps closer to two, since she had last made love to a man. Their coupling had been awkward and sloppy. Then again, sex usually was.

The creaking of stairs announced Daniel's approach. She feigned a yawn as he entered the sitting room. She could imagine how he must have felt, how he likely would have escaped through a downstairs window had there been one.

"I smell coffee-bean soup," he said.

"Instant stuff the thieves must have missed, or maybe left behind on purpose — just crystals, nothing too exciting. Consider it a tepid coffee-like substance rather than actual coffee."

"No complaints here."

She bent toward the pot on the camping stove and poured most of the remaining water into a plastic mug, its bottom lined with shiny brown crystals. He immediately wet his lips.

They stood silently at the window. Songbirds flitted in the branches of a Japanese maple on the side yard. A sparrow alighted on the window frame. It cocked its head, regarded them both, and flew off. Daniel nudged the fin-shaped shard. It toppled forward and shattered against the hard ground.

"I've always loved the quiet of morning," she told him. "I don't miss the rush of the world."

He drained his mug.

She felt the need to fill the silence. "Life could be worse."

"Much worse."

She emptied the pot into their mugs. Just drips and dribbles, not a drop wasted.

"I have to tell you something, Jillian."

Bam. She took a deep insulating breath. She had expected as much: the "it's been fun but," the "thanks but no thanks," the "we can still be friends." She had gotten used to the hurt. This time would be okay though. No reason to be sad. They had been through a lot together in a short amount of time, had a bit of fun, and now it was time to part ways. Simple. The way it was supposed to work.

"I have to leave," he said. He let a beat pass before adding, "But I'll be back."

"Oh!" She snapped her head in genuine surprise. "Good. I'm glad."

"I...I won't be alone."

"Okay." She wrinkled her brow. "Meaning?"

He took his time, seeming to not quite know how to say what he had to say. Something hurtful no doubt, something horrible.

"You're married," she said, saving him the trouble. "I just fucked a married man, right?"

"That's not what I was going to say. Listen, Jill. I'm not from around here. I told you that already. But I'm not from Boston, and I honestly have no idea what a broker does. I work in private security in Scranton, Pennsylvania, or at least I used to."

"You're a bodyguard? Or a mall cop?"

"Listen to me. I like it here, in Pell. In fact, I like it a lot better than everywhere else I've been living since this mess started. And that's what I'm going to tell my tribe."

"Your *tribe*." She had used the exact same word to describe the group of people she had always wanted to belong to, the group of like-minded individuals she had not yet found and likely never would. The word sounded foolish aloud.

"I don't know what else to call it. Nomads, we are, looking to settle down. We've been on the move since those squid things turned shit upside down, picking up more weapons and stragglers along the way. I'm telling you this because I want you to be safe. The last thing I want is for you to get hurt."

"I don't understand what you're saying," she said, though she had an idea. She wanted to hear him say the words.

"We're going to take over Pell."

And there it was.

Kip Detto had been right, the simple son of a bitch.

Her face became hot.

"Why?"

"Simple," he said. "What someone else has, they want — especially when we're talking about someplace like Pell. The bay right there, easy access in and out. Whole town ringed by a crown of hills, protected from the elements, so the winters probably aren't too bad. Still, wouldn't surprise me if they tore up Pell, chased the chickens from the coop, and kept moving, keeping eyes out for another place to raze to the ground. Continue the slaughter."

Jillian imagined a band of wild-eyed barbarians, with spiked clubs and studded codpieces, laying thatch-hut villages to waste. Brain the men and seed the earth with their entrails, ravage the women, and enslave the young.

"If it were up to me, I'd stay right here," he added. "That's what I told them, even before I met you."

"This is all a sick joke, right? This kind of stuff just doesn't happen."

"Listen to me: It's happening as we speak. No bullshit."

"You *can* stay, and you don't even have to torch the place to do so. You're no one's slave." She blushed as she considered the color of his skin. "We live in a free world, Daniel, and you're a free man."

"You'd think."

"Stay here, with me. Tell your assassin buddies to keep moving."

"Nah." He closed his eyes and scrunched up his face as if he smelled a dead fish. "There's no way to stop what's coming, no way to talk anyone out of it. They understand one thing: brute force."

"Good! We'll fight!"

"C'mon, Jill. Be real. I can't deter them by myself, and you ain't built for that kind of dirty work. You couldn't even put a bullet in the roly-poly priest who straight up told you he was going to eat the fat off your ass."

Jillian's eyes moved to the floor. He was right, but his words still cut.

"Let me paint a picture for you: Thirty men armed to the hilt, all camoed up, moving through the forest like they weren't even there. All led by a guy named Raz." He paused. "Raz, they call him. Mountainous. Charismatic. Merciful at times, sadistic at others, probably bipolar. Because of him, I have played a part in ending a lot of lives, most of them human. Fucked-up shit. Drowned 'em in cages. Set 'em on fire. Dropped 'em off buildings. He's a madman, a devil."

"You're not like him."

"I'm more like him than I am like you."

"You can become someone else. So can I."

Her implication: They could become different people together. He offered no response. His silence told Jillian everything she needed to know about his state of mind.

"Why did you bother coming back for me?" she said. "At the seminary."

"Because it was the right thing to do."

She nodded and pursed her lips, wishing he had said something else.

"You've shown that you have the capacity to do the right thing. What's stopping you from doing it again?"

"Self-preservation."

"Okay. You've been honest enough with me. Allow me to return the favor. Pell has its own militia. If you try to invade, your *tribe*" — she used the index and middle fingers on each hand to make air quotes, though the index on her right hand barely bent — "is going to get cut to ribbons."

"You're talking about the ragtag group of yahoos over at the old folks' home? Yeah, we know about them. We've got it covered, Jill. Serious firepower. A lot of our guys are ex-military, and they love their toys."

"Oh my God," she said. "You're doing recon."

He nodded. His hazel eyes fixed on hers, and the edges of his mouth curled into a slight smile. She broke away and turned toward the open window.

"Good people live here, you know."

"I don't doubt it."

"But you're just going to come in and spray the place with bullets and bombs until no one is left standing."

"Only the opposition, most likely. We're not looking for a fight. There's risk in every fight. But we'll do what we have to. That's what I'm telling you."

"Why?"

"Look: I just want to spend however many days I have left someplace quiet, someplace nice. But the other guys, the other nomads, I can't say they want the same thing. Some of them just want a war. It's all they know."

"What about when life goes back to normal?" She remembered Sev's warning about the Ochos' looming return. "*If* life returns to normal. You're going to have to answer for the things you did. All of us will."

"We came up through New York. Whole damn city looked like a warhead went off. Skyscrapers gone. Bridges shredded and lying at the bottom of the Hudson. Lady Liberty, no sign of her. Nothing's going to get back to normal, not the normal you remember. No good guys coming to save the day. This is life now, and we're starting over from the ground up. Here in Pell."

"I'm just supposed to pack my shit and leave?"

"I'd recommend it. Pell will be a different place inside of a week."

She felt a jab of disappointment in his failure to ask her to stay. How foolish to think such a thing, but humans were nothing if not foolish.

Daniel removed the pistol from his belt and offered it to her, butt first. Like he had done before, when he invited her to murder the priest. It all made sense now. His matter-of-factness. His secrecy. His violence.

She kept her back to him.

"Take the gun, Jill. I want you to have it."

"Such a sickly sweet gesture, Mister Saint-Pierre. Aren't you going to need your precious weapons for the looming takeover?"

"I have plenty more where this came from."

She stared out the window, holding the empty coffee cup to her lips so she didn't have to say anything else.

Daniel placed the pistol at her feet and left the parlor. Her peripheral vision suggested he lingered by the front door. She shut her eyes tight. The doorknob squealed and the door hinges creaked, followed by the soft click of a lock finding its seat. She didn't want to open her eyes, but she knew ignoring reality would change nothing.

He had gone, and she was alone...again.

She peeked around the window frame, hoping for one more glimpse of him, hoping to see him look back longingly, knowing he had made a grave mistake by leaving her behind. Something did move across her field of vision, but it wasn't Daniel.

An alligator, with a whitish-pink scar where its right eye should have been, waddled across the lawn and into the street. Perhaps eight feet long from its gnarled snout to the tip of its dragon-like tail, the alligator was likely heading for the salt marsh and the bay just beyond. Perhaps to feast on fiddler crabs and fatten up for winter.

She took the reptile's arrival as an omen, far worse than a yellow-eyed black cat crossing her path. Somehow life was about to become even grimmer than the darkest days of a dim and distant past.

Chapter 25
Homecoming

Jillian sank to the floor in a pile. Her body shook with each sob. It felt unnatural to cry, like falling apart, stitches coming undone. She hadn't felt so alone in years. The hollowness in her chest reminded her of the day she left Dracut for Still Lakes Center for the Mortuary Arts in Providence, when she had said goodbye to her father, abandoned her hometown, and left behind the adolescent memories of her first love, Timmy Labreque.

Even when she was trapped in the seminarians' meat locker, she had hope to keep her company. She had lost so much: a life she had begun to love, her livelihood, and every possession she had ever earned, plus Albert, Laurie, Sev, and now Daniel. Now she recognized hope as a poison, and she no longer wished to imbibe.

Death suddenly didn't seem so bad. At least then she would feel nothing.

Between sobs she heard an insistent metronome, like drops of water falling from a dizzying height. She lifted her eyes to see a small globular mass by the stairs leading to the basement.

A suckered arm tapped the tip of a grease pencil against the bare wood.

"Sev," she said quietly, almost as if to convince herself.

She crawled across the floor on hand and knee and lifted him in her arms. His mottled flesh flashed blue. His tentacles slithered across her face, her throat, the back of her neck, suckers pulling gently on her flesh, until one found its place on the center of her forehead. She repeated his name, practically screaming it this time.

"Your arm," she said. A new arm, small and thin, had sprouted to replace the white nub left by her scalpel work. "It grew back."

Your face, she heard him say.

"Just bruises. Just scratches. You're alive!"

Fit as a fiddler crab.

"What happened to you?"

Call it a journey endured. I escaped the backpack and came ashore to wait for you, but you did not emerge. After more time than I care to admit, I followed the stream to the mouth of the sea, and traveled down the coast, toward home — your home. Enjoyed some delicious crabs along the way, purely to heal my tattered spirit. I have been waiting for you here ever since.

"I thought I'd never see you again!"

I knew we would be together again as long as you survived your imprisonment. I could see you, your cell, but I could not see beyond the walls that held you any better than you could. I would have come for you otherwise.

"What in the blazes are you talking about?"

When we spoke, during your confinement, I was with you. You recall our conversations, of course.

"I thought I imagined that — my crazy brain being crazy."

Our bond deepens until our hearts stop beating. Joy overtook me when you came down the stairs last night.

"You...saw that?" She remembered her torrid night with Daniel and felt a pang of shame. The positions they put themselves in, the things she had instructed him to do, the noises she had made — Sev had seen and heard it all. "Mighty surreptitious of you. Downright creepy and sneaky even."

Credit the Maker for bestowing me with the gift of camouflage.

"Someday you'll have to teach me that trick."

Words cannot describe my elation at seeing your face, bruised and battered though it may be.

"Did you see who ransacked the place?"

Negative.

"The sons of bitches nabbed everything worth taking," she said. "But we have bigger problems. Bad things are about to happen in Pell — humans coming to drive the natives out. War is inevitable."

Not for long. The conquerors' return draws near. All men will have bleaker battles to fight and lose.

"Are you sure?"

As sure as I can be. The sharp edges of my senses have dulled.

"That settles it then." She paused. "I have to tell Laurie. She deserves to know what's coming so we can all get out of here before the shit hits the fan."

Just speaking her old friend's name caused her gut to spasm. Would Laurie give her the cold shoulder? Would she welcome her with a loving bear hug? Would she slap her across the face and tell her to get lost or dole out an even harsher punishment? None of these reactions seemed beyond the pale. Sev's silence on the matter suggested he thought the same.

"Laurie will listen," she added. "Part of me wonders if I should talk to Kip. He's been preparing for an invasion this whole time, so he'll be a willing audience."

The unenlightened.

"I suppose."

Let them perish.

"How can you say that?"

Search my three hearts and you will find no trace of hatred toward humans, but I welcome the downfall of your race with a clear conscience. You should too.

"I don't give a shit about Kip, but Laurie..."

They will not understand, or they will choose not to understand. Either way, they will not believe you. Fruitless efforts. A waste of your time and talents.

Sev was probably right, but she didn't want to hear it.

"If I know Laurie, she'll hear me out. I think."

Why do you want to help this person?

She opened her mouth to speak, but no words came out. To her surprise, she didn't have a good answer. Perhaps, if she were being honest, she wanted to prove to herself that Laurie's friendship had been real, that she had succeeded in leaving a lasting positive impression on at least one fellow human in her life.

Do what you must, and I will stand with you. Just know that you do not have much time. The final purge is imminent.

"Define *imminent*, Sev. Give me a date, time, and location."

Nothing comes to me clearly now. When my flesh touched yours and our minds became one, the act diminished the strength of the link to my race — the mind-speak. I can no longer see or hear with clarity, only dim voices and blurred images. I know this: Their return nears. To make a home of your oceans, tame your lands, and enslave or destroy your people. To rule as divine beings.

"Yes, yes, all that. I promise to be quick."

I will come with you to meet Laurie and the son of a bitch Kip. I will protect you.

"Like hell! They'll put you in a pot and serve you on skewers. Your job is to stay here and dream up a plan of escape. Think about where we go and how we get there. I'll handle Kip and Laurie."

They do not concern me. I worry about what is to come.

Jillian considered every fresh hell lingering beyond the lockless door and glassless window. Whatever came to greet her, she would deal with it.

We should stay together, for both our sakes.

"We've already been over this, Sev. Where I'm going, you're not welcome. Stay put."

We should leave now. The stalks of his eyes seemed to scan the sky.

"Not until Laurie has heard me out. I won't be long."

She trusted Daniel's warnings. She wanted to believe Sev too, but her brain preferred to think the Ochos were gone for good. Either way, they would need to leave Pell and make a home elsewhere. The funeral home had come apart anyway, unable to be salvaged.

You just returned. Stay here with me.

She had uttered the same words to Daniel. Her heart hurt.

"You'll be fine without me," she said. "Wish me luck."

Luck, he said.

Good or bad, luck would find her. First she needed to find some shoes.

And, just to be safe, fetch Daniel's gun.

***

Dried leaves crunched underfoot as Jillian skulked through the forest. Unsure of the proximity to her target, she winced from the clatter of each step. Kip and his thugs wouldn't be expecting her, and there'd be no telling what they would do to her if they discovered her creeping through their back yard.

She rested a hand on the butt of the pistol tucked into her waistband. She abhorred the sensation of the gun's steel skin against her own. The metal seemed to sweat against her bare belly.

The wooded terrain sloped downward, and soon she saw swatches of red brick between breaks in the foliage. She estimated two hundred feet between here and there, maybe two hundred fifty. With her eyes fixed on the building, she tripped over a mound of soft earth and fell to the ground. The stench of decay found her nose. As she looked back, she saw a skeletal hand poking through the leaf litter. She brushed the leaves away to reveal the corpse, its leathery flesh shriveled and black. Tangles of thin white hair flowed from the crown of the hollowed-out skull. Empty eye sockets stared back. Withered lips exposed the nubs of stained-brown teeth. The name RUTH was scrawled onto the fabric of her gown's right shoulder. The woman had been ancient at the time of her death.

Jillian noticed several more mounds nearby. Nineteen in all. She approached the nearest one and kicked away the leaf litter. Another corpse. Then she realized what she was seeing: the shallow graves of the former residents of Birch Meadows, the old folks. Kip hadn't even had the decency to give each of them a proper burial, just left them to rot in the middle of nowhere, not even a stone or marker to designate each body's final place of rest. She just hoped they had been long dead when Kip decided to drop them there.

She sat on the forest floor and unlaced her tight-fitting shoes, plundered from the pile in Cozen's spare bedroom, and decided to carry them the rest of the way. In her mind, doing so would make her steps more deliberate and, hopefully, mask her presence behind enemy lines.

Burs and shed bark dimpled her feet as she moved from one tree trunk to the next. Birdsong and the music of rustling leaves from a light wind filled her ears. Thirty feet from the forest's edge, she felt the gentlest of snags across the top of her foot. She looked down to see a thin black wire strung across the forest floor, maybe six inches off the ground. Her eyes traced the tripwire's path to a small green box at the base of a towering oak: an IED perhaps, or a signal flare. Either way, nothing good would come of setting it off. She depressed her foot into the soil, backed away, and took an exaggerated step over the tripwire.

Her chest throbbed as if she had just run for her life.

She leaned her shoes against the oak's trunk as a marker, then approached a sycamore near the edge of the woods. She stood in a gully that had likely once been a small stream, and listened to the staccato of hammers sinking nails and the wheeze of a handsaw biting through wood — construction noises. The rise prevented a decent view of the building's front, though she detected movement by the building's rear. She crept closer and found a trio of women tending a would-be vegetable bed. After a moment, two of them stood in unison and went inside, leaving the third all alone, kneeling in the soil.

Laurie.

A blue bandanna held up her hair, and a patina of yard dirt sullied the front of her teal tank top. Jillian smiled, as she never figured Laurie for the gardening type. Minding the tripwire, she crept to the tree line, a mere fifteen feet from her friend. She was ready to step into the open when she detected movement on the roof: a sentry in an olive t-shirt and brown-and-tan camo cut-offs, holding a shotgun at the ready. She waited until he turned and walked back in the other direction, his feet moving almost in time with the distant whacking of a hammer.

"Laurie!" she said in little more than a whisper, and then again. The third time got her attention. She inched her head around the curve of the thick trunk.

Laurie swiveled her head and locked eyes with Jillian. She checked over her shoulder to see who might be watching. Three beats later she dropped her spade and walked into the trees.

The voice came from above: "Where do you think you're going?"

The sentry cleared his throat and spat a ball of mucus that landed in the middle of Laurie's vegetable bed.

Jillian gasped. She turned with her back to the trunk, arms at her side, ready to bolt for home.

"Got to take a piss, mouth-breather," Laurie told him. "Now do something useful and fuck off."

She peered behind the sycamore trunk and came face to face with Jillian. She waited until the sentry loped back toward the roof's opposite end before whispering, "Hey, stranger. Where the hell have you been?"

"Long story," Jillian hushed. "Listen, you have to get out of here. Bad things are about to happen. Real bad — the worst. You have to trust me."

"Like what?"

"Believe it or not, Kip was right. People want to take this place from you. Thugs and killers. Lots of weapons. They're coming, if they're not here already."

"Kip's no dummy. This place is better protected than you think."

"A few machine guns — no big deal compared to what's on the way," Jillian said. "Please. You have to find a way to bust out of here."

"Bust out? I'm free to leave whenever I want." Laurie smiled and cocked her head to the side. "You look...different."

"So much has happened. Too much, in fact. I wish I had time to fill you in." Jillian paused and added, "How are things going here?"

"Oh, they're going. Not exactly what I expected."

"I can't say I'm surprised. People like Kip—"

"Don't."

"What?"

"As much as I appreciate you coming here just to say, 'I told you so'..."

"Don't put words in my mouth," Jillian insisted. She raised her voice to prove her solemnity. "You have more to fear than humans with bad intentions. The Ochos — the monsters — they're going to return. Any day now, I'm told. This time they're going to level the place. I came to ask you to leave, to come with me."

"Thank you for your concern."

"I'm sorry about what happened between us, Laurie. I wish I better understood what hap—"

"All in the past, Jill, which means it no longer matters. I could've handled myself better, I'm sure."

Laurie patted Jillian on the cheek and turned to leave.

"Come with me, Laurie. I'm begging you. Wait until dark and then slip out the door. Meet me at the funeral home. We'll be miles from this place before anyone notices you're gone."

"I'm glad to see you're okay, Jill." Just as Laurie readied to step onto the grass, she wheeled around and added, "But, Jill..."

"Yeah?"

"Don't come here again."

Jillian's spirit sagged as Laurie returned to the vegetable bed.

"Hope you remembered to wipe," the sentry hollered from the roof.

"Why don't you come down here and check?"

She kneeled into the dirt and churned the soil with her spade.

Jillian stayed there for a moment, staring at her friend, wishing they could lock eyes once more so she could implore her, with one knowing look: "I miss you, thank you, and good luck." Yet Laurie refused to lift her eyes from the holes she made in the earth.

"Fuck," Jillian hissed. She had failed.

Jillian retrieved her shoes and stepped deeper into the woods. Out of respect, she stopped at the burial mounds. So much life lost, and for what purpose? She wagged her head in disgust. After a moment, she discovered the gently worn path that would lead her back to the funeral home.

No matter how much she wanted to, she would not look back.

***

Jillian found Sev on Cozen's front porch. His tentacles surrounded one word scrawled into the tired wood: *Crabs?*

"Maybe tomorrow." She remembered the alligator she had seen a day earlier, presumably headed for the salt marsh to feast on the same prey she would be hunting for Sev. "I'll fetch a few crabby crawlers for you tomorrow."

Tomorrow may never come.

"I'm too tired and aching to go traipsing through the marsh, especially with Sasquatches, cannibalistic seminarians, and other hunters on the prowl."

Your gentleman friend has taken leave of you. Does this make you grieve?

"I'm just glad you're here with me."

She picked him up and hurried inside. As she perched him on her shoulder, the tip of a tentacle slithered onto her forehead.

As humanity falls around us, we can escape, you and I, into the waves, into the comforts of the abyss.

"I have a life here, Sev. A terrestrial life."

Then I will stay with you, no matter where you go. One thing remains clear: We must flee.

"Tomorrow," she pleaded. "Let's discuss it tomorrow. Mama needs some shuteye."

As you wish.

Jillian collapsed onto the couch in the sitting room. The pistol skidded across the glass coffee table. She was glad to be free of it. Sev settled in the crotch of her armpit. His cool, clammy flesh warmed to hers. They stared through the hole where the plywood-covered bay window had once been, and watched clouds streak the sky.

Hours passed in silence. The pale blue sky turned orange and purple. She closed her eyes as the moon came into view. Together they slept.

***

Jillian woke to the shock of raindrops blowing in through the glassless bay window. Dawn had lit up the sky, but lingering cloud cover obscured any trace of the sun.

"How long have I been dead to the world?"

She remembered falling asleep with Sev close by. No trace of him now. Then came the clamor from the kitchen. She crept off the soft cushion, springs creaking beneath her, and padded into the kitchen. She found Sev on the counter, rummaging through the drawers.

"What are you looking for, my dear?"

He lashed a tentacle onto her shoulder and slithered up her arm. His tentacle kissed her forehead.

I wanted to surprise you with the gift of sustenance. None to be had.

"Blame the looters for that," she said. "Never fear. I wouldn't be a survivor if I didn't have a few more tricks up my sleeve."

She closed the pantry's yawning door and retrieved a step stool. She climbed to the top step, extended her arm as high as it would go, and felt around the unseen space atop the pantry. She pulled down a plastic bag filled with two unopened packages of Pop-Tarts and a small tube of old-fashioned oats, generic, stowed as a "just in case." She slid a Pop-Tart out of the box, tore back the foil, and took a small bite. Its stale crust aside, the pastry tasted glorious. She broke off a piece and placed it on the counter for Sev. A tentacle deftly lifted the treat toward his beak. He nibbled and almost immediately dropped it to the floor.

Unimpressive, he whispered.

"Beggars can't be choosers, Sev. As soon as the sun shows its face, I'll head down to the marshes and net a few creepy crawlers for you."

She instinctively went to the back door to retrieve her sickle. She found it — or what was left of it — on the floor, its blade detached from the hickory handle.

"Son of a whore," she spat. She pictured Kip standing in the funeral home's mudroom, bending the metal until the blade snapped.

Nothing of hers was whole anymore. The bucket had a crack in it, unable to hold water, but it would imprison fiddler crabs just fine. She held the Pop-Tart in her teeth as she cleaned up some of the mess. Bucket in hand, she slipped out the back door, headed down the driveway, and hurried toward the marsh.

Dull clouds painted the sky the color of iron. The humid air made her lungs fight for every breath. Other than the gentle swish of tall grasses, nothing stirred. No sign of the alligator she had expected to find lurking in the mud. Her heart thrummed in her chest as she imagined the massive reptile springing from its hiding spot. She could practically feel its teeth stabbing her calf and taking her off her feet, could almost smell the brine as she pictured her face meeting the soft mud. If that happened, nothing and no one would be able to save her. The alligator would simply drag her through the quagmire, as her fingers carved ruts in the formless mud, and wrestle her into the sea. As gray-green waves crashed over her, the icy water would fill her ears, mouth, and lungs. The light would go dark and then...nothing. Gone. The fiddler crabs would emerge from their marshy burrows, unmolested, to resume doing whatever crabs did when there were no humans left to keep watch.

Alligators hunting humans in coastal Rhode Island — crazy.

She closed her eyes and listened to the wind and the far-off growl of waves lapping rock as she tried to convince herself that none of her worst imaginings would come to pass. Besides, there were far more ignoble deaths than getting dragged, drowned, and pulled apart by a modern-day dinosaur.

As she stepped into the marsh, her foot cracked the mud's brittle skin and sank up to the ankle. She tossed the bucket ten feet in front of her, where she would place the crabs once caught. Far fewer crabs scurried in the marsh than she remembered, but she didn't know whether they had died off or simply disliked cooler weather. She didn't want to consider a possible third option, that perhaps they sensed the Ochos' imminent arrival and would hide until the storm passed.

Only a trio of crabs circled the basin of the bucket by the time Jillian decided she'd had enough. Sweat dripped from her forehead and pasted her t-shirt to her glistening belly.

"Sorry, you guys," she told the three crabs. "As for the rest of you, today's your lucky day."

She looked up the coast, toward another stretch of salt marsh, where the corpse of her Hyundai rusted to pieces. Perhaps she would have better luck hunting crabs there. She extricated herself from the mud and walked the road, talking to the crabs at the bottom of the bucket, until she could see her old car up close. The marsh had nearly finished consuming the vehicle, only the pane of its tarnished roof visible.

As her right foot sank into the mud, she heard a familiar click behind her.

"And who's this pretty little lady?"

She did not have to turn around to realize that she was caught.

Chapter 26
A Lit Fuse

"We've had all eyes out for you for weeks," the man said.

He was maybe sixty years old and as fat as a rhino. Jillian could outrun him, but not the reach of his long gun. She could smell his body odor. She imagined the tang of old cheese wafting from his walrus mustache.

As she eyed his heavily bandaged left hand, she recalled Jen Cates' story about the prick she had stabbed for trying to break into her home and abscond with her daughter. She remembered the hint of a name.

"Are you Christian's father?"

He smiled and responded, "Clay Ingersoll. My reputation precedes me."

"So does your smell. How do you live with yourself?"

"That supposed to be funny?"

The half-a-size-too-small flats cramped Jillian's feet. The front of each shoe abraded her toes, slowing her steps.

"Quit stalling," he said, and nudged her with the butt of his rifle.

She realized she should have been thinking about things other than the discomfort in her feet as she stepped onto the asphalt driveway leading to Kip's compound. The rock-and-panel sign for Birch Meadows had been swabbed in red paint with the words THE CITADEL. A metallic click echoed overhead. One of Kip's goons was perched on a deer stand among the heavy branches of a London planetree. A black mask hid his face. The barrel of a rifle rested on the stand's metal rail.

"Bring me the head of Kip Detto," she hollered. She did her best to hide the bulge in her waistband.

"Shut up, smartass," Ingersoll said.

The man in the deer stand maintained a hard stare, saying nothing.

A curve in the driveway brought Kip's so-called "Citadel" into view. Rows of raised mounds lined the front lawn, women on their hands and knees sifting the loose soil between their fingers. Bombed-out vehicles lined the front of the building, a simple blockade, wheels removed and stacked as bollards to protect the main entrance. A man with a spear paced the roof. The butt of the spear clicked against the gravel substrate in time with each step. Another sentry hunkered behind a wall of sandbags. The lethal end of a machine gun projected from a slit in the sandbag wall, almost daring any intruder to step into its sights.

A high-pitched whistle shrieked from behind her — the man in the deer stand, alerting others to Jillian's approach.

The Citadel's residents lifted their eyes from their work. Some faces looked familiar — including that of Jen Cates, the woman who had knocked on Jillian's door seeking sanctuary for her teenage daughter. The woman bent her neck and returned to digging in the soil.

"Keep your ass where I can see it," Ingersoll said, and then waddled into The Citadel.

As Jillian walked toward Cates, Chinh advanced from his post at the line demarcating lawn from forest. The same high-pitched whistle escaped his lips.

Jillian knelt beside Cates and said, "You never came." She knew to keep her voice down.

"Our luck ran out," Cates replied. "They came for us that night."

"Oh." She wanted to say she was sorry, for doubting her, for not being able to help, and for their misfortune. "Is your daughter here with you? Amelia, was it?"

Cates drove a balled fist into the soil.

"They broke her," Cates said. "Broke her every way they could."

A howl issued from the building's entrance. Jillian turned to see Kip Detto fastening his belt buckle. Fresh off the toilet perhaps, though Jillian figured he might have been doing something else with his pants off.

"Well, look what the three-legged alley cat dragged in," he said. Clay Ingersoll stood beside him, and a small group fanned out behind them.

The last was Laurie.

"Jillian, Jillian, Jillian," Kip said. "We all thought you'd run off and gotten yourself killed. Fell into a well or something. Such a pity, we all said. Didn't we?"

He turned to his acolytes for their assent.

Jillian stood and said, "You didn't waste any time ransacking my place."

"Two weeks and not a sign of your pretty little face. No disrespect, but we couldn't let anything go to waste."

Laurie stepped away from the crowd. Jillian detected no discernible emotion in her friend's face — a study in indifference.

"Look," Jillian said. "I came here to warn you about what's coming. And to let you know that you were right."

Kip smirked. His expression suggested a hybrid of delight and surprise.

"Bad people have their eyes on you," she said. "Bad people with big weapons. They know who you are, know where you are, know your vulnerabilities. They're probably watching right now."

"Oh, I think we'll be just fine," Kip said. He tapped one of two pistols tucked into his shoulder holster. "We've got enough fireworks to light up the inside of a black hole."

"You don't get it," she said. "These people are military — or ex-military. They're coming to take what doesn't belong to them, just like you said. They want what you have. They want Pell. If you don't give it up, they'll wipe this place off the map. I know. I met one of them, and I've seen the damage just one man can do."

Daniel. The memory of his angular face flashed into her mind.

"We're safe here," Kip said curtly. "The adults in the room have all the bases covered. You can stop talking."

"That's not all. The Ochos — the creatures — they will return to tear down whatever's left standing, whoever's left standing. What you've built here will be rubble soon enough."

"Okay, crazy lady, talking crazy."

"So now that you have what you want, you no longer give a shit?"

"Stop talking." Any trace of charm or humor had left his voice. He motioned toward the lone figure at the edge of the woods and said, "Do the honors, Charlie."

Chinh moved on Jillian. His speed and directness unsettled her, bare feet making no sound. She backed up and prepared to run, only to find three men behind her, blocking her escape. She pulled the pistol from her waistband. Chinh froze in place.

"You walked right into the lion's mouth this time, sweetheart," Kip said. "What did you think would happen when you came here uninvited? You'd just waltz in here, run your mouth like you always do, and everyone would just bow down in awe and gratitude for sharing your infinite wisdom? That's not how this story ends."

Laurie stood by the building's entrance, unaffected. Maybe Sev had been right, Jillian thought. She wished she had heeded his advice.

"Suddenly the cat's got your tongue?" Kip said. "Any other time you would talk, talk, talk, cluck, cluck, cluck, and not know when to shut the fuck up. Maybe now you'll see that running your mouth has consequences."

"Funny," she said. "I was thinking the same about you."

Someone laughed.

Jillian steeled herself as Kip stormed toward her. Her brain shouted: *Don't move. No matter what, don't let him know you're about to piss your pants.*

He towered over her by nearly a foot. Tears welled in her eyes, but she willed them not to wet her cheeks.

"You've been a boil on my ass since the day I met you," he said, his voice little more than a whisper. "I could slit your throat right here and no one would bat an eye."

"Do it then," she said. "You're so tough, go ahead and do it."

He reached for the knife on his belt and eased it out of the sheath. Steel hissed against leather.

She cocked the pistol.

"You shouldn't provoke a man who has nothing to lose," he said. "Drop the weapon before you shit yourself." He held the knife up to his right eye. The thickness of the blade obscured his pupil.

She had to give him credit: He was a showman, full of blare and bluster.

"You know what?" she told him. "I hope the marauders do come. And I hope someone takes that knife and shoves it so far up your ass it tickles your tonsils."

"Leave her alone, Kip."

Jillian swiveled to see Laurie tramping the lawn. She lowered the pistol and eased down the hammer with her thumb.

Kip turned to face Laurie and said, "No one asked you."

"I'm telling you anyway," Laurie shot back. "She's leaving and never coming back. Isn't that right, Jill?"

Tension floated on the soft wind. People chattered. The crowd seemed to sense a shift in the balance of power.

"You can go, Jill," Laurie told her. The hint of a smile lit her face.

"Like hell!" Kip said. "She tries to walk, I plug her ass with a forty-five."

Laurie stepped between Jillian and Kip. He adjusted his posture, kicking one leg out behind him. Jillian had always suspected that Kip felt intimidated by Laurie, and his reaction proved her suspicion.

"Go back inside," he dared, "and make yourself useful."

His words lit a fire in Laurie. The crude, crass, and loud she-demon who had once trained her ire on Jillian now had Kip in her sights. She unleashed a barrage of insults, each landing with surgical precision. A finger wagging in his face. Her lips close enough to spit in his eye.

"...ball-less moron...little man in big shoes...a schoolyard bully who never grew up...a failure at everything you ever tried...tiny-dicked prick..."

The spectacle gave Jillian enough of a window to slip through and escape Kip's attention, which she suspected had been Laurie's intention. As she backed away and turned for the driveway, she smacked directly into a brick wall named Chinh. His hands clamped onto both of her shoulders and bulled her off her feet. She landed on her backside with a cushioned thud. Her finger depressed the trigger.

The fired bullet obliterated Chinh's little toe. He gritted his teeth in agony, though he barely made a sound. He bunny-hopped in a circle, as if trying to shake off the insult. Jillian apologized profusely.

The Dying Man, her cold-hearted hero, would have been ashamed.

Chinh came around to face her, his face reddened, his expression monstrous. As he bent toward her, either to lift her off the ground or to throttle her, another gunshot pierced the air. Chinh fell backward in a cloud of red haze — a bloody mist. The ground seemed to shake from the impact.

A flare shot up from a break in the trees. Then came another, thirty feet away, followed by yet another.

A second later the whole place ignited.

***

A fireball incinerated the tilled beds. Clumps of dirt fell to the ground in hollow thumps. A blade of shrapnel bit into the soft space between Jillian's breast and left shoulder. The pistol fell away as she crawled toward a boulder at the edge of the driveway, her hand tight to the wedge of metal jutting from the hole in her chest. Blood trickled through the seams between her fingers.

War had come to Pell.

She shielded her ears from the gunfire and shrieks of human targets. Bodies dropped around her. Women, children, and most of the men hurried to The Citadel's chute-like entrance — Laurie among them — and fought to cram inside.

A faint *click* came from the roof. A second later the weapon behind the wall of sandbags unleashed its fury. Liquid metal gushed from the machine gun's muzzle and tore up the trees and bushes hiding an invisible enemy. Between bursts, Jillian heard the gunner shout, "Come on out and get your chicken-shit asses torn up!"

An orange projectile discharged from the woods, trailing embers, and zeroed in on the man atop the roof. Sandbags flew in the ensuing explosion. Pieces of the ruined machine gun — and meaty pieces of the gunner — clattered onto the driveway. Sand flowed off the roof like water. Tongues of fire licked the tree limbs above.

With the primary threat erased, incoming fire sprayed The Citadel's façade. Windows shattered. Brick turned to dust. Shredded tree branches dropped to the earth. One by one the enemy guns went silent, until the bullet spray ceased entirely.

Jillian peeked out from behind the boulder. A baseball-shaped projectile rolled to a stop at the edge of Chinh's vegetable beds. Yellow smoke hissed out and spread slowly across the lawn.

"I'm speaking to whoever's in charge in there," the voice boomed. "I'm coming out. To talk. You should do the same so we can get this mess settled."

A moment later a towering figure, decked out in black and green, pierced the smoke screen, a ghost appearing out of thin air. His hands rested on the butt of a rifle that looked as if it had come from a warzone in Afghanistan or Iraq.

"Come on out now," he added. "Don't be shy."

The Citadel's front door cracked open, and out stepped Kip. Both pistols remained stowed in his shoulder harness. In that moment, Jillian's opinion of Kip improved greatly. The two men came together, standing close enough for her to hear the back and forth.

"Fellow military man, I presume." Kip introduced himself and added, "U.S. Army Reserve, corporal."

"Whatever you say, tough guy," the man said. "Listen, we've got the whole building surrounded. Each of us has an M4 or an XM-15, with a full mag in the well and plenty more in reserve. We don't want the building or whoever's in it. We just want you gone. How that happens is up to you."

"Raz, is it?" Kip asked. Jillian assumed Kip had read the nameplate stitched onto the man's chest. "Look, man. We've got plenty of firepower too. Let's not make this ugly."

"Here's what I know, tough guy. You have maybe a dozen men, a handful of women who might put up a fight, none of them battle tested. Give one of my snipers thirteen shots. Problem solved."

Kip had no response. He wasn't bullshitting his way out of this one. Jillian almost felt bad for him — almost. He turned to notice plumes of smoke rising from The Citadel's roof. Wood crackled as it burned.

"Look," Raz said, "I could have terminated every one of your people seven times over in the thirty seconds we've been yapping. Lucky for you, I'm feeling magnanimous. You have five minutes to clear out. Take one second more, we bring the walls down and no one leaves here alive. Understood?"

The spiteful part of Jillian loved to see a strongman making Kip feel as small as he had made her feel. If only she weren't in the middle of a would-be firefight — and already wounded gravely — she might actually have enjoyed his comeuppance.

"So," Raz said. "You ready to be a good little shepherd and lead your sheep out of here?"

Flares shot up along the perimeter, in every direction.

Bursts of gunfire. Screams of terror cut short.

As Raz turned toward the commotion, Kip pulled a sidearm and fired twice. Both bullets landed — one in the throat, another through the left cheek. Raz stumbled backward and choked on his own blood.

Men in camouflage sprinted through the fading smoke screen, heading straight for The Citadel. One by one, Kip's fighters picked them off. The only two to escape the onslaught darted past Jillian's boulder and made a hard right down the driveway, fleeing the melee.

Something else came right behind them.

The ground trembled. A low grumble built into a roar. Jillian refused to believe the scene her eyes showed her.

A horde of ape-like beasts thundered toward The Citadel. She estimated a dozen or more, perhaps as many as twenty — Sasquatches. One of them carried a rifle as if it were a spear. Another picked up a flaming car tire and hurled it through the nearest window. A woman shrieked as if being torn apart. It might have been Laurie. Handguns discharged in quick succession.

Jillian bolted for the driveway. Her chest ached from panic, if not from the shrapnel lodged in her flesh. Ponderous footsteps echoed behind her. She didn't want to look. Her only desire was to escape the bloodbath.

Then her feet left the ground, lifted by her hair. She could hear the strands tearing, could feel the follicles fighting to cling to her scalp. An atrocious smell, somehow familiar, assaulted her nose. As she opened her eyes, she stared into the gold-glinted pupils of an ancient beast.

The Sasquatch smiled. A line of spittle dampened the fur on its scarred chest. The creature brought her closer to its face, smelled her, licked her cheek — perhaps in remembrance, from the altercation at the sporting goods store and the ensuing chase through the woods that ended in the breath-stealing rapids of Otter Pelt Creek. It gave an approving growl.

The Sasquatch's grip suddenly loosened, and Jillian fell to the ground. Her left foot absorbed most of the impact. The ankle folded and sent daggers shooting up her leg. The Sasquatch tumbled to its knees, howling. Its face contorted, body shuddered, as if reeling from unseen blows. From behind the beast stepped a man holding a massive knife with serrated teeth along its silver spine. Thick blood dripped from the blade's keen edge. The man then plunged the knife into the side of the creature's oblong skull. The blade landed with a heavy *thunk*. The man turned to Jillian and said, all too calmly, "Run."

It took her a moment to recognize him through the mask of black-and-green grease paint, but there was no mistaking him: Daniel. He pulled a sidearm from its holster and unloaded five shots into the beast's middle.

The creature roared to its feet and snatched Daniel in its claws. Inhuman noises slipped from his mouth. Bones cracked in the beast's crushing grip. She sat there, useless, as the beast battered Daniel against a dying pine tree. Confusion wracked her brain as the creature released Daniel, yet he remained aloft, hovering above the earth. A branch protruded from his gut. Arterial blood painted the dusting of pine needles at the tree trunk's base. He peered down at her, gurgling, and repeated his plea: "Run." He raised his sidearm once more and fired a final shot into the Sasquatch's forehead.

The creature's body crumpled to the earth in time with the sidearm falling from Daniel's limp hand.

She could not move, paralyzed. Listening to the breath leave his lungs. Waiting for the postmortem spasm. Watching his liquids gather beneath him — a blood meal for the soil.

An inferno consumed The Citadel. The roof caved in with a roar, putting an end to the dwindling screams and the occasional gunshot. *Laurie.* Jillian took a halfhearted step toward the flaming wreckage, only to realize she could do nothing to help.

Thunder cracked overhead. As she turned to run, a gust blew her off her feet. A starburst split the sky, and the clouds turned red. Rain fell in blinding sheets. The drops stung her eyes, briny on her lips — salt rain. Pendulous globs fell to the earth, some exploding on impact. One landed on the patch of grass beside her, and she watched it unfurl into a small blood-red octopus, not unlike Sev.

Fighting the pain in her ankle, she stood and limped down the driveway. Dozens of octopuses, each of them colored a blazing red, scrambled across the macadam. One lashed out and caught her calf, and a toothed sucker bit into the muscle. It burned like hot iron, but she kept running until the leg went numb from calf to ankle. One foot clipped the other, and she tumbled. Her chin bounced off the asphalt.

The octopus scuttled up her leg, toward her core and, to her horror, toward orifices it would surely consider points of entry. A vision flashed into her mind — the creature prying her jaws open and filling her mouth, then sliding down her esophagus, tearing and clawing and infecting as it went. She tried to kick it away, swat it with her hands. Her foot connected with the octopus' mantle. The blow seemed to stun the creature.

A green-black blur shot from beneath a rhododendron at the driveway's edge. A second passed before Jillian recognized the alligator, nearly eight feet long from snout to tail, one eye absent — the same beast she had seen skulking toward the salt marsh only days before. She braced for the impaling, for the feeling of its conical teeth rending her flesh. A tug on her leg made her open her eyes in time to see the reptile's jaws tear the octopus from her leg. Only a tendril of one of its scarlet arms remained, wriggling and spurting blue blood onto the arc of her pale shin. As the octopus slid down the alligator's gullet, Jillian had the presence of mind to utter a word of thanks to her unlikely rescuer.

Numbness spread to the tips of her toes and up to her pelvis. She could barely bend the leg, yet the surge of adrenaline coaxed the useless limb awake. As she limped forward, a gargantuan mass formed in the sky above her. With an audible *pop*, a tentacled monster slipped through the portal — she could see the edges of the doorway, glowing a brilliant purple against the pale orange beyond — and entered her world. It reminded her of the gory act of a newborn sliding through the birth canal.

Tens more portals cracked open in the sky above Pell, each delivering an obscene gift. A hundred squirming tentacles reached for the earth.

The Ochos had returned, just as Sev had predicted.

Ancient pines, birches, and alders crashed to the ground. A tentacle landed like a hurled boulder and reduced a Cape Cod to kindling. Otherworldly roars filled the air behind her.

All Jillian wanted was to limp the few blocks back to Cozen's, find Sev, and collapse into a cocoon of warmth and softness. If the end came — *when* it came — they would experience it together.

***

She found Sev on the funeral home's porch, gazing into the boiling clouds. The scarlet sky, writhing with black tentacles, seemed to transfix him.

Return, he scrawled on the damp wood.

"No shit, Sev!" She scooped him up and hurried inside. The tip of a tentacle kissed her forehead.

You have injuries.

"I'm fine," she said, almost forgetting the shrapnel wound and the barb lodged in her anesthetized leg. "We'll ride this out in the basement."

"Not this time," said a gravelly voice behind her.

Kip Detto filled the open doorway. Blood and soot streaked his face. Gray dust colored his hair. His eyes seemed ablaze. A wild man gone mad.

"I see it now," he said, nodding toward Sev. "Everything is clear as a goddamn bell."

She stuttered a wordless response.

"*You* caused this," he said. "All this time you've been on their side — the wrong side — a fucking traitor to your species."

She turned for the basement, knowing she could lock them in and wait out the storm. Kip had a straighter path. He tackled her and went for her shoulder. She howled as his fingers twisted the torn flesh of her shrapnel wound.

"Treason bears a stiff penalty," he growled.

The pressure relented suddenly, and the intense pain eased. The sharp jag lessened to a measured throb. She opened her eyes to see Sev attached to Kip's face, his tentacles constricting her enemy's throat. Kip yelped as Sev's stony barbs tore into his cheek and bled venom into the marrow of his bones.

Sev would make quick work of him. Or so she thought.

Kip pried Sev from his face. A tentacle snapped and fell to the floor. The severed limb writhed on the wood until it reached the top of the basement stairs and tumbled off the edge, into the inky darkness. As Kip mashed Sev into the door, an inky spray colored the nearest wall an opaque black. A stunned Sev stayed fixed in place. Slowly, as his suckers lost their strength, his battered body slid down the door's face.

Kip reared back and lined up his target.

"No!" Jillian lunged for Kip's arm.

His fist collapsed Sev's mantle.

The air gusted from Sev's body. He tumbled to the floor and landed with a pronounced *flop*. A puddle of ink gathered beneath him.

Kip shook his head, as if trying to clear the haze. Sev's venom would have already begun its work: first, a subtle tingling; followed by progressive paralysis, the body shutting down, system by system and organ by organ; and then, assuming Sev had delivered an ample dose, the numbness of death. He kicked Sev's body into the far wall and slammed the basement door. He then stumbled into the center of the room, standing between Jillian and the front door.

"Time to pay the price for your betrayal," he slurred.

As she bolted for the kitchen, a thunderous blow shook the house from its foundation. A portrait fell from its hook. Pots and pans clattered to the kitchen floor. The impact sent her sprawling to the shattered tile.

He was on her immediately. Brushing aside her knees, kicks, and claws, Kip climbed on top of her and clamped his hands around her throat. She sank her fingernails into his wrists, but his grip only tightened. His eyes looked inhuman, demonic. She gurgled and spat, but the fight began to leave her. Pinpricks of white formed at the edges of her vision. She could feel the tunnel of light closing, the end drawing near.

Another blow rocked the house. A patch of red sky opened above her as a monstrous tentacle tore through the roof.

Hands clamped around her throat, Kip lifted her and slammed her back to the floor. Her head bounced off the tile. A sense of euphoria overcame her. Calmness settled in, and her hands loosened from Kip's wrists.

"This was supposed to be my time — *mine*," he groaned. "You had every chance, every opportunity to help me build something here. But you had to *fucking* ruin it. I had *everything* in my grasp, and you *ruined* it!"

His grip eased, enabling her to draw a breath.

"I loved my brother, *loved* him," he continued. "But you have no idea what it was like to grow up with him, with Perfect Kyle, to stand in his shadow your whole life. No, you couldn't possibly imagine."

"I know how it feels to not be seen," she said. "To be invisible."

His body shifted as he seemed to consider her words. He sat with all his weight on her pelvis.

"God gave me a do-over," he said, his voice cracking on the last word of the sentence. "It was like he reached down from the clouds and said, 'Okay, kid. Try this one on for size, see if it fits any better,' because he knew I was a fuckup. Kyle had something I didn't — *everything* I didn't. With him gone, it was like all the talent he hadn't yet used up just sort of fell into me."

She swallowed hard and said, "There, there, Kip."

Glass shattered upstairs.

"I can die happy knowing I rebuilt Pell, knowing that what I did here would have endured if not for those *things*," he said. "People will remember that. Can you say that about anything you did? No. You can't say shit. All you can say is you did your best to thwart me at every turn. Worse than that, turns out you were in league with those *things* all along. I don't know why they chose you, of all people, but that doesn't change the fact that they did."

He leaned forward with his left hand braced against the floor, likely to keep from falling over. Ringlets of hair hid his face. He seemed to hover over her, likely pondering what to do with her, how to kill her. As the target came into view, The Dying Man's words returned to her: *Either accept oblivion or lead someone else into its icy mouth.* She had to strike before he could.

"There's no one left to remember you, Kip. The world has already forgotten."

Jillian thrust upward and clamped her teeth onto his Adam's apple. Her incisors sank in until she tasted iron — borrowing The Dying Man's finishing move, "The Last Word," for disabling an opponent.

Her hero would have been proud.

Kip planted both palms on the floor, trying to pull away, but she would not relent. His screams turned into something else as she felt the crunch of thyroid cartilage. Her jaws came together. Warmth and salt filled her mouth.

As she unclenched her jaws, Kip reared back with his hands to his throat, spewing blood. She reached blindly for a weapon of any kind, and her fingertips found the rim of a cast-iron frying pan. Her grip closed around the handle. She swung, and the pan's base connected with the point of his chin. A resonant clang filled the enclosed space. He sat upright, straight as a pin, and then slowly toppled backward.

Jillian turned onto her side. Each labored breath burned her throat. She shook the fog from her head and crawled across Kip's body. She left him splayed across the splintered slat separating the kitchen from the sitting room.

She found Sev where he had fallen, in a spreading puddle of blood and ink. His mantle rose and fell weakly as he struggled for air.

"Sev." She couldn't say anything else.

A terrible sound fluttered from his siphon.

"You saved me."

A trembling tentacle reached for Jillian's forehead. She bent toward him.

Returning the favor.

Outside, the Ochos raged. The ceiling caved, and much of the second floor merged with the first. A porcelain bathtub crashed into the sitting room.

"I'm not ready," she told him. "I don't want this life to end."

Disrobe, please.

"A horny old goat, right to the very end." She smiled through her tears. "Now is not the time, Sev. I don't know—"

This is not the end. Not for you. Trust me.

His tentacle slipped from her forehead.

She stood before him and unzipped her pants. Her wounded shoulder flared as she removed the remnants of her torn and bloody shirt. Her pants, bra, and underwear formed a small pile. She stood before him, completely nude, as the world beyond the walls came undone.

She kneeled next to him. Red-tinted light filtered through the hole in the roof, revealing the extent of Sev's injuries. He wasn't going to make it. She reached for his limp tentacle and held it to her forehead until the sucker responded.

"You're hurt so bad."

My dear Jillian Futch. Take me into your arms.

She complied. His cold, wet flesh chilled the bare skin of her belly. They stayed there for a moment. She felt comforted by the bond, hoping he felt the same as he neared the end.

Place me on your shoulder.

Again, she complied, having no idea what he had in mind.

You will feel as though you cannot bear the pain, but you must.

"Tell me what you're—"

A barb pierced the skin on the back of her neck. The spur bit into the bone of her cervical spine.

Untold horrors flashed before her eyes — the grotesque profiles of otherworldly creatures, all claws and scales and bat-like wings, humanoid beasts rending each other limb from limb, wails of unimaginable suffering, depths of inky darkness no light could penetrate — as she saw into his mind.

She collapsed as the venom coursed through her body. Every fiber of her being felt as though it had caught fire. She begged him to end her life.

***

The Ochos undid Pell's fragile remains. Roofs caved and walls collapsed. Tentacles as long and thick as telephone poles pitched fleeing humans into the sea. Some of the invaders shambled up Main Street to scour nooks for burrowing bipedal prey.

So enthralled were they in their destruction, they paid no mind to a riderless bicycle pedaling down the driveway of the Cozen Family Funeral Home and Crematory. The bicycle turned right and veered into the street, only to crash into the door of a charred Ford F-150.

The bike then righted itself and shakily pedaled past inert bodies and canyon-like craters. It continued north, up the coast, leaving the roiling tempest in its wake.

Chapter 27
The World Eater

An icy wind raked the road as Jillian stopped to tighten the drawstrings of her hooded windbreaker. She pulled on a pair of fingerless gloves. Winter grew near. The farther north she went on barren roads, the less forgiving the weather became. As she placed a foot on the bicycle's pedal to resume her journey, her hand found the pistol holstered to her belt. The weapon had become part of her, like a fifth limb.

The remnants of a recent meal burned in the furnace of her belly — fuel for the miles ahead. The bicycle had been holding up all right in the weeks since she had escaped Pell, but a broken chain or flat tire seemed imminent. If or when such a scenario came to pass, she could walk. Until then, she would keep pedaling — the wind in her face and the reminders of her former life cramped into a ratty old backpack.

"Another twenty miles or so and we'll stop," she said.

Sev's voice whispered in her ear.

Crabs?

The backpack shifted with Sev's excitement.

"We'll see what we can find. But likely, yes."

The sustenance of crabs had kept him alive all these weeks, even when his end seemed inevitable. After Sev had injected her with his venom — showing her the horrors of his existence and the awesome yet awful secrets of his species from generations past — she was all but certain he would die from the injuries Kip Detto had inflicted. For nearly a week he lingered in the space between worlds, near death, and she felt his suffering — actually *felt* it. Each crab minced in the teeth of his beak drew him another step away from the brink. The arm she had severed with her scalpel had regrown entirely, the only evidence of the event being her memory of it. That, too, had begun to fade. Likewise, the limb Sev had lost in his battle with Kip had sprouted a feeble frond destined to grow into a suitable replacement.

Just as Jillian could see his wounds healing, in time with her own, she could feel his energy returning, however slowly. Whatever substance Sev had injected into her body had not only infused her flesh with the temporary gift of camouflage — invisibility — but it had also created an unshakeable bond between them. Symbiosis. Each could see directly into the other's mind. Because of magic or chemistry or some combination of the two, they no longer needed his grease pencil or the physical connection of his tentacle against her bare forehead to communicate.

Jillian saw her life's purpose differently than she had prior to fleeing Pell. Either Sev's venom had reshaped her perspective, or the world had. She had done things in recent weeks — terrible, awful, illicit things, however necessary — that former versions of Jillian Futch would not have imagined in her most nerve-rattling nightmares. Survival at all costs.

Like Sev, she had learned to savor the briny taste of crab. They would stop at a coastal marsh and hunt for an hour, enjoy a feast of handheld crustaceans — raw for him, boiled in a tidy pot for her — and then lounge so Sev could rest. Putting miles behind them became secondary. She plucked any remaining blueberries from bushes dotting the roadside. An able scavenger, she scoured abandoned cars and crept into empty houses for food, clothing, ammunition — whatever resources she could haul. The houses weren't always empty, but she always came away with what she needed. Someday, she realized, she would have to deal with the blood-spattered recollections of the wrongs she had committed in order to procure the resources she took, but for now she concerned herself only with living through the day.

Nomadic life came with its share of stressors and obstacles, but she had no choice in the matter, so she did her best to enjoy the journey. Her mind had settled on a destination: Guillemot, the small village in Maine she had visited as a child, where she had been brought back from death's doorstep on the shore of a tea-colored lake — and, she believed, where she forged her lifelong fascination with the macabre. She could return and make new memories to wipe away the bad ones. She could become someone else. Few people had made a home of Guillemot during normal times, let alone now, meaning the Ochos' wandering tentacles would likely seek more densely populated areas to tear to pieces. And, she posited, Maine's famously unkind winters would deter them.

Use your voice, Sev whispered.

"Two plus two equals goldfish."

Your mathematics is poor.

As they rounded a bend obscured by a downed tree, Jillian had to swerve to avoid the cliff's precipitous edge. She ditched the bike and skidded across the asphalt. The bike tumbled over the ragged lip, clicking and clacking all the way down. She exhaled in relief at yet another too-close brush with death. The burn in her leg suggested road rash. Sure enough, the macadam's infinite teeth had removed the top layer of skin and most of the stubble of her leg's outer edge, from the lower calf to the middle of her thigh.

"You all right back there, pal?"

Peachy, Sev said. *What happened?*

She stood and shook the ache from her bones, and then rotated her left shoulder. The joint had yet to fully recover from the shrapnel wound earned during the firefight at The Citadel. She tiptoed to the cliff's edge. The coast had been torn away and swept into the sea, leaving a chasm more than a hundred and fifty feet deep and perhaps a half-mile across. Her bicycle sat at the bottom — the frame slick with mud, the front tire submerged, and hopefully unbroken. Ponds of murky water lined the basin, either pulled in from the sea or seeping up from the earth. There was no going back, so she had only one option: climb down the cliff's ragged face, traverse the ravine, and scale the bluff on the far side.

"Hang on, Sev. We have a hard road ahead of us."

She sat on the edge and leaned over. Rocks, tree roots, and assorted detritus jutted from the clay-like mud — an obstacle course all the way down. She took one breath and pushed off the ledge. Wind brushed her cheeks as the ground rose to meet her. She landed on all fours on a rocky protuberance, but she nearly lost her grip on the mud-slicked surface. Rocks and roots provided handholds to take her most of the way down. She slid the last forty feet and splashed into the chill of a briny puddle. She wiped the mud from her eyes and fetched the bike, amazed to find no damage other than a twisted seat, a cracked pedal, and slightly bent handlebars.

Hours slipped away as she managed the gauntlet of mud and water. Her feet sank as she walked. She held the bike aloft as she waded into chin-deep pools whose bottoms she could not see, eyes out for ripples or rogue shark fins. At one point she passed a mud-caked casket absent its deathly cargo. She mourned her former life until the moment passed.

She scanned the high wall on the far side and saw the full scope of the devastation. A meteorite or an A-bomb — nothing else could have wrought such calamity.

Night fell as she finished scaling the opposing bluff. Exhausted and hungry, cold and wet, she collapsed on the first patch of soft earth she could find.

She awoke with Sev swatting her cheek.

Do not waste the day, he told her. *Crabs.*

After peeing in the bushes and changing into semi-dry pants, she straddled the bike and tested its road-worthiness. She took one last look at the chasm and pressed on. The road veered on a slight downward grade, meaning she could coast — a rare blessing, gratefully accepted. They followed the curve and passed a reflective green road sign that had been knocked from its post. Though damaged, the sign was intact enough to let her know they would soon reach a familiar New Hampshire destination.

"Two miles to Portsmouth, Sev."

Do we like Portsmouth?

"I was a young girl when I was there last."

She told him a story about the day she and her father had stopped in Portsmouth on the drive back from Guillemot. Father and daughter had enjoyed lunch on the patio of a fancy restaurant by the marina, though the event's tenor changed when her father's cardinal-red lobster arrived at the table. She watched in horror as he pulled the crustacean to pieces, like a savage, and sucked the buttery meat from its blistered shell.

You never talk about your mother.

"You've never asked."

Where is she?

"Long dead, like the rest of the world."

The road veered back toward the coast, and the vista opened up. Piles of broken timber and crushed brick suggested another dead community, a town erased from the map by the Ochos.

"Holy hell," she gasped. "Sev, look."

She braked hard and swung the backpack off her shoulder. A zipper unzipped, and Sev poked his gnarled head out of the main compartment.

In the distance, far out to sea, miles-long tentacles fanned the heavens and roiled the seas, as if stirring a pot. The spectacle exceeded any absurdity her mind could have conjured.

Empress.

Lightning erupted from the belly of a storm cloud and outlined a fraction of the creature's impossible silhouette. A dark halo encircled the great beast. Jillian fished a pair of field binoculars from the backpack. As she trained the lenses on the horizon, she saw hundreds of Ochos undulating in the sky above the waterline, as if caught in a gravitational field. Each Ocho likely measured two hundred to three hundred feet long, from the crest of its mantle to the tip of its longest arm, but each looked insignificant in the shadow of the Empress. Her unending tentacles glistened with a metallic sheen. Her jet-black mantle would dwarf the state of Rhode Island, Jillian figured. She imagined the great beast burrowing to Earth's core and eating the world from the inside out.

She recalled snapshots of the chasm she had crossed the prior day. The Empress' work, she now understood. Even a glancing blow from one of her gargantuan tentacles would have turned the coastline into a crumbling ravine.

Movement in the surf, just beyond the rocky shore, caught Jillian's eye. She pedaled closer for a better vantage point. The scene defied sense. Dozens of naked humans — survivors — swayed in the waist-deep surf, arm in arm, facing the churning sea and the tentacled leviathan beyond. The water temperature would be no warmer than fifty degrees. Each member of the human chain had a blood-red octopus the approximate size of Sev latched onto his or her back.

Exalting.

The Ochos had won. Mankind had reached its end.

She sighed. The exhalation felt like a lifted weight, for it meant she could stop pretending to care about the end of her species' dominance. Men, women, children — humans of every age and gender had hurt, frightened, or disappointed her too many times, and now her species was getting its due. In her mind, the reckoning would make the world a kinder, gentler place.

A different fate awaited her. She would keep moving, nomadic, spending the rest of her life learning from Sev, plumbing the secrets of his species, and exploring the fantastic truths of a realm few, if any, humans had ever seen. Some day in the not-too-distant future, she would follow Sev to the rim of the nearest portal and step through the doorway separating her world from his. The Sasquatches — air-breathing primates, much like herself — had accomplished this feat, so she was certain she could too. She would see his home, breathe its air, and feel its dusty soil beneath her feet. She would wander its forests. She would climb its mountains. She would cast her eyes upon the amphibious lizard-men along the coasts. And one day, after age had turned her weak and worn, she would wet her feet, follow him into the surf, and paddle past the breakers. Then, with Sev clutched to her breast, she would take one final gasp and descend into the briny deep to meet her end in the world that shaped him.

The first twenty-nine years of Jillian's life had passed with her standing on the edge of the lightless void. She had since become one with it, consumed by it, a ghost peering out of the abyss.

She stomped the gear-side pedal to get the bike moving and pressed on to Portsmouth. The crank arm groaned beneath her, squealing for fresh grease. Her overworked calves burned with each rotation. She had miles of barren asphalt to put behind her before she could rest again. Other than Sev's delicate freight in her backpack and his thoughts swimming in her brain, she would have the road all to herself. And she would be glad.

A knife-sharp gust drew tears from her eyes. The first flakes of winter would fall soon enough.

Acknowledgments

I extend my gratitude to the following humans for their time, support, and thoughtful criticism, all of which helped make this story better: Donna Schoener Donahue, my wife, partner, and best friend, for critiques of early drafts, among other things; Don Swaim, founder and leader of the esteemed Bucks County Writers Workshop, as well as past and present BCWW members Lindsey Allingham, Candace Barrett, Chris Bauer, Beverly Black, Bob Cohen, Ef Deal, Daniel Dorian, Natalie Zellat Dyen, Jim Kempner, Wil Kirk, George MacMillan, Jackie Nash, Bill O'Toole, John Schoffstall, Ashara Shapiro, Alan Shils, David Updike, and the late John Wirebach; authors G.L. Davies, Vaughn A. Jackson, Candace Nola, Grant Price, Steve Stred, and Schuy R. Weishaar, for dropping some well-placed breadcrumbs of guidance and encouragement; and every person who took the time to read and/or review one or both of my first two novels. Also, many thanks to the JournalStone team, particularly Scarlett R. Algee, for picking up the story and twisting, turning, and hammering it into "a thing."

Finally, I am indebted to the nonhumans in my life — Marbles, Crash, Baxter, and Sprout, as well as the many kittens Donna and I have had the privilege to foster through the nonprofit Forgotten Cats (forgottencats.org) — for providing the best possible kind of disruption while I was trying to write or edit pages.

About the Author

William J. Donahue is an editor, features writer, and kitten foster who has not been the same since watching John Carpenter's *The Thing* as a ten-year-old. His prior novels include *Burn, Beautiful Soul* and *Crawl on Your Belly All the Days of Your Life*. He lives in a small but well-guarded fortress in Pennsylvania, somewhere on the map between Philadelphia and Bethlehem. Although his home lacks a proper moat, it does have plenty of snakes.